I0577533

HOTT SHOT

A STEAMY RUSH CREEK ROMANTIC COMEDY

HOTT SPRINGS ETERNAL
BOOK 1

SERENA BELL

Copyright © 2023 by Serena Bell

All rights reserved.

Jelsba Media Group

ISBN 978-1-953498-28-1

No part of this book may be reproduced in any form or by any electronic or mechanical means, including information storage and retrieval systems, without written permission from the author, except for the use of brief quotations in a book review.

This book is a work of fiction. Names, places, and incidents either are products of the author's imagination or are used fictitiously. Any resemblance to actual events, locales, or persons, living or dead, is entirely coincidental.

Comb-and-scissor icon created by Freepik from www.flaticon.com

1

QUINN

As a scientist, I'm used to predicting outcomes, taking every variable into account. But sitting with my siblings around the big conference table in the lawyer's office, reading my late grandfather's letter, I'm not a scientist at all. I'm just a sucker-punched guy— and there's *no* way I could have seen this coming.

Okay, Quinn. You think you're such a hot shot? Let's see how you handle a completely different kind of business.

I look up to find my sibs staring at me with expressions ranging from total confusion to barely veiled amusement.

"What does that mean?" my brother Rhys demands.

My brother Preston shakes his head in disgust. "It means the man couldn't help himself. He can't let death stop him from making trouble. What a total dick move."

"Language," the lawyer chides. "There are ladies present."

Arthur Weggers is my granddad's attorney. He's a short, balding, sixty-something guy with pasty skin who I had no reason to dislike before today but who I would happily donate to science right now.

"This woman doesn't give a fuck," my sister, Hanna—eight months pregnant and sporting a watermelon front and center—says with a shrug.

"Keep reading," the lawyer urges.

But I've had enough. I thrust the letter back into Weggers's hands. "He can't do this."

"He can," Weggers says. "We've been over this, Quinn. He made sure the will was airtight. He had two different medical professionals attest to his soundness of mind and body. He had me review the no-contest clause with three other lawyers."

Rhys, who's also an attorney, mutters something next to me.

"What's that?" Weggers says.

"Deadhand control," my brother repeats louder.

The two men glare at each other across the table.

Rhys turns to us. "It's what it sounds like. Most states won't let people just keep exerting infinite control after they're dead."

Weggers scowls. "If you'd like to take a shot at contesting the will, that is, of *course*, your prerogative."

Rhys scowls back. "Believe me. I'm looking into it."

He's taking this will extremely personally.

But not as personally as I'm taking it.

My granddad's will leaves the ranchland we grew up on to the six of us: Hanna, me, and our four brothers. But it also contains what Weggers calls *conditions* and I call the Asshole Clause. We have to hold the land for two years before we can sell it, and during those two years, we have to comply with any "additional instructions" my grandfather provides.

"What does he mean, 'additional instructions'?" Preston demanded when Weggers first read that clause to us, two days ago, after all of us had been summoned back to Rush Creek for the funeral. "It's not like he's around to tell us what to do."

"I'm afraid I can't say more," Weggers said, loftily. "It will make more sense *in time*."

He deposited those words into the air like a television chef sprinkling finishing salt—the first moment when it became clear he wasn't on our side.

Today, apparently, is "in time." Weggers summoned us with a group text: *Your first instruction is to appear in my office at 5 p.m. on the day following your grandfather's burial.*

When we were assembled, he handed me a letter-sized envelope containing a single sheet of paper, typed and signed in my grandfather's arthritic lifelong rancher's hand. "Read it out loud," Weggers said.

"I'd rather read it to myself first."

He shook his head. "Out loud."

It's like my granddad is speaking through a pushy, bald medium. Weggers just needs a crystal ball and some patter about the spirits from beyond, and he could be a fortune teller in a back-alley tent.

Now he pushes the sheet of paper back into my hands. "Go on."

I continue reading from where I left off:

You'll work as the Hott Springs Eternal spa and salon recep-tionist for sixty days, starting no later than forty-eight hours from the date of this letter. The spa is open six days a week from

10 to 6; you'll sit at the front desk for those hours, minus a thirty-minute lunch break. You'll live in Hott Springs staff housing for the duration of your duties. And lest you think this is an opportunity to phone it in, the spa must operate profitably during your tenure, *without your personal financial contribution.*

The numbers swim in front of my eyes, so it takes a minute for the full meaning to sink in. Receptionist. Front desk.

People. Polite small talk. All day long.

Way to hit me when I'm down, Granddad.

I close my eyes, half hoping that when I open them again, this will all be a bad dream.

"It doesn't have to be Quinn, does it?" Preston asks. "One of us could do it. This is so not Quinn's thing."

He's right about that. I think of Freya's words to me: *I'm a people person, and you're a things-and-ideas person. It would never have worked long term.*

Those words hurt like hell when she delivered them, but she was only telling me what other people in my life had already taught me. Better to know your limits, right?

I give Preston a half nod of thanks.

"It has to be Quinn," Weggers says. "Your grandfather is very clear that the instructions have to be followed to a *T*. We'll set up a webcam so I can check on Quinn periodically to make sure he's fulfilling the terms."

"You'll—what?" Rhys's mouth hangs open.

"As your grandfather's lawyer *and* his executor, it's my job to make sure the conditions get met."

"And if the conditions *don't* get met?" Rhys asks.

"Then the land passes to Blue Iron Mining."

"Are you—are you *shitting* us?" Preston demands. "Why the hell would he…?"

But he trails off because the answer's obvious. Even though we don't want to live on the land, Granddad knew exactly how much we'd hate the idea of stripping it for profit.

Just like that, I get it. I understand my grandfather's game. And I think my brothers do, too, because when I look up, they're all looking back at me with alarm on their faces.

"We're next," Preston says. "Aren't we? Because he couldn't get us back to Rush Creek any other way, he decided to do it from beyond the grave. If he's gonna do this to Quinn, he's gonna do it to all of us." He turns to Weggers. "He's got some equally evil scheme up his sleeve for each of us. Doesn't he?"

Weggers smiles, mean and pleased. "I'm afraid I can't say. Your grandfather was quite clear that all this happens on a need-to-know basis."

This guy is enjoying himself way too much.

"Look," I say, trying to calm myself down because throwing a temper tantrum won't get me anywhere. "I can see he's trying to make a point. Forcing me back to Rush Creek. Humbling me or whatever."

Because the letter echoes the fight my grandfather and I had when I finally told him that, like my older brothers, I wasn't coming back to Rush Creek to run the ranch.

C'mon, Quinn. If you can establish a multibillion-dollar biotech company, surely *you can handle this job.*

Unless you can't.

From beyond the grave, my granddad is still trying to best me at a game I never agreed to play.

"Did you know about this?" Preston asks Hanna. Not accusing, exactly, but wary.

She's pale when we all turn to look at her, her skin even lighter than usual against the backdrop of her short, nearly black hair. "No. God, no. Swear I didn't. I knew he had something up his sleeve after none of you guys showed up for his eighty-fifth birthday party, but then when no evil plan materialized in the last two years, I thought…" She closes her eyes. "I underestimated him. Or overestimated him."

There's a collective sigh of relief. Hanna's constitutionally incapable of lying, and we all know it. None of us wanted to believe she would've let this happen, but it's still a relief to know she didn't.

Because…Jesus, what a mind fuck.

My brain jumps around, trying to find a way out, but there isn't one—not that I can see.

This isn't like jury duty. I can't claim that I'm so essential elsewhere that I'm exempt. And truthfully, now's not the worst time to take a break from my company, MedThena.

But that doesn't mean I belong at Hott Spot, either. Especially not if it means taking someone else's place.

"I can't steal a receptionist's job," I say.

For a moment, this freezes Weggers. Apparently he's not such a dick that he can take pleasure in someone losing their job over my grandfather's twisted joke.

Hanna coughs. We all turn to look at her.

"Actually, our receptionist hasn't shown up for the last five days," she says quietly, rubbing her temple as if her head hurts. "We're not sure what's up with her. The staff's been filling in till we sort it out—but it would be great to have you there. And if she does come back, we could always have her work up at the main resort desk. There's going to be plenty of work with me heading into maternity leave."

She sounds weary, and for the first time, I register that her exhaustion isn't just grief. My sister has always been the strongest, healthiest person I know, but right now? She looks like someone wrung her out. A knot forms behind my rib cage. My brothers are right: I'm not a people person. And I've been a bad brother. But holy God, I love my sister. As a kid, she was a stubborn, often-angry spark plug of a tiny human who drove us halfway to distraction, but growing up in Rush Creek wouldn't have been the same without her.

God, I wish we'd done better by her. I flick a look at Preston, wondering if he feels any guilt for the chain reaction he started when he left Rush Creek, but he's staring at his phone. Of course he is. Preston's always working.

Hanna sighs. "I've been trying to help out up at the spa where I can, since everyone's filling in at the reception desk."

"On top of all her other jobs," says a voice from the doorway. Easton, her husband, leans there, handsome, well dressed, and usually easy going, but his expression at the moment is anything but.

"Easton, please, not right now," Hanna says.

"They need to know. They need to know how it is for you. How you took care of your granddad. How hard you work."

Hanna presses her fingers to her forehead, wincing.

Easton's at her side instantly. "Is the headache back?" he demands.

"Yes, but—" She leans down, groaning. "God."

"What? What is it?"

She's gray.

Something turns over in my brain, an alarm signal. I'm not a doctor, but I spend an absurd amount of time in medical offices and hospitals, and I've read every warning poster so many times they're engraved on my soul.

Hanna moans. "Ow," she says, cradling her head in her hands.

"For fuck's sake," I say, panic kicking into high gear. "Call 911."

2

QUINN

"You shoulda said something," I growl at Hanna. She's sitting up in her hospital bed, looking immensely pregnant and very tired but much less gray and woozy. It's a huge relief to see her more or less herself again. They're letting us in to see her—but only one at a time, to keep her stress levels down. I think it's a good choice: Five Hott brothers at one time would send anyone's blood pressure through the ceiling. Having spent several hours with the four others in the waiting room, pacing like caged wolves, I'm qualified to speak to this.

"Quinn," she says, smiling at me. "You were worried, huh?"

I don't answer; we both know I was, and we both know I won't say so. Instead, I sit down in the chair next to the bed. And then, unable to help myself, I bend my head down to her belly and rest my cheek against the curve of it, above where the fetal monitor is sending a steady heartbeat to one of the machines at her bedside.

I sit up to find her giving me a hard but sympathetic look.

"Give me your hand," she commands. "She's turning somersaults."

She takes my hand with her IV-free one and clasps it to her abdomen. As soon as she does, I feel her belly give a seismic roll, almost a bounce. And holy shit. There's a person in there.

Of course, I knew there was, but experiencing it first-hand is still deeply pleasing, the way all confirmation of hypothesis is. That's part of why I love science so much.

My eyes prickle, and I pull my hand away.

"She's fine, Quinny." Her voice is tender, which is surprising because Hanna is one of the most sarcastic people I know. She's also the only person who calls me Quinny—the only person on earth I'd allow to do it.

"I've been a bad brother."

She sighs. "Not the worst. You sent me a wedding present."

"I should have been there." The wedding was eighteen months ago. Only Tucker and Shane were there, the rest of us mired in work, convinced we were too busy to make the trip. A decision I now wish I could take back.

"You send Christmas presents."

I whisper, "My assistant sends Christmas presents."

She smiles. "Because you tell her to."

I close my eyes tight. "I told her once, and she made it a repeating item in her calendar."

"You're too honest. You could've just taken the compliment."

"I couldn't. You know I couldn't." Because in a lot of

ways, Hanna and I are two peas. Blunt, unpolished, gruff, prone to saying the wrong thing at the wrong time, not great at showing love. All the Hotts are a bit that way—but Hanna and I are the king and queen.

"I know," she admits, shaking her head and laughing.

Jesus, I've missed her. And I meant what I said: I've been a bad brother.

"May I?"

I hold my hand out again in the direction of her belly. She takes it and positions it over the pitch and roll of my niece.

"You're such a softie." She says it very quietly, like she knows I wouldn't want anyone to overhear.

"I'm not."

"You need to let more people see this side of you."

I shake my head because I gave that a shot with Freya, and it didn't work out so well.

"This is what you and I do. We assume people don't like us. But what I'm learning is that sometimes it's *us*, building walls so we don't get hurt like we did when we were kids. You have to take it on faith that they *do* like you and proceed accordingly."

I squint at her. "That feels like a bad bet."

She gives me a sharp look.

"Unscientific," I add.

She shrugs. "People aren't very science-y."

We're quiet for a minute. Then she says, "You don't have to do it, you know."

"Do...?"

"What Grandfather said in the will. I'll be fine, no matter what. I was fine before—working for the Wilders."

"But you love this more—working at Hott Springs Eternal."

"Yes," she says. "I do. I love it because Granddad and I did it together…"

Grief streaks across her face. She loved our grandfather. She saw a heart of gold under his crusty, manipulative surface. Part of me had hoped she was right, but the will proves she wasn't.

She collects herself because she's Hanna and growing up with five brothers taught her not to show weakness. "…and because it's on the family land, and because for the first time in my life I've built something that's—well, that's *mine*. My efforts, my results. And people come to me and tell me that I've given them a wedding weekend they won't ever forget, and—" She lifts her shoulders, palms out. "For all the reasons. But," she says, "I get it. You can't walk away from a multibillion-dollar business and come here and sit at a reception desk—that was just a fantasy Granddad had, that if he got you here, somehow…"

She trails off.

"I'd stay."

She sighs. "Yeah. I mean, I'm sure that's what he was thinking."

We don't look at each other. When Preston left, we were all in it together. But as each of my brothers shook off Rush Creek, there were fewer of us left behind. Hanna and I were the last two standing, and then…well, then I left her, too. And it's hard to forgive myself for that, especially now. Because maybe Easton's right and we let this happen to her.

"Easton's full of shit," she says, reading my mind. "This isn't your fault. Preeclampsia's a common pregnancy risk.

I'm glad you guys are here, and I hope you'll stay—well, as long as you feel like you can." She runs a hand through her short hair. "But I don't want you to give up your life for me. What about MedThena?"

"I'm overdue for a vacation."

"This is more than a vacation."

"A sabbatical, then."

She's still squinting suspiciously at me.

I don't want to tell her the truth—that in the waiting room, I made a bargain with God. If Hanna was okay, if the baby was okay, I'd do...well, anything.

Even figure out how to people.

I wonder if Rhys made a similar pact with whatever being he prays to. He stopped muttering about *deadhand control* and contesting the will right around the time the doctor came into the waiting room to tell us Hanna and the baby would be okay.

"My company will be fine without me for two months," I say. "We're waiting on the results of a clinical trial."

"But will you be fine without your work?" she asks, narrowing her eyes.

Hanna's always been able to read me better than anyone else.

"Don't you worry about that."

"You don't have to fix anything. Or...atone for anything. You don't *owe* me anything.

"I'm not doing this for you," I say.

"Like hell you're not."

"You have to trust me."

She frowns. "You all used to say that when we were kids before you tied me to a tree and tickled me."

I laugh, remembering. "We were awful."

We were, like most siblings, but also...

Well. There were other times, too. The time when Rhys's new bike got stolen and we all pooled our savings to get him a new one; the time when Preston got dumped and we decided the best way to cheer him up was to subject him to a week's worth of bad pranks...

It worked, I'll add. Although we never got the ketchup out of the sheets.

Maybe she's remembering a similar moment because her grin deepens then disappears. "You don't have to do this."

I know she means it and that she'd forgive me if I turned around and went back to Boston, but that's not the point.

I think about the vow I made and broke—the first and only one. The original one. Maybe it wasn't my fault, but I still hold myself one-fifth responsible. And I will never break another one. Especially not one made on my sister's and niece's lives.

I'm still pissed as hell at my grandfather for putting me in this position. But I can do this. I don't have to be *good* at it —in fact, I might be extra bad at it, to spite my granddad. But I can still do it. For Hanna. And...the little spud.

"I do," I say. "And I will."

3

SONYA

I've been looking forward to my birthday celebration for weeks, and not only because it's an opportunity to soak in the hot springs with my favorite people. Because I have A Plan. Possibly the Best Plan Ever. If I were a comic villain, I'd be wringing my hands and cackling, but instead I'm biting my lip and biding my time.

"Why did it take us so long to think of this?" my friend and surrogate mom Bella cries, holding up her glass of champagne, curling her toes happily as she stretches her legs under the steaming water at Hott Spot, the day spa where most of us work.

My coworker Reggie rakes fingers through her damp multicolored hair. "Because it's too obvious," she says. "Like when you live in the same place for years but never go to the museum there because that's a thing tourists do, plus you can do it any time, so you just don't."

"Oh God," Serenity, another coworker, groans. "I lived in DC for four years during college and never once set foot in the Smithsonian. I can't tell you how many times I've kicked myself since then." She touches her champagne flute to Bella's, and we all follow suit, clinking glasses and beaming at each other.

We're sitting on the edge of the spring, legs in the water, cooling off with a glass of champagne. Today is both my birthday and Bella's, and we always celebrate together. The last few years, we've enlisted some of our friends and coworkers to make things even more festive. Last year we did that iFly thing, the one that's like skydiving over a giant blower, and the year before we did a super-fun glamping trip organized by a local outdoor adventure outfit. Three years ago, we rented one of those beer bikes and pedaled around Bend, getting slowly sloshed on microbrews.

This year, we needed to celebrate on a budget, so I floated the idea of a party on the broad stone patio next to Hott Spot's pools. Even though all of us but Bella work at the day spa and salon, I was the only one who'd ever been in the hot springs. Shoemaker's children and all that.

So here we are, enjoying cheese and crackers, champagne, and chocolate-covered strawberries under the stars of a mild June night in Rush Creek. Candles flicker around us, supplemented only by the underwater lights and a few solar-powered lamps spaced out around the gorgeously landscaped patio.

"Open your presents," Serenity instructs Bella and me.

"I don't want to get them wet!" I protest.

"I gotchoo," she says, jumping up.

"I want that bathing suit," Lily, our other coworker, tells her.

"It's *hot*," I agree.

Serenity puts a hand on a hip and twirls to model her

vintage suit for us—sweetheart neckline, thick straps, boy-cut hemline, the cranberry vivid against her cool brown skin. "Maya's Wardrobe, baby."

"We could be one of those lineups in *Cosmo* or something," Lily says. "'Does your bathing suit reflect your personal style?'" She mimics the breathless style of a glossy magazine headline.

We all look at each other and burst out laughing. She's right. Our suits *are* us: Not just Serenity's find but also Bella's functional racer-style one piece, Lily's teeny-tiny string bikini, Reggie's board shorts and repurposed sports bra, which bares pale skin mostly obscured by colorful tattoos. My suit is vintage, like Serenity's, a gingham high-waisted bikini with a cap-sleeved top.

"Who knew you could express your whole personality with half a yard of fabric?" I ask.

"Seriously," Lily says.

Serenity folds a towel on the stone next to us. Reggie and Lily get into the action, too, drying their hands so they can grab the small collection of presents from the table nearby and set them down on the towel.

"You go first," Bella says. "Youth and beauty before old age and wisdom."

"Forty-eight's not that old," I remind her.

"I'm the oldest out of all of you! And you"—she points at me—"are a baby!"

"I'm almost thirty," I point out. "Mei and Catalina are both younger than I am." Two more of our coworkers who couldn't be here tonight.

Bella rolls her eyes.

"The rest of us aren't that far behind you," Reggie reminds her.

"You're almost ten years younger than I am!" Bella says, pushing curly ash-blond hair out of her brown eyes. "I feel like I'm a million years old." There are big circles in the pale skin under her eyes and a tautness around her mouth that's been there for months. I hate seeing it—I'm so glad I can help make it go away.

She pushes a gift at me. "Open it."

I untie the ribbon and carefully remove the tissue paper while my friends all groan impatiently and urge me to hurry it up.

Reaching in, I pull out a handful of cloth. It takes me a moment to figure out what it is—then I understand. "Bella! You shouldn't have!"

It's the expensive blue-and-white Japanese fabric I admired the last time she and I were in the quilt store together. The one I said reminded me of a shirt my mom always wore when I was a kid. The one I said I couldn't/wouldn't/shouldn't buy because I had no idea yet what I would do with it and I'd forbidden myself to impulse-buy fabric.

"'Course I should have," Bella says. "Anything for my baby girl. And your mom would definitely have wanted you to have it."

She reaches out and takes my hand, her smaller but strong fingers wrapping warm around mine, and tears fill my eyes. Bella not only took the best possible care of me after my own mom died when I was eleven but she's kept my mom alive for me more than anyone, telling me stories of the two of them working together in my mom's salon, giving me the advice she thinks my mom would have wanted me to have, buying me gifts that remind her of my mom. Bella's said on a few occasions that I feel more like her daughter than her own does, and while that makes me sad for both of them...it also makes me feel anchored in the world, in the best possible way. Losing my mom so young was hard—but the way Bella stepped up for me has always been all silver lining.

"Quit it, y'all—you're going to make us weepy," Reggie grouses, and Bella and I give each other one last squeeze and let go.

I open the rest of my gifts—teas from Reggie, a hilarious memoir about a woman who works in the beauty biz from Lily, nice soaps from Serenity that I recognize as ones I've admired openly from the Hott Spot stock. Then it's Bella's turn. Lily's given her a different book by the same author, Reggie's bought her a cookbook, and Serenity's gotten her a scarf that I also recognize as being from Hott Spot's retail selection.

"Supporting product sales," Serenity says when she sees me smile at the scarf.

"Good girl," I say.

We've been working hard to boost the spa's retail sales the last couple of months, and I appreciate her after-hours enthusiasm.

"Now yours," I say to Bella—I've been waiting all night for this moment. I hand her the small pink bag tied up with loads of curling ribbon, and she reaches in and extracts the envelope from among the tissue paper.

I hold my breath. I'm ninety-nine percent sure this is

going to be a huge hit, but it's a bit of a flier...and I don't know for sure.

She slides a finger under the envelope flap, tips it up, and slides the card out.

And bursts into tears.

I rush to give her a damp hug, her arms and cheeks still warm from the hot springs but her bathing suit cool where it touches my bare skin. Her shoulders shake. She's not just crying—she's sobbing, and I'm suddenly alarmed. Maybe I've done the wrong thing. Maybe this was a misguided idea...

"It wasn't supposed to make you cry!"

She pulls back, taking my arms. "Sonya, sweetheart, you have *no idea* how much this means to me."

I almost swoon with relief.

Holding the card up, she lets the rest of us see it.

"It's a job offer," she sniffs. "Start date—two months from today. Starting salary same as my last assistant manager position. Hours—flexible."

There's a collective gasp, followed by, "Oh, wow," and "Holy shit, Sonya," and "God, hon, that's so cool," and a ton of big hugs. I've kept this a secret from the rest of my staff, too, wanting to make a hundred percent sure I could make it happen before I got anyone's hopes up. Reggie, Bella, Serenity, and Lily were the A-team at my mom's salon, back in the day, but they haven't all worked together in one place since. So this is a big deal to them, too.

And it's a huge deal to me. I've been working toward this for...well, for years. Ever since we sold my mom's salon and her people—*my people*—scattered to the winds. Now the last of them will be back in the fold.

Bella grabs my hand again. "Oh God, Sonya, you have no idea. I—"

Now she's crying harder.

"Shh," I say, arms around her. "It's okay, Bell."

"It is *now*," she says. "But—"

She lets her hand fall to her lap, swipes the back of her other across her eyes. "You saved my ass. You wouldn't believe how good your timing is, hon." She bites her lip. "I lost my job at the dollar store yesterday."

Reggie makes a soft sound of dismay. "What happened?"

But we all have a pretty good guess. Bella's daughter dropped off the radar a couple of years ago—substance-use issues—and surfaces only to ask for money, so Bella's raising her two grandkids. Plus her mom has Alzheimer's and has started wandering. When one of them needs Bella's help, she has to be there—and that's been a big problem for her bosses at her last few jobs. So much so that for the last nine months, she hasn't been able to get a beauty industry job at all—even though she's one of the best, savviest salon managers I've ever known.

"I got a call from school that Abel had gotten in a fight," Bella says.

We all nod.

"I had to take him to the ER for stitches. And then home for a come-to-Jesus."

"Of course you did," Lily says.

"Mr. Fuckweed told me not to bother coming back to work. I said, 'For the rest of today?' and he said, 'Ever.'"

"Jeez, Bella," Serenity says. "What the hell?"

"He was a dick," she says. "But...it's okay now. It's okay. Because Sonya—oh my God. Best birthday present *ever*."

She hugs me again and whispers, "You're the best."

I hug her back. "You know I've been wanting to hire you since you left Beatific," I say. "I wish I could start you sooner than two months, but that's literally the first date when I can make a paycheck happen."

The whole product-sales initiative, the one that Serenity supported by giving Bella the scarf, has been about this. Two months from now, the product sales will finally have increased enough that I'll have the cash flow to bring Bella on. In the meantime, I've pinched every last penny from our budget to make this happen. I've had my fingers crossed for weeks that I'd be ready to make my announcement for her birthday.

"No, it's perfect," Bella says. "I have just enough savings to carry me through till then. But Sonya," she says, her voice shaky, "I won't be reliable. Not the way you deserve. There'll be times I can't—"

"You'll be reliable enough for me," I break in. "I know your constraints, and I can set us up to share the load in a way that will work for me. No more getting fired every time some little thing goes wrong, okay? We're gonna have your back now."

Like you had mine all those years ago, I don't say out loud, but I think it so loudly that it feels like I've said it.

And Bella must know because she clutches my hand again, and this time she doesn't let go.

THE NEXT MORNING, I'm eating a bowl of granola with milk, nursing a mild-to-moderate champagne hangover, and admiring my new fabric when my phone rings.

"Hello?" I say.

"This is Detective Faranheim at the Rush Creek Police Department," a woman's voice says.

My heart pounds. My dad. It's gotta be my dad. Is he—

"Have I reached Sonya Rossi?"

"Y-yes," I stammer.

No. It can't be my dad. They'd show up at my door, right, if he were hurt or worse... *Calm down,* I coach myself. He just must have gotten himself in trouble. Which makes sense. It's been a while since he went off the rails. I've been subconsciously waiting for the other shoe to drop.

"Did you recently employ a Maura Stall?"

I'm so startled that it *doesn't* have to do with my dad that for a moment I can't answer.

"Uh. Yes. She's the receptionist at the spa I manage—"

"Ms. Stall is a person of interest in our investigation of money embezzled from Rush Creek Presbyterian," Detective Faranheim says. "We have some questions for you about her—to aid in our investigation. Nothing to do with you personally or your business. At least...we hope not."

Oh jeez. I take a moment to catch my breath. Not my dad. Whew. "I could come down—yes. In a half hour or so? On my way to work?"

She tells me how to find her—it won't be hard in Rush Creek's small police station—and we hang up.

I'm in the process of packing up my stuff when my addled brain finally catches up with the news I've received.

Maura. My receptionist for the last eight months.

A suspected embezzler.

Which explains why she didn't show up to work this week. Without phoning in. I texted her a few times then called and left voicemails, but no response. At first I hoped it was just a bad case of the flu, but yesterday Hanna and I admitted to ourselves that she's probably gone. Detective Faranheim's new info sheds a lot of light.

I pause—feeling wildly unsettled, unpack my laptop, and set it on the kitchen table.

I open it, slowly, the way you do when you don't actually want confirmation of what you already suspect, and navigate to my favorite spreadsheet, which is named *Yes We Can Hire Bella!* It's based off a report generated by...yup, Maura.

The spreadsheet shows our steadily rising product sales: shampoo, conditioner, soap, lotions, creams, makeup, T-shirts, scarves—you name it, they're the key to my being able to hire Bella and finally bring the whole team back together. To achieve my goal, I brought in loads of new products, put my people through product-sales training, and deputized Maura to track how well sales were going.

Answer, according to Maura's report: *Amazingly! Product is flying off the shelf!*

Except looking at this spreadsheet, something's off. I scroll through the numbers, my heart speeding up. I do some math, then some more math.

It's not adding up.

I start ticking through boxes, scrutinizing formulas... and that's when I find it.

What the fuuu...?

And then... No.

Oh hell no.

My blood pressure spikes. The skin on my forehead tightens painfully.

I copy the spreadsheet, fixing the formulas in the second version. And...oh *shit*.

I have to give Maura the benefit of the doubt—innocent until proven guilty. It could be an honest mistake. I text her: *Can we talk about the product spreadsheet?*

My phone dings immediately. Whew. If she'd done something, she wouldn't have replied so quickly—

New phone. Think you have the wrong person.

My heart sinks. *You're not Maura?*

No, sorry!

Then I remember I actually know Maura's roommate, a woman named Gia who I took a kayaking class with one time. I dig up her number and text her.

This is Sonya—we took that kayaking class together? I can't reach Maura, can you have her get in touch with me?

The three dots appear immediately.

Sorry, she didn't leave me forwarding info

A pause, then three dots wriggle, disappear, wriggle again.

If you find out where she is, let me know because she owes me rent

I try not to panic, but it's practically impossible.

Will do, I text back, but I'm pretty sure only a police detective is going to find out where Maura is...and maybe not her, either.

The math on my spreadsheet is off by an outrageous amount. More than half my product has somehow gone missing. The woman in charge of that product has also gone missing...and apparently she's suspected of embezzling money from a house of God.

Someone who'd steal from a church might not balk at toying with the numbers at a for-profit beauty spa. At disappearing tens of thousands of dollars of revenue.

I compare the two calculations—Maura's and mine—one more time.

The difference between the revenue I was expecting and the revenue that shows up when I fix the rigged formulas?

Almost double what I'd budgeted for Bella's salary for her first few months.

My throat tightens.

Okay, I tell myself. *Okay. It's going to be all right.*

But at the moment, I'm having trouble seeing how.

I DRIVE from the police station to the spa, heart heavy. My whole body feels leaden.

Detective Faranheim took my statement about the product sales, copied both the spreadsheets, and snagged screenshots from our sales management software. She didn't seem surprised by what she saw; she just nodded. Apparently they think Maura's main game was pilfering my products, not embezzling from the church, which Detective Faranheim called an "opportunistic add-on."

From what they've been able to suss out about Maura—not her real name, of course—she's part of a well-run ring. Ring members pilfer beauty products wherever they can put a staffer and resell them on the gray market. It's been almost impossible to track down individual culprits, and while they're making some progress on the leaders, they don't think they'll have answers for months still.

And I definitely won't get the money back anytime soon. I can make an insurance claim, of course...but there are no guarantees, and these things take time, especially when there's an actual investigation in progress.

Definitely more than two months.

Which means that even if I don't rehire for the receptionist position, I still don't have enough money to hire Bella.

The thought of telling her that turns my stomach.

I can't accept it.

I *will* make this work, somehow. I *will*. For Bella, for her mom, for her grandkids. Because she's as much family to me as anyone left in this world, even my dad.

I'll just double down. Bring in even more, better product. Increase incentives for my people. Upsell the shit out of everything I can at the front desk. I'm suddenly thankful I'm our temporary receptionist because even though a lot of sales get made by stylists and aestheticians, the receptionist seals the deal. We need someone at the desk who knows the clients, who knows the products inside out, and who has a lot of experience with customer service. I wouldn't want to be breaking in a newbie kid right now.

I. Can. Do. This.

I won't let you down, Bella.

I drive the curving roads that lead onto the ranchland owned by my boss Hanna's family. For years, it was a working ranch, but a couple of years ago, Hanna and her granddad—the only two family members still living on the land—decided to take advantage of the hot springs that had recently burst to the surface. They converted the ranch to a wedding venue with its own spa. The whole operation is called Hott Springs Eternal, and I manage the day spa and salon—Hott Spot.

I pull into the spa parking lot and unfold my already weary body from the front seat, trundling toward the spa's waiting area, which is where we have our reception desk and retail operations.

I'm not the first one in, which isn't super surprising. Lily, who's our attendant and in charge of room setup and cleanup and handing out robes and towels, often beats me here for morning prep.

But when I step inside, there's someone else sitting in my chair at the front desk. Which makes no sense because Maura's gone—and also because the person behind the desk is a stranger.

It's a man with long, wild reddish-brown hair, a beard that hasn't seen a trim in probably months, and thick, assertively male eyebrows with a whole zip code of their own. He's sprawled out, wide legged, in the receptionist's chair, dwarfing it.

He's also vaguely familiar, which means he's probably the groom Hanna said she'd send my way, a guy whose bride put her foot down at the eleventh hour and demanded he spend a day getting "the works." Lily must have left the door open when she came in, and he helped himself to a warmer place to wait, even though it's not yet ten.

"There are plenty of chairs in the waiting area if you need a place to sit!" I call out cheerily, gesturing at the comfy armchairs on one side of the room. "That one's mine." I approach the desk. "Let me block some time out for you. You're in luck because we've got plenty of room for walk-ins this morning. I've got someone who can do the hair and beard, and I can do your eyebrows if you want that, too."

His eyes widen. "What's wrong with the hair, beard, and eyebrows?"

Yikes. I definitely got the wrong end of that one. "I'm so sorry! I was expecting a client with a beard this morning, and I totally assumed you were him. But you're...obviously not. You must be here for something else. Massage? Or a dip in the springs?" Ugh—it's never good to start the day off insulting a potential client, even if he's *sitting in my chair.* "There's a ten-percent-off coupon here with your name on it, an apology for my making assumptions about who you were—"

"No." He scowls. "I'm not here for any of that. I'm here because due to circumstances beyond my control and yours and probably even God's, I'm your new receptionist."

I laugh, reflexively. And then I realize I'm the only one laughing and my laughter sort of...falls off a cliff.

"Yeah," the bearded stranger says. "It's not even remotely funny. Although I think my grandfather would have disagreed. I'm pretty sure he's laughing all the way to hell."

"Your grandfather," I repeat. I'm so lost, I couldn't find my best self with a compass and map.

He stands and holds out a hand. And I realize he actually wasn't manspreading. He was taking up all that space in the chair because he's legitimately huge—at least six-two and built like a warrior god. He wears worn jeans and a T-shirt that reads, *I'm a chemist. To save time, let's assume I'm never wrong.*

"Quinn Hott," he says. "Hanna's brother, Fox Hott's second-youngest grandkid. And your new receptionist."

A lot of things happen all at once. First, I realize why this guy is so familiar—because he looks vaguely like my boss who also happens to be his sister and because he graduated from my high school a few years ahead of me. But mainly because I've seen him in the news from time to time. He's not famous like Elon Musk or Mark Zuckerberg, but because he's a local boy turned science genius and successful business owner, he's taken his turn in the *Oregonian*, the *Rush Creek Gazette*, and the *Bend Bulletin*. If I remember right, he figured out how to get rid of the side effects of an ALS drug, founded a company with a friend, and raked in money.

Second, automatically, I take his hand. It's ridiculously huge, because he's huge, and extremely warm. My hand disappears inside it as we shake, and entirely against my will, something goes molten in my lower belly.

"But you *have* a job," I say stupidly. "You founded a company." And then, recovering some brain function. "Sonya Rossi. Spa manager. How—what—? *Receptionist?*"

This must be Hanna's doing, but that makes no sense because Hanna was clear from day one that she wanted to give me complete autonomy in the spa. She's *never* once butted in, and definitely not by installing her brother at my front desk.

Her brother. Co-owner of the land this business sits on. I'm not sure whether he's a co-owner of the business—I don't think so, so he's not actually my boss—but at the very least, he has my boss's ear.

This day has gone from disastrous to…

I swallow a whimper. "Did Hanna send you?"

"She's in the hospital," Quinn says.

"Wait, what? In the hospital?" I practically lunge for my phone. I set it on Do Not Disturb during my meeting with Detective Faranheim, but I can see now that there's a message from her.

Please don't worry, totally okay, but in the hospital. My brother's coming in to help at the front desk. Long story but he has to. I'll let him explain.

Oh God! I quickly type out, *Hanna so glad you're okay! Hugs!!* then turn back to Quinn. "Is she really all right?"

For the first time, his scowl softens a bit—but his voice is still gruff. "She's fine. Preeclampsia. High blood pressure. They caught it early."

"Can she have visitors? I'll go over there at lunch. I can stop and pick up— Do you know what she needs? Does she have everything she wants from home? Does she need real food? Hospital food is a nightmare." I'm already planning the stops I'll make on my way to the hospital—her house for anything she needs, Rush Creek Blooms for balloons and flowers, Rush to Read Books for something to make bed rest suck marginally less.

He gives me an impatient look. "Easton brought her stuff. She's fine. She'll be home later today. She doesn't need visitors right now—she needs rest."

I flinch—but I shouldn't be surprised. Quinn is Hanna's brother, and Hanna's not exactly known for her diplomacy. Apparently it runs in the family.

Hang on. I need a rewind here.

"You're my new receptionist," I say slowly. "Hanna's text says you *have to* work at the desk. What does she mean by 'have to'?"

Because my plan calls for *me* to be at the front desk. Spreading sunshine and upselling like crazy and narrowing our product deficit slowly but surely.

He raises his eyebrows. "Hanna didn't tell you about the will?"

"Your grandfather's will?"

"Yeah."

I shake my head. I hugged her at Fox's funeral, both of us crying, but we didn't get a chance to talk.

"If my siblings and I want to keep the land, we have to do whatever he tells us."

"The land...? You mean *this* land?"

He nods. "And in my case, what he told me is that I have to be the Hott Spot receptionist for two months."

I'm having trouble tracking. "'He'? You mean your grandfather told you? How?"

"Letter," he says succinctly. "He wrote me a fucking letter. He had a sick sense of humor, and he thought it would be a howl to put the guy who's definitely not a people person on a front-desk job."

I bite my lip. Because he's just expressed my worst fear out loud. This is the worst time possible to put a "not a people person" at this desk. When I desperately need sales to go up, not down.

At the same time, I'm not going to say that out loud to a guy who's clearly going through some stuff of his own.

"I bet you're better with people than you think you are," I tell him.

The look he gives me is ripe with scorn. "No need to butter me up," he says. "I know who I am."

"I wasn't—"

"Look," he says. "You've already told me I need a haircut and a beard trim—and what was the other thing? Oh yeah. Eyebrows."

"Please—forget what I said about the hair. I thought you were someone else."

"Who obviously needed a haircut."

"No, I—"

"It's fine. We both know I'm not pretty enough for the job," he says.

It's true he doesn't look like any receptionist I've ever hired for a salon or spa front desk before. More like a cross between a mad scientist and the mountain man you get snowed in with in a romance novel. In the tiny one-room cabin on the mountain with the real bearskin rug, the blazing fire, the super-rich dark chocolate, and only one bed. The one whose alphahole demeanor turns out to be just what you needed during sex.

Not "pretty," no. Something else entirely.

"You were probably hoping to hire someone like you, with the makeup—and the hair—" He gestures with a blunt finger, a twirl to describe the shape of the curls that I spent twenty minutes ironing into my hair this morning.

If things weren't already bad enough this morning, I might call a time-out and say, *Hey, dude, I look like this because it's part of my job to look like this, and it's no better for you to judge me for the time I put into my appearance than for me to judge you for the time you haven't—which I didn't, by the way.*

But I haven't made this spa a huge success by losing my cool when people are difficult. Hott Spot is what I've come to think of as a high-emotion spa. Half our customers are locals, but half are wedding parties—and they're always full of the feels when they come to us. Taking care of them at the reception desk is a customer-service job through and through; you have to smile and chat clients up and make them feel heard. Even when *you* get sworn at by a mother-of-the-bride who's been pushed past the point of no return. This may or may not have happened to me. Approximately a hundred times.

My staff and I have worked hard to perfect the calm, soothing atmosphere here, to make it an escape from the ups and downs and stresses of weddings. Pale walls, soft music, beautiful and comfortable waiting-area furniture, shelves filled with luxury products and gifts to pamper yourself with.

I take a deep breath. *Just another difficult customer,* I tell myself and find that part of me, deep down, where there's always a smile for someone who's having a tougher day than I am. But when I aim my best smile at him, all I get back is a deeper frown.

"I—I still don't understand," I tell him. "About the receptionist thing. And the will. Can't you just...say no? I didn't think you and your brothers even wanted the land."

Even if I hadn't become good friends with Hanna—and even gotten to know Fox a bit—over the last year, I'd know the story—it's Rush Creek lore. The Hott brothers all left Rush Creek over their granddad's fierce objections to seek their fortunes—and they all made it big and never came back. He tried pretty much everything in his power to get them to return home and take over the ranch: bribes, threats, blackmail, coercion—but no dice.

And now it looks like he's getting his way—after death.

I wished Fox had warned me that I was going to be a pawn in his game.

Quinn's scowl deepens. "It's not about what we want. It's that we have to hold the land for two years or we lose control of it. If I walk away, it's not only me who doesn't get the land. If I don't follow my grandfather's instructions, *none* of us gets the land, including Hanna."

I shake my head, not understanding. "Where does it go?"

His expression darkens. "To Blue Iron Mining."

I flinch. "That's the company that destroyed Jed Wyer's land." I can see the carnage in my mind's eye—stripped forest, the enormous pit, the leaching apparatus—the whole thing abandoned when all the uranium had been extracted, but the land and water no longer usable for... anything, basically. Everyone in town knew about it, and most of us still feel ashamed that we didn't do more to prevent it.

"Yes," he says simply. "The will says that if we don't fulfill all his requirements, the land passes to Blue Iron."

"Why would he do that?"

He throws up his hands. "Because he was smart. Because he knew us. He knew he had to make the consequences intolerable to us or we'd ignore his instructions."

"He was—" My mouth hangs open, all the words

feeling too crass for this pretty, airy room. *A sadist. An asshole. A sadistic asshole.*

"Yes," he says again. "Whatever you're about to say, he was that. Also a man who loved a game of chess. I think that's what this is. A game of chess. And I'm in checkmate."

"So...that's that?" I say helplessly. "You're...?"

He nods. "Your new receptionist."

Guess that's me in checkmate, too.

4

QUINN

She crosses her arms. "Okay," she says briskly. "We've got this. We can make this work."

Her eyes—big and long-lashed—travel from my hair to my face and down my body. They stop on my T-shirt, but she doesn't comment on it. She just bites her lip.

I know what she sees because it's the same thing most people, including Freya, see. A guy who doesn't quite fit. In this case, we're talking about a receptionist job, not a life-time of marital bliss, but the point's the same. A six-foot-plus guy with a shaggy beard and hair and a science T-shirt doesn't make any sense at the front desk of a beauty salon, no matter how much you squint at him.

And it's not surprising that I'm not up to Sonya's standards.

She's beautiful, like a supermodel or an NFL cheer-leader. She has tan skin and long, dark, glossy hair that curls in perfect corkscrew ringlets. Her makeup is eye catching. I don't know shit about women's makeup, but there's glitter on her eyelids and a dark line that wings up at the outer corners of her eyes. Her lashes are thick, and her lips are the color of a reddish plum. She's wearing a wrap dress that swerves deep into a narrow waist and out over delicious curves.

She doesn't look anything like Freya, who was pale and blond, but they're both cut from the same cloth. Shiny, polished, upbeat, sunshine-y. That's why I don't trust Sonya's smiles and politeness. It's so easy to wear them on the surface.

"So the will says...what?" she asks.

I've read the thing over so many times, I have it memorized. "'You'll work as the Hott Springs Eternal spa and salon receptionist for sixty days, starting no later than forty-eight hours from the date of this letter. The spa is open six days a week from ten to six; you'll sit at the front desk for those hours, minus a thirty-minute lunch break.'"

I don't tell her the part about living in ranch housing, since it doesn't affect her.

"And that's it? Nothing about what you have to do while you sit there? And it doesn't say you have to sit there alone, or anything like that?"

"No. That's it."

"Oh—good," she says, perking up, her shoulders slumping a bit with what has to be relief. "Then we're set, I think. So you can just *sit* here, and I'll basically do the rest."

Fifteen minutes ago, *just sitting here* was exactly what I thought I wanted. I should be filled with relief because *just sitting here* means not having to make small talk or explain the benefits of a bottle of shampoo. I should be saying, *Thank you.*

But small insults have a way of building up. Getting

summoned to a town I never intended to come back to. Getting checkmated by Grandfather at a game I never agreed to play. Having to walk away from work just as our efforts on the new drug are paying off. And now this. Two months with Sally Sunshine. Who thinks I need a haircut and, apparently, a personality revamp.

So what comes out of my mouth is, "I can do the job."

"Oh, I'm definitely sure you can. It's more that—"

"If I can explain the benefits of a complex drug to MDs, I can sell scented hand cream."

If I thought that would get under her skin, I was wrong. Her bottom lip curves like she's trying to hide a smile, and she says, cocking her head to one side, "Is that what you think we do? Sell scented hand cream?"

"Isn't it?"

The smile gets bigger. "There's a lot more to it than that. We're not only selling services and product, we're in the business of making space for people to take care of themselves in whatever way feels best to them."

"What does that mean, even?"

"It means exactly what it sounds like," she says.

"And you believe that."

"Yes," she says evenly. "I do. I believe that sometimes people need to feel pretty. And sometimes they need to feel pampered. And that it's important for us to make a place for that. So even if you don't believe that, I need you to..."

She squints at me again.

"Cut my hair?"

She sighs and rolls her eyes, and it gives me a funny sort of pleasure, to have made her grumpy, even if only for a split second, before the expression vanishes. "No. I just need you to...be polite to customers."

"I'm always polite," I say.

She cuts me a well-earned suspicious glance. "Friendly, then," she says. "I need you to be *friendly*." She eyes me again. "And maybe not wear T-shirts with words."

"I don't have any other kinds of shirts."

"You seriously talk to doctors about complex medications in screen-print T-shirts?"

The truth is I haven't talked to doctors in a long time, not since the incident where I went into too much detail about a little-documented side effect and my partner, Banks, gently suggested we pull me off the marketing rotation and let me focus on "doing science"—which is his phrase, not mine.

See also: *not a people person*.

But I don't tell her that. Instead, I shrug. "Doctors like scientists. They like feeling like the people providing their pharma know what they're talking about."

"Well," she says, a smile flirting with the edges of her mouth again, "people coming for salon-and-spa services don't like T-shirts with words. They want to feel like they're walking into a zone of calm and neutrality. They don't want to be confronted."

"You think my T-shirt is confrontational."

"I think it's...not the atmosphere we're trying to create here."

She gestures at the room, and I let my eyes follow her fingers—the products in their neutral and black and white and gold boxes, the bright-colored be-ribboned soaps, the scarves twisted artfully around a sculpted tree.

I don't care what she says, there's nothing calming or neutral about this room. It smells like a garden went to war with a bakery. And the music is probably supposed to imitate the ripples of a waterfall or something, but it's aggressively soothing, like an adult talking down to an angry teenager. Fingernails on my mental chalkboard.

Two months.

Fighting the inevitable—or Sonya—is only going to make this harder.

She's right. The smartest thing I can do here is sit down, shut up, and let her work. Though there are some concessions I'm not willing to make. I do have my grandfather's stubborn streak.

"Okay," I say. "I'll do exactly what the will says and let you do the rest. But I'm not cutting my hair, trimming my beard, or waxing my eyebrows."

Her eyebrows go up. "I didn't say—"

"This is me," I say. "Hair. Beard. Eyebrows. The T-shirts are possibly negotiable. My grooming, or lack thereof, is not."

She closes her eyes tight, then opens them. They're amber, with streaks of lighter and darker brown. I've always been a sucker for pretty eyes.

I look away.

"Deal," she says.

"Deal," I say back.

Her hand's out again, and, grudgingly, I take it and shake. The cool smallness of her hand in mine leaves me with an ambiguous pleasure, like the first drops of too-hot water falling onto bare skin in the shower.

The door swings open. Her gaze snaps to the door, and

her expression flashes instantly into a buoyant smile for our first customer of the day.

I was right; she does wield those smiles like weapons. She can turn them on and off at will.

The knowledge doesn't feel like a victory, though.

Because I'm the one left staring—at her slightly upturned nose and lush mouth, at the fall of her hair over her shoulders.

At that light-up-the-room smile.

It takes me longer than I want to admit to turn away.

5

SONYA

It's a no-win situation.

Obviously I can't tell Quinn he can't sit at the front desk. Doing so would screw him, me, my staff, Hanna—pretty much everyone I care about.

But letting him sit there will, quite possibly, screw Bella. No win.

As soon as I finish checking in our first customer and send her back, I tilt my head, considering him and his six feet of muscle. Mass of chaotic curls. Thick beard.

"What do we tell customers? About why you're here?"

He shrugs. "Security."

It's the first time I've thought he *might* be teasing, but there's no sign of humor on his grim face. Or at least not that I can see around the facial hair.

"No one will believe that."

One of his eyebrows goes up. "What, I don't look like I could protect you?"

Actually, he looks like he'd be equipped to break the

face of anyone who messed with me. That shouldn't be a sexy thought, but sexy thoughts suck at following rules.

No, he's plenty big. And rough looking. He looks like he could take on pretty much any guy I've ever met, which doesn't fit the scientist-businessman mold at all. I guess that's the thing about stereotypes—they do exist for a reason, but if they were always true, we wouldn't need to break them.

"Not all security guys are clean shaven," he grumbles.

"I wasn't thinking that!"

He shrugs. "We don't have to explain me," he says.

"Customers will want to know why you're here."

"New receptionist," he says, shrugging. "The truth is usually the best."

"Okay. Truth it is. Tour first, I guess. Getting you oriented."

Most of my staff's still not in, but I introduce him to Lily and do a quick fly-through, showing him the luxurious interior lounge, the large locker area with its curtained-off stalls and changing rooms, the deck leading out to the hot springs, cold pools, and saunas, as well as the salon, the mani/pedi room, and the treatment rooms.

When we're done with that, I send him back to the front desk, then drag a chair from the staff break room to the reception area and set myself up right next to him. "We can start with the desk stuff," I say.

"It's a phone and a computer. How hard can it be?"

"I'm sure you know there's more to it than that," I say. "You have to learn how to use the point-of-sale software and the scheduling app, too."

He scowls back. "I stand by my question."

"Of course you do," I sigh. I reach for the phone hand-set, then hesitate. "I'm not sure you'll even need to know any of this. I'll be right here the whole time."

"I'm capable of filling in for you while you use the restroom," he says, his scowl deepening. "I won't ruin every-thing in two minutes. You could even take a lunch break."

The idea of leaving Mr. Grumpy Pants alone at the desk for the duration of a lunch break worries me. "I can eat at the desk."

"Right," he says. "Don't leave Quinn alone. He might scare the customers."

"I didn't say—"

He glares. "Yes, you did."

In fairness, I *was* thinking it.

I sigh. So does he.

Okay. So we're not going to be friends. We're just going to...do this. I figure I'll make it as quick and painless as possible. I run him through the phone system, the POS system, and the scheduling app. To his credit—and unsur-prisingly—he's a fast learner, instantly picking up on how to do the easiest tasks and intuiting what else the system might be able to do. Which was never my concern. I know he can handle all the technological components of the job. I just don't know what happens when—

As if answer, the door opens and a client comes in.

"Hello, Nan!" I call out. She's a local, a regular, and a character.

"Hi, Sonya! I'm here for my mustache. Oh!" she says, spotting Quinn. "Who's McDreamy?"

To my surprise, Quinn blushes, splotchy red above the line of his beard.

"Nan," I chide.

"I'm sorry!" she says. "I forgot my manners there for a moment. Right. No objectifying, not even the hot guys. Are they still doing firefighter calendars? Or do we have to give those up, too?"

"I saw that the firefighters in town are putting together a winter fundraiser that includes a calendar where they're all shirtless and cuddling dogs that are up for adoption," I tell her. "So I think calendars are safe for a bit longer."

"It's so complicated," she grouses. "So, McDreamy, what are you doing at Hott Spot? Besides improving the view?"

She winks at Quinn.

"You're incorrigible," I tell her.

She shrugs. "Just seventy-three and fresh out of fucks."

Since Quinn shows no sign of answering Nan's question, I answer for him. "New receptionist. I'm, um, training him. Nan, this is Quinn Hott; Quinn, this is Nan—"

"I know Nan," he says gruffly.

"Quinn Hott!" Nan says, surveying him. "Well, I'll be damned. You've changed a bit since you were last around. I'd heard the Hott boys were back in town—" She stops, chuckling. "Hott boys, hot boys...it never gets old." She points a finger at him. "You're the one who doesn't talk."

"I talk." But the blunt rasp of Quinn's voice more or less proves her point.

"Didn't till you were almost three," she says. "I remember your mama would come into the bakery with you and your brothers, and the rest of them would be chattering and wrestling and begging me for free samples, and you'd be just standing there, quiet, like you were taking it all in."

She cocks her head. "You back for your granddad's funeral? Sorry I wasn't there. Well, sorry-not-sorry. Fox and I didn't see eye to eye on much. So, back in Rush Creek, huh? Funny, I thought you were doing something with science. Was I wrong about that? Different brother? I used to be able to tell all of you apart. The Wilder boys, too. Now it all blends together. Getting old, I guess."

Quinn has frozen, clearly paralyzed by Nan's monologue, but just then, Catalina, who's our other esthetician besides Serenity, slips into the archway that leads back to the rest of the spa, saving him from the need to respond. We all turn to look at her—Catalina always turns heads, with long, thick dark hair, light brown skin, and a wardrobe of ModCloth dresses that look like they were tailormade for her hourglass body. "Hi, Nan! I'm ready for you," she says.

She spots Quinn and shoots me a *what the fuck* look.

Later, I mouth.

"Bye, Quinn!" Nan says. "Come get a cookie and catch me up on what's going on with you!"

Quinn grunts.

As soon as Catalina and Nan are out of earshot, I turn to him. "Remember how we talked about being *friendly*?"

"Friendly isn't in my...repertoire," he says.

"Could you at least pretend?" I ask.

He looks at me blankly. "That *was* me pretending."

I'm sorry, Bella, I think mournfully.

6

QUINN

Sonya hurries into the body of the spa and returns with a thick printout of all the products, their purposes, and their ingredients, which she hands to me. "When I realized we could be selling a lot more product than we were, I made this for everyone," she says, a note of pride in her voice.

"Will I be quizzed?"

I mean it to sound teasing, but it comes out belligerent. I feel a quick pang of regret, but she only shrugs, like she's resigned herself to me. Most people do, after a bit.

"Of course not," she says. "It's just in case it's useful. I don't make my people memorize it or anything."

I flip through her printout. It's impressively detailed. Sonya definitely runs a tight ship.

"We display the products by brand," she tells me, gesturing to the shelves. "I did a lot of research and quite a bit of testing, and it turns out that when I organize the products by brand—maybe because they look neater—we sell more. So it's harder to find stuff, sometimes, but for customers who are just browsing—and we get quite a few of those, especially around the holidays—we do better this way."

Her tone is brisk. She's given up on trying to be friends. No more flattery, and definitely no more of those light-up-the-room smiles—which is for the best.

Pointing out products, she leads me around the reception area, and I leaf through the printout as she goes, committing everything she says to memory.

"This is our premium smoothing oil," she says, indicating a small ivory-colored box adorned with gold leaf.

"So, similar to the Lean In kitoko oil," I say.

She flashes me an incredulous look. "Uh, yeah. How did you...?"

"Eidetic memory," I say. "What they used to call photographic."

"That's so cool!" I'm gifted with the full-on Sonya smile. Her eyes light from whiskey to amber.

I like her compliment too much, probably a leftover wound from spending high school getting teased for being nerdy. It didn't help that my last name provided endless fodder. I was the only Hott brother who, well, wasn't.

Since then, I've gained nine inches of height and a hundred pounds of muscle, made a key scientific discovery, and started a business, but apparently you never quite leave high school behind, as I was reminded when Nan pushed the Hott-hot button earlier.

Sonya's given up on getting a response from me and returned the small box to the shelf. "The Lean In is a less expensive product. And you tend to get what you pay for. Don't say that to customers," she adds quickly.

I raise my eyebrows. "Do you really think I would?"

The look she gives me back is all the answer I need, and I honestly can't blame her. Brutal honesty is definitely a hallmark of the two youngest Hott kids.

She reaches across my body to grab a bottle from a shelf, and even in the cacophony of spa smells, I catch her scent. For some reason I expected it to be expensive and rarefied, but it's actually homey—vanilla and cinnamon and apple, like a fresh-baked pie or my mom's gingerbread and applesauce. I find myself leaning in to catch more of it, and when she stands, her hair brushes my face, flooding me. There's probably a product in this room that's responsible for making her smell edible, and for a brief, foolish moment, I want to know which one.

Which is ridiculous because what would I do with that knowledge? Buy it and sniff it?

It's getting close to lunchtime; that's all. The human brain is tuned to seek food smells when the body's hungry. It's purely chemical.

"Did you get that?" she asks.

I return to planet Earth to find her staring at me expectantly. She pushes a lock of thick hair back from her face. Her lashes are long—and, I don't think, fake.

"Quinn?"

"Uh. No."

She gives me a *sorry if I'm boring you* look, and I want to explain that it was the opposite—

But I don't think that will help the situation.

Patiently, she repeats herself: *really good for dry hair, very saturating...*

"Do any of these claims have any scientific basis?"

She presses her lips together. "Product testing isn't like drug testing," she says. "Cosmetic manufacturers are legally required to make sure their products are safe. But beyond that, if the product makes people with dry hair feel like their hair is less dry, then it works."

"That's pretty flimsy," I say. "But I guess it's not about science." I think of what she said to me earlier, that I need to talk the talk even if I don't actually believe the party line. "We're in the business of making space for people to take care of themselves in whatever way feels best to them, right?" I say.

Her eyes snap open. "Are you making fun of me?"

"No, I—" I begin, but it's too late; she's shoved the bottle back onto the shelf and moved on to something else.

I wasn't making fun of you, I want to say.

But I'm used to this, the way words twist themselves between my brain and my mouth. All the times I ticked off a friend or family member by saying the wrong thing, then had to retrace my steps to figure out where I'd gone wrong. How often, when I tried to fix it, I made it worse.

And the times I couldn't see it, no matter how hard I looked.

I might be missing that gene.

Sonya holds up another product, and for the rest of my product training session, she powers us through, not making room for conversation.

Which is a good thing. Simpler. Cleaner.

The smiles only confuse things.

7

____

SONYA

By the time Quinn takes off at six, I'm exhausted.

I leave the spa and walk back to the Hott Springs cabin that I've been calling home for the past year or so.

The Hott land is ringed by mountains and forest, but most of the land itself is sprawling grasslands separated by scrub and occasional windbreaks. On my walk home, I pass the wedding barn, the stables—now recently converted staff housing—and the lodge, which is where most of the guests stay. Another path leads down a hill to more staff housing and a sprawling campground, both on the edge of a beautiful river.

When I reach my "house," one of the staff cabins, I can hear Gus barking inside. Gus is a rescue, a chaotic mix of breeds that has resulted in one straight ear and one floppy one, a tuft of white hair on his otherwise brown head, and a tail that's too long for his body. He greets me like I've been gone forever, jumping up and trying to get close enough to lick my face, which he can't—being only medium sized—until I lean down and let him give me a kiss.

"Hey, bud," I say. "Didya miss me? I missed you. It wasn't the same without you."

Many days, Gus is at the spa with me. He's comfortably middle aged and well trained, and his only desire in life is to follow me everywhere. When I can, I indulge him. Today he was home so the mobile groomer could come by.

"Could have used you at work, bud. It was a tough day. You wouldn't believe this, but there's this guy, Quinn—you'll meet him tomorrow—and he has to sit at the desk for the next two months or his family will lose the land the spa's built on. The lawyer even stopped by this afternoon to install a *camera*. I have to hang out with this guy for two months! And he's—"

Gus has followed me into the kitchen and now watches me scoop his food with big, eager eyes, tufty head tilted to the side. He's an extremely empathetic listener.

"He's *grumpy*. So grumpy. I don't know what to do with him. How am I supposed to fix things for Bella when he's so grumpy with the customers? I don't know, Gus. He's not making it easy, that's for sure."

Gus tips his head the other way.

"Also," I say, lowering my voice to a whisper, "he smells good."

Quinn, I discovered, smells like Oregon forest on a dry summer day, plus something spicy and male. It's the kind of thing we could make a fortune selling if you put it in a bottle. I'd wager, though, that it doesn't come from a bottle. Quinn seems way too aggressively low maintenance for that.

"I wasn't smelling him on purpose," I tell Gus. "I mean, not the way you doggos do. He was just *there*."

He's a big guy, so we kept getting in each other's space at the desk. He tried to wheel out of the way when I stepped in to quickly use the computer, but there wasn't anywhere for him to go. If he stayed seated, he was staring at my ass; if he stood up, he towered over me.

Either way, I was on edge, my whole body on high alert, a million cells aligning in his direction despite my aggravation with him.

"Does that ever happen to you, dude? That you feel attracted to someone you don't even *like*?"

Gus licks my hand.

"Thanks for listening, buddy," I tell him.

He dives into his food while I strip off my makeup, twist my hair up into a clip, and change into yoga pants and a baggy sweatshirt that's overdue for a trip through the laundry. Once Gus has slorped down his food like it's his last meal ever, we head out for a walk.

When we get back, I heat up a tortellini-and-pesto bowl for my dinner. The smell of garlic and basil fills the kitchen, and my stomach growls. I didn't get lunch today, nervous about leaving Quinn to his own devices, afraid he'd grunt a client into bailing on product. Or worse. But tomorrow maybe I'll ask Lily to keep an eye on Quinn when I can't be around so I can sneak in a bit of work in my office or grab some lunch.

The microwave dings. I grab my food and plop down onto the couch, cueing up the second season of *Sex Education*. Gus climbs up beside me and drops his head into my lap.

"Give me a minute, buddy. Have to finish eating before I can do the scritches."

He gives me a baleful look but rests his head and patiently waits.

I've made it halfway through my dinner—finally starting to feel like myself again, when I hear something. I pause the TV and freeze.

Someone is jiggling a key in the lock of my front door.

Gus jumps off the couch and tears toward the door, barking. My heart pounds so hard, I think I'm going to be sick.

I reach for my phone to call 911. I start jamming on the Power button, rising to my feet so I can defend myself if necessary, looking wildly around the room for a weapon. Frying pan, maybe, I think, edging toward the kitchen area.

The door opens and—

"What the *fuck*?"

The deep voice is familiar enough to stop my frantic button pressing.

Quinn Hott is standing in the doorway. Filling it. And as big as he is—and as much as I'm pretty sure he's not my fan —he doesn't look like he's planning to murder me. He looks confused and taken aback and off balance from Gus's frantic jumping and...licking.

Some guard dog I've got.

"What are—what are *you* doing here?" Quinn asks. One of his hands reflexively reaches for my dog's head, his big hand cupping, fingers working their way into the fur behind Gus's ears. Gus stills and accepts the treatment as his due.

"I live here," I say. "What are *you* doing here?"

He looks down at the key in his hand, then back up at me. He scowls, the deepest one I've seen yet. And then, on a heavy sigh, he says, "Apparently I live here, too."

8

QUINN

"I don't understand," Sonya says.

She looks completely different than she did when I left her at the spa an hour and a half ago.

Her hair's up, and she's taken off her makeup. I was right—the eyelashes *are* real. She looks softer and younger and less intimidating. Just as pretty, but...different.

She's wearing black leggings and a baggy Tierney Bay sweatshirt that's definitely seen better days. There's a big hole where the neckline meets the body of the shirt, and one of the sleeves looks like it's been shredded.

She doesn't look glamorous.

She looks cute.

Aargh. I don't want to think so, any more than I want to have noticed how good she smells. I want to get in, do my two months, and get out. I don't want to sniff, crush on, or even *notice* Sonya as anything other than my "supervisor."

And now things have gotten infinitely more compli-cated—because apparently she's my roommate, too.

She's still staring at me, waiting for an explanation. "I—

uh. The will says I have to live in ranch staff housing. Easton said to ask at the main desk at lunch for a key, and they gave me this. They said it was empty?"

"It's *not* empty," she says.

"It's a one-bedroom?"

She bites her lip, a white pearl of a tooth digging into soft, pink flesh. "Well. No. Not exactly."

"Then...?"

"My stuff's in the other bedroom."

"What kind of stuff?" I ask.

She wrinkles her nose. "My sewing stuff— Look, it doesn't matter. There's got to be another empty room somewhere in staff housing, right? I'll call the main desk."

She lifts and dials her phone. She rests her weight on one bare foot while we both listen to it ring, wearing an expression I've already come to know well: exasperation. I turn away from the frustration on her face and slowly take in my surroundings: a great room with bare header beams and wood walls and big windows. Dusk is falling, but I can see that Sonya's view looks out over a span of grassland ringed with stubby trees and rising up to peaks that are still snow-topped in June. There's a living area, including a stone fireplace and a big TV, on one side and a kitchen area on the other.

It's strangely familiar, probably because my brothers and I used to disregard our mom's orders and play in the cottages when they were empty, but maybe also because the whole room smells like Sonya: vanilla and cinnamon.

"Hi, Julia!" Sonya says, sparkly as white sand in the blazing sunshine. "How are you? Everything good with the kids?"

She listens.

"Aw! Is there a photo up on your Insta?" And then, "Give him a hug from me! Hey, so, I apologize in advance for making things complicated, but I think Josie or someone must have booked Quinn Hott into my cabin while you were at lunch. Wondering if you can find him someplace else. Yeah. He needs to be in Hott Springs housing, but—yeah."

She's quiet again, and I can hear Julia's voice indistinctly on the other end of the line. No words, but even from here I can catch the tone. Apologetic.

"Oh, wow. Jeez. Yeah. That's..." she says, and then, after a pause, "No, I get it. Totally not your fault. These things happen." Another pause. "Seriously? Nothing? Okay, thanks. Yeah." She kicks a foot out, catching the edge of the couch. "Yeah. We'll do that."

She hangs up and shoots me a rueful glance.

"She says she's so sorry but whoever did it didn't have a record that I was in the house—maybe Hanna knew but didn't get it in the books. They thought it was empty, which is why they sent you over here. Apparently they have eight cabins and two bunkhouses under renovations right now. She said she'll keep an ear open and let us know as soon as she hears someone is moving out, but the first vacancy she knows is coming is in"—she presses her fingers to her forehead—"three weeks. I can't believe this is the *only*..."

She lifts her phone again. "I'm going to call Han—" She freezes. "Shit. No. I'm not. We can't bother her right now."

"Yeah," I say. I'd already thought about that and dismissed it. Hanna's on bed rest, and I'm not going to add to her stress load. Obviously Sonya's had the same thought.

We stare at each other. It might be the first time today that we're truly on the same page.

"I'll scare up a tent," I say. "I'll text Easton, tell him not to say anything to Hanna—"

"God. No. I can't make you sleep in a tent."

"You worried I won't be able to find a place to shave? Or change into my button-down and slacks?"

Her eyes comb my face. "Did you just—make a joke?"

"It happens," I say. "From time to time."

She looks doubtful, but her shoulders relax. "Do you…" she begins, then stops. "Do you have a girlfriend who's going to be pissed if you shack up with a woman?"

"No." And then, because even I can tell it came out short and mean, "I don't do relationships."

"What, like, ever?" Her eyebrows draw together, like what I'm saying doesn't compute for her.

"Take my word for it," I say. "I've tried. Call me married to science."

She's still looking at me like she thinks there's more to the story, but then she sighs. Shrugs. And says, "Look. We're not going to solve this tonight. We'll find you a place to stay tomorrow. Tonight you can crash here. I'll clear out some space for you in the other bedroom."

She takes a step toward the stubby hallway. Her derpy dog trots past us and jumps up onto the couch. There's a clatter of remotes, and then the TV springs to life. On screen, a couple is having athletic sex, the girl bouncing on top of the boy. Sonya lunges for the couch. A remote slides onto the floor, sending the plastic battery cover skating across the room. She chases it, grabs it, aims it at the TV. The girl bounces faster, the boy's face stretches into an O—

"Fuck," Sonya says. "The battery fell out—"

She gets down on all fours; it's hard to know where to look because neither the television nor Sonya's backside is a safe bet. In a desperate effort to distract myself, I crouch, too, spot the battery, and lunge. Our heads smack, and we both leap back. Sonya comes up with the battery, jams it back into the remote, slides the cover on, and stops the onscreen action. Her face is red. I'm sure mine's worse. The visuals from the screen have left me semihard.

"Sex education," she says.

"I definitely feel educated," I say drily.

"No. That's the show. *Sex Education*. I wasn't watching, like, porn or something."

"I wouldn't have judged."

"I mean, not that I'm judging, either. If you do… Oh. God. I'll shut up now." She rises to her feet. "I'll go get that bed ready. For. You. To. Sleep. In."

She scurries toward the bedrooms.

"Do you want some help?" I call to her.

"No!" she calls back. "Stay there. I'm fine."

But I don't. I drift toward the hallway. There's a bathroom straight ahead and a door to each side. She pushes open the door on the left, and I see what she means when she says the room isn't empty. It's barely big enough to hold a dresser, two night stands, and a double bed, and the bed is covered with bags. I don't know much about bags, but these are all shapes and sizes—the kind women fill up with stuff for a day, the kind they carry to the grocery store, the kind they hold in one hand when they go out to dinner. Purses, I guess, and tote bags, and I've never seen this many in one place at one time except for once when I was a kid and I followed my mom into a leather shop. But most of these bags are made from fabric, not leather.

"You sewed all those?" I ask.

"Yeah."

"Why?"

Her skin turns pink across her nose and cheekbones. "I was hung up," she says, "on finding the perfect bag for every occasion. The right size, the right pockets, the right configuration of zippers and clasps."

I get that. Not specifically about bags, but the precision of the right tool for the right task. The need to perfect a thing or a process.

"And I could never find the perfect bag, so I started sewing them, thinking if I made it myself I could get it right. But there was always something I felt like I could do better."

Yep, I get that, too.

"Okay, yeah, you don't care about any of that," she says, sweeping an armful of the bags off the bed.

That's not true, I want to say, but she's halfway out the door, so I say "Let me help" instead.

"I've got it," she tosses back over her shoulder, and her tone doesn't leave any room for further argument. "You go get your stuff."

I go out to my rental car and come back inside with my backpack. She's coming out of the bathroom with her arms full of bottles, a shower tote stuffed with more bottles, a hair dryer, something that looks like a cattle prod, and several pretty patterned bags. She juggles them, almost dropping a bag; I catch it as it slides and follow her into her bedroom, where we deposit everything onto her bed and dresser, which is already crowded with hair clips, scattered jewelry, and tubes of makeup.

Somewhere in this array of cosmetics is the key to why she smells so damn good.

Her eyes light on my backpack.

"That's...it?" she asks, pointing to my backpack. "That's all your stuff?"

"That's it," I confirm. Two pairs of jeans, six T-shirts, socks, underwear, soap, deodorant, toothbrush, floss, and toothpaste.

"You and I are basically two totally different species of human," she says, the corner of her mouth tipping up.

That's right. We are. And I need to remember that fact, especially when her scent makes me hungry in ways that can't be fixed with a trip to Rush Creek Bakery.

9

———

SONYA

Quinn's gone when I get up in the morning, which is a relief. I can shower, dress, feed myself and Gus, and walk him in peace without having to figure out how to maneuver around a big, scowly grump of a man.

Because he is those things. Big. Scowly.

Did I mention big?

You know how people put coins or paperclips in photos of online products to show scale?

Having Quinn in my space last night was like that. I didn't realize how much space he took up until we nearly collided in the hallway. Until he helped me carry my stuff into the bedroom. And then I was aware of the walls feeling closer, the ceiling lower. It left me breathless—which I'm chalking up to claustrophobia.

Gus and I amble our way back to the spa, where I find Quinn already sitting at the front desk. Gus trots to him, noses into his hand, and settles on the floor, his face hooked over one of Quinn's feet.

Traitor!

"Huh," I say. "He doesn't do that to anyone other than me, usually. Maybe it's because you slept with us last night." I squeeze my eyes shut. "Slept. In. The. Same. Cabin. With. Us."

I can feel myself blushing, my chest, throat, and face heating. Quinn raises an eyebrow, so slight it's almost undetectable, and the flush deepens. Damn it. That's the second time in two days I've gone all blushing bride on him for no good reason.

"I'm going to go get a stool," I say and flee, relishing the cool air moving over my hot face.

I poach a spare stool from the nail salon and wheel in next to Quinn.

He gives me a look under lowered brows. "Are you going to sit there all day?"

"You're still in training."

He scowls. "I don't need more training."

"You haven't handled customers by yourself yet," I say as reasonably as I can. The combination of a still-hot face and Quinn's grump routine is fraying my patience.

"I did. Yesterday afternoon. But you kept jumping in."

I breathe deeply and count to three. "Because you're still having..." I strain for the right word. "Some challenges..." I wince as his scowl carves deep lines into his forehead. "With the friendliness factor."

I would have said it was impossible, but his eyebrows scrunch closer together. "No one can live up to your standards on that front."

Patience. Deep breaths. Just keep smiling, just keep smiling.

One of our regulars, Cole Davis, pushes through the

front door. A seventy-ish man with cross-cropped salt-and-pepper hair and warm brown skin, Mr. Davis never misses his weekly facial.

"Hey there," he says to Quinn. "You're not Maura."

"No," Quinn agrees.

"I'll plop myself right down over there and wait my turn," Mr. Davis says, and does.

I shoot Quinn a meaningful look. Eyebrows up. *Talk to him.*

He shakes his head like a pitcher shaking off the catcher's signal. I raise my eyebrows higher. He looks away.

"How are things going for you, Mr. Davis?" I ask, just before the silence in the room pushes me over my breaking point. I reach over Quinn to check him in on the system.

"Not too bad, not too bad," our client says with an amiable wave of his hand. "You, Miss Sonya?"

"Things are—"

I accidentally make eye contact with Quinn, who's watching me, one eyebrow raised in what looks like challenge. Like he's daring me to lie.

"Delightful," I say. It comes out tight as a knot.

Serenity appears. "Mr. Davis!" she exclaims with delight. She gives him a hug and sweeps him back into the spa.

I turn on Quinn, arms crossed. "I rest my case," I say.

"What?" he demands.

"How hard is it to make conversation?"

"It didn't need to be made," he says with a shrug. "I looked at the schedule. He's been coming here every week since you opened. You think he's going to stop because I don't chat him up?"

"That's not the point!" I cry. "I don't think it's unfair to expect a brilliant scientist to engage clients with more than monosyllables!"

A flicker of something—maybe surprise—crosses his face and then is gone. He folds his arms. "Look," he says, "you don't want me to try to chat people up. It's not in my skill set. Much better if I just say what needs to be said and do what needs to be done."

I want to weep. I make myself take another deep breath. Regroup.

"Okay," I say when I can finally organize my thoughts. "How's this? At a minimum, call out a greeting. Be friendly. Make sure you ask how their day's going so far. Point them to the fruit-infused waters and snacks. If the wait's long, thank them for their patience. On their way out, ask how their service was, if they want another appointment, and whether we can help them with anything else. Ask if they want any of the products we used on them. What are you...?"

"Writing it down," he says, pulling a services brochure toward him and scratching something illegible on it in pen.

"You have an eidetic memory, but you have to write that down?"

"I wouldn't want to forget any important elements," he says.

I can't tell if he's being earnest or snarky.

The door swings open to admit a first-timer—or at least someone I don't recognize. A thirty-something woman decked out head to toe in expensive athleisure.

She approaches the desk as the seconds tick by,

stretching in my head to become interminable. She's almost to the desk. I can't stand it a second longer.

I nudge his arm. "Greeting," I whisper.

He shoots a glare at me, then says, "Can I help you?"

She looks from him to me, puzzled, her gaze locking on me. "Hi!" she says. "Do you take walk-ins for haircuts?"

"Yes," he says, glancing down at his notes. "How's your day going?"

"Not bad! Yours?"

He shrugs. "I've had worse."

I groan inwardly, but she smiles at him. A flirty smile. "Well," she says, "sounds like there's some room for improvement. Hope things look up."

"Thanks."

There's a long, awkward silence. "I'll see if one of our stylists is available," he says. "Our waiting area's over there. Please help yourself to fruit-infused water and some snacks."

She watches his rear view as he disappears down the hall.

"He's in training," I whisper to her.

"Yeah?" she says. She's still peering down the hall after him. "Huh. Okay. Yeah. Makes sense."

"Let me grab your info and enter it into the system," I say, sighing.

As I finish that up, Quinn comes back with Reggie at his side, and she takes over the interaction, leading her new client into the salon. I find myself blowing out a held breath.

Quinn plops into his chair like he's run a marathon.

"Okay?" he asks, eyes challenging me to disagree.

But I'm not going to back down. This is my day spa, Hanna's business, Bella's future.

"You could still be more...open. Friendly. Upbeat. To build rapport. It's especially important with the first-time custo—"

"Sonya." His rough voice cuts across my instructions, dragging my gaze to his face. It's grim. Grimmer than usual, that is. "It's not me. I can't be perky or peppy or a bundle of sunshine. And not everyone wants sunshine blown up their ass—"

I start to interject that yes, most people *do*, but he shakes his head. "And even if they did, I'm not that guy. I can't do it."

"You can—"

He shakes his head. "*You* can. You're good at it. But me? Nope. Not gonna happen. Not for two days, and definitely not for two months. At some point, you're gonna have to let me do it my way."

I open my mouth to object, but my argument melts away.

He's right.

We're driving each other nuts.

He's making me feel like a control freak, and I'm making him feel like a failure.

I have to accept that he's not going to magically become my dream receptionist.

And either he can run the front desk without torpedoing my plan...or he can't—but giving him a hard time over everything that comes out of his mouth isn't going to fix that.

His eyes take in my hesitation. "Trust me," he says.

"Remember, your boss is my sister. I don't want to screw her. Or you," he adds.

The last bit softens my frustration. I nod. "Okay."

"Okay?" He's obviously surprised.

"Okay. I'm going to take a lunch break."

It's only half an hour. Nothing terrible can happen in half an hour.

Especially not if I send Lily in to keep an eye on him.

10

QUINN

A week or so after Sonya grudgingly leaves me to my own devices, I come back from my lunch break to find her hunched over the computer muttering, "Shit. Shit. Shit. Shit."

Her shoulders are slumped, her head bent, and something in my chest goes sideways.

None of your business, Quinn, none of your business, none of your business.

She stopped hovering after I asked her to, but now Lily, the spa's red-haired, freckle-nosed attendant, is in the front room every chance she gets. She fusses over product on the shelves—even when she just rearranged that shelf an hour ago. I know she's bringing intel back to Sonya.

But it's better than having Sonya herself there, not only because Lily is good company and willing to do enough talking for both of us, but also because if Sonya and I aren't stuck behind the desk together, her scent can't crowd out rational thoughts like, *We're basically two different species of humans.*

I'm still grateful for that reminder.

It's why I've spent most of my evenings this week at Oscar's Saloon and Grill, nursing a single beer and the dinner special of the night, why I've gotten up early to shower and leave the house before she's even awake. Because there's no need to tempt fate by finding out what happens when Sonya's shower weaponizes her scent into steam. Or whether she wears a robe or a towel when she emerges from the bathroom in said cloud of steam. Or how her skin looks when it's flushed from the shower's heat.

It's bad enough that I know she looks cute in sweats without her makeup, that she talks all the time to Gus as if he were a person, and that she sits on the couch at night and works on sewing projects, wrinkles forming in her forehead as she squints at her stitches.

The wrinkles are there now, too, as she frowns at the computer screen.

None of your business, Quinn!

"What's wrong?" I ask, unable to stop myself.

Her head turns at the sound of my voice, and she blushes like I've caught her watching *Sex Education* at work.

Her blush is a pink light behind a scattering of freckles over her nose and cheeks. Today she's wearing a long-sleeved scoop-necked blouse that bares an expanse of creamy skin. One edge of lace has snuck over the top of the neckline, and I force my eyes away from it and the hint of pink in her skin.

Instead, I glare at Weggers's camera, hoping he hasn't caught the microsecond drop of my gaze into her cleavage, then turn back to her.

She sighs. "I've been trying to order these high-end

products that you can custom brand to the salon, and I got confirmation yesterday that they were shipping, but now it says they're back-ordered. And I really—I really need them."

She bites her lip, hard enough that I want to reach out and stop her—but I don't.

"Why do you need them so bad?"

She hesitates, like she's not eager to explain. "The last receptionist...she..." She squints into the distance. "Pilfered? Embezzled? Not sure what the right term is. She stole product and resold it on the gray market."

"Jesus," I say. "Does Hanna know?"

"Yeah. I waited as long as I could to tell her, but even Easton thought she'd be livid if we kept it from her. So she knows now."

"Did you go to the police?"

"Yeah. And I filed an insurance claim. But the thief also messed with the books, and I was going to use the money next month. To hire a woman—someone who really needs the job. Someone...important to me." She screws up her face. "I was hoping to make this work out with the branded product, and now..." She doesn't finish the sentence, just closes her eyes and presses fingers to her forehead.

"Oh," I say because I suddenly get it. Why she's so over-the-top eager to whip me into shape. "I'm—sorry."

She opens her eyes and waves it off. "It'll be okay. I'll figure something out."

"No," I say. "I mean I'm sorry I'm here. With my bad hair and shitty people skills. I'm sorry I'm fucking up your plans."

"You're not—"

I raise an eyebrow.

Her mouth turns up a tiny bit at the corners, and I feel like I've won a prize for a scientific breakthrough. "It's not my ideal scenario," she admits.

We're both quiet for a minute. Then she says, "It's obviously not your ideal scenario, either."

"No," I agree. "Can you find a replacement for the products? Or get them from another vendor?"

"You wouldn't believe how many vendors I tried before I found one that wasn't back-ordered. Other spas know custom branding is big money, too."

"How does it work—the custom-branded thing?"

"A cosmetic company makes the product, but they put your label on it."

I think about that a minute. "How many products?"

"I was going to start with just a few. Shampoo and conditioner, maybe? Grow it if it worked?"

My brain has jumped ahead. Sifting through ideas and contacts. Building a tentative plan.

She resumes staring at the uncooperative computer screen, her fingers frozen on the keyboard, shoulders slumped.

I want to fix things for her.

Quinn... a voice warns. *This is an in-and-out operation. You're not supposed to get involved.*

Especially not with a woman like her.

I'm not getting involved with her, I tell the voice. *I'm tackling a very specific business problem. It's for Hanna. Helping the spa helps Hanna's business.*

Mmm-hmm, says the voice. *Suuuuuure.*

11

SONYA

I trudge home, discouraged.

It's more than a week since I discovered that the custom-branded product was back-ordered. I've been combing through product sites, but I still haven't been able to find anyone who can supply what we need. And I haven't found anything else that'll give us the money to hire Bella.

I've already pinched and scraped every penny I could out of the budget. There's nothing else that can be sacrificed.

I'm going to fail Bella, and it makes my stomach hurt.

All I want to do is heat up some takeout, glom it in front of the television, and fall into bed.

But when Gus and I get home, I'm greeted with an absolutely terrible smell.

Quinn is in the kitchen. He has what looks like a kid's chemistry set spread out over my counters, and he's blending something by shaking it in a jar.

"What on earth...? Are you doing *science* in my kitchen?"

I've startled him, and he scowls at me.

There are beakers and flasks, test tubes in racks, a small Bunsen burner. He's wearing goggles and—no joke—a white lab coat. Not a mountain man. Definitely a mad scientist, with his hair flying out in all directions.

Having Quinn's science invade my sanctum is the last straw.

"It smells—awful!" I start opening windows. I wave my arms, trying to disperse the smell. The kitchen is littered with open bottles and bits of torn plastic and paper.

"Sonya—"

I throw up my hands. "You know what? I'm gonna get dinner in town. Text me when whatever this is—is—done."

"Wait—stop!" he says, grabbing my wrist.

I freeze at the feel of that big hand, cuffed around my wrist. My eyes come up to meet his, obscured behind the reflective glare of his goggles.

He instantly lets go of me, but I can still feel the strength and heat of the grip.

"Sorry," he says, pointing to my wrist. "I just—I'm— damn." His shoulders slump. "I'm—developing shampoo. And conditioner."

"You're—*what?*"

He pushes the goggles up on his head. His eyes are a striking shade of blue green, with flecks of every color you can imagine in them. For a second, I can't look away.

"So you can custom brand them. I was thinking about the situation. You said you needed a high-end product that you could custom brand."

He holds his hands out, as if in surrender.

"Oh," I say. "God. I'm so dense. You're doing this for—"

I was going to say *for me*, but then I stop myself. Because of course he's not. He's doing it for the spa. For Hanna.

But regardless, the end result is that if he can do what he says...I'll be able to hire Bella as planned.

I get a flash of the expression on her face when she opened my birthday gift—wrecked and grateful at the same time, and I want to throw my arms around Quinn and tell him how much this means to me.

He picks up a measuring cup and fidgets with it. "I figure I'm not bringing anything to the table—or front desk, I guess—with my people skills, so I thought I'd take a page from Mark Watney in *The Martian* and science the shit out of it. So. Hott Spot's own hair care. Well. Not yet. But soon."

He tries to run a hand through his hair but is stymied by the goggles, which tumble off the back of his head and onto the floor. I bend, pick them up, and hand them back to him. Our hands touch. A spark jumps his skin to mine, bright and delicious.

"Quinn, this is—really nice."

His eyes slide to mine.

I could hug him.

I could *kiss* him for what he's doing.

And I think I might have liked it better before, when he was just the grumpy pain in my ass. This is *waaay* more complicated. And his blue-green eyes on my face aren't making it any less complicated. I feel like he can see through me to my confusion, and...I want him to see.

"Do you—know how? To make shampoo and conditioner?"

"I know how to treat ALS," he says. "I think I can figure it out."

I cough out a laugh. There's the Quinn I know.

But I can't hear him the way I heard him even a day ago. Because I'm starting to understand something about Quinn that I didn't realize right away: He means exactly what he says. What he said really *isn't* bragging. He's telling me what he knows. He's assessed his abilities, and he should be able to create shampoo.

And I'm sure he's right.

"Okay," I say. "I'll leave you to it. Do you mind if I use the microwave to heat up a frozen dinner?"

"I can clear out of your cooking space if you want," he says.

"I don't really *cook*."

"You don't cook?" he asks, giving me an incredulous look.

"I can make eggs, pasta—on a good day, and oatmeal."

"Salad?"

"Yeah. I can make salad."

"What about following a recipe? Just...do this, do that, do this thing?"

"Here's my secret," I tell him. "I'm super organized and with-it at work. But for some reason, as soon as it has to do with food preparation, I'm a complete disaster. You'd be surprised how often, even when I'm completely alone and undistracted, I ruin perfectly easy recipes."

He gives me a look that I now recognize: he's sizing me up. Trying to make sense out of me. Like Hanna, he's slow to warm up, blunt, not particularly good at reading people, and absolute crap at sugarcoating his responses.

But definitely not an asshole.

Maybe even a good guy.

He gives me one last assessing look, then pulls his gaze away and squats, eye level with one of the Pyrex measuring cups that came with the cabin. He's put the goggles back on, and his coat is spread out behind him. It pulls across his broad shoulders and back, and it's too tight to be comfortable over his biceps. Lab coats are apparently not manufactured for scientists with mountain-man bodies.

Mmm. It's a nice combination.

"Quinn?" I ask. "Can I help?"

12

QUINN

"I think I've got this operation more or less under control," I tell Sonya. "Stench aside. But if you don't mind, you could heat food up for me, too."

I address my words more or less to her chest because I'm squatting. I can't say I regret the focal point. She's both slim and willowy and gloriously gifted in the chest department, her breasts hugged by a fitted blouse, a glimpse of cleavage visible above the second button. I want to bury my face there and maybe dip my tongue for a taste—

No.

No.

I do not want to do that because that would be a terrible idea.

"On it," she says, and for a second, I think she's addressing the image in my head, not the reality of our conversation, and oh man, I like that.

Quinn, my friend, you are in trouble.

Two different species!

I don't think my caveman brain speaks reason.

She heats us up two tortellini bowls. I drag mine far away from my work so I don't cross-contaminate. She sets hers on the big blond-wood kitchen table and sits down.

"So what's the current status?"

"Shampoo: possibly viable. Further testing required. Conditioner: utter failure."

"Oh, that sucks," she says.

"Nah. It's the nature of science. I have all day Sunday when the salon is closed to experiment."

We fall silent. Normally not talking is almost as awkward for me as talking—my head fills up with all the small talk I *should* be making—but for some reason, eating in silence with Sonya feels okay. I think it's the fact that we've also been sitting in silence behind the desk at work. Silence with Sonya makes sense.

As I finish up eating and go back to titrating, she says, "Lily told me you were a superstar with Yolanda Hubert today while I was out at lunch."

I look up from tweaking the flame on the burner. "Did you ask Lily to spy on me?"

She blushes and looks away, down at her food. "I'm sorry. I just—"

"It's fine," I say. "I get it. I'm not good with people. You want to keep an eye on me."

"According to Lily, you were 'charming' with Mrs. Hubert."

"I don't know about charming. I was honest."

"What did you say to her?"

"I don't remember."

"You sure?" she asks, her mouth turning up at the corner.

"Lily told you, huh?"

"Uh-huh," she says. "She said you checked Mrs. H in for a lip-chin-brow and told her, 'If there are stray hairs on your face, I *definitely* can't see them.'"

"It was the truth," I say.

"It's also very charming," she says.

I fidget with my fork. "No one has *ever* accused me of being charming before."

"Lily also said you were great with Sandy Wellington. That you told her not to waste her money on the skin cream Serenity recommended—"

I wince because obviously this isn't going to go well in the retelling. Good receptionists don't tell people not to buy product. This story is exactly what Sonya was afraid of.

"—and she ended up spending fifty bucks on makeup," Sonya concludes. "Plus when her post-service survey came in, she gave a five out of five for customer service."

Something is happening to my face.

Sonya's staring at me. "Quinn. Is that a *smile*?"

"Nope," I say.

That makes her smile. Not just at the edges, but all out, like she smiles at her staff and her customers. And holy shit, I like it.

"You can cut my hair," I say abruptly.

"What?" Her fork, which had been en route to her mouth, stalls in midair.

"You can cut my hair. If you want. If you think it would help the spa."

She stares at me. "I could have sworn you said, 'You can cut my hair.' As in, you would trust me with a sharp object near your head."

"That's what I said. I've been thinking about it, and the shag's a liability. I don't want to turn your customers off."

"Wait," she says. "This isn't because you still think I want you to cut it, right?"

I work my face into a mock scowl. "You did say I needed a cut and beard trim and—"

She sticks her tongue out at me. And. Oh. First of all, tongue. I have to not think about that. But also...she's teasing me. We're teasing each other.

My face is warm.

"It's actually because Lily told me it would look good shorter. She showed me photos."

Sonya's lips curve up. "Mmm-hmm." But then she relents. "We'll get Reggie to make time for you next week."

"Not Reggie. You."

Her eyebrows go up. "Me?"

"You do haircuts, right?"

"I have my hair design license, yeah."

"So you do it. Tonight—before I change my mind."

She tilts her head to one side, like she's trying to figure me out.

"I've never liked getting my hair cut," I admit. "I used to kick and scream when I was a kid."

"Whereas now you act like a big, grumpy..."

"Tantruming kid," I admit and am gratified when the corners of her mouth lift. "All I'm saying is don't give me a chance to back out."

"Okay," she says quickly. "Tonight."

I bite back a smile.

"My tools are at the spa."

"We can walk back there." She still looks hesitant, so I say, "Mmm, starting to have second thoughts…"

She frowns. "It's not my usual MO to let people cut their hair on impulse. Letting them back out is part of the process."

I raise my eyebrows. "You usually don't have me working as your receptionist, either."

That makes her smile. "True. Okay. We'll finish eating, clean up, and head over to the salon. Usually when I sneak over there at night, it's to use the hot springs, not to surreptitiously cut hair."

I don't let myself think too much about that—Sonya sneaking over to the spa to slide her lithe, curvy body into the steaming hot water. Or the feel of the word *surreptitious*, slippery and warm, like tendrils of steam wrapping themselves around her as her mouth opens in an O of pleasure.

I like the idea of being Sonya's surreptitious something.

When we've both finished eating, I clean up the mess I've made of her kitchen and we head for the spa. Gus trots alongside us, out of the cabin and along the paths that connect the various parts of the ranch. Past the other cabins, which are clearly in various states of being revamped. Past horse stables and an enormous barn in mint condition—obviously recently renovated—to the spa. She unlocks the side door, and we slip in, Sonya turning on lights till we reach the salon room.

"If you want to take a seat over there…" she says in what I suspect is her "hair stylist" voice, cheerful and certain.

She points to the chair in front of the first sink, and I sit. Gus finds a corner and plops down, settling with a contented sigh. Sonya sets a towel in the lip of the sink and guides my head back.

On the way over here, I'd steeled myself. I figured this would be like other haircuts—uncomfortable. Too much touching by a stranger, too much unsolicited closeness, someone's coffee breath in my face. The uneasy too-much-but-also-too-light touch of fingers in my hair, ticklish and lasting an indeterminate, *interminable* amount of time.

But this is different from every other haircut I've ever gotten, which makes it a whole different kind of torment. Sonya's hands on the side of my head, her fingers in my hair. She seems to intuitively understand that for me, not enough is too much, and her fingers don't tease or tickle; they're firm and sure. Warm water flows over my scalp, her fingers massaging shampoo into my skin. I sigh involuntarily, relaxing deeper into the seat. She leans over me, and I close my eyes so I'm not staring at her breasts a few inches away, cupped under her top and bra. I don't close them fast enough, though, and I see the tightness of her nipples.

Her breath brushes my face, lemongrass and something else I want to taste. Her.

I don't want the hairwash to end, but it does too soon, the water shut off with a small clunk of pipes beneath us, her hands rubbing a towel through my hair. That feels good, too, the brisk rub and caress. Firm enough again, like she knows that's what I need.

"Sit over there," she instructs, pointing at one of the stylist's chairs.

I know it's the way Sonya's touch riled up my body, but

her bossiness at that moment feels like a challenge, one I want to take. I'd rather be the one delivering the instructions. *Lie back. Open your legs. That's right, let go for me.*

Jesus, Quinn, I think. *That escalated quickly.* I'm grateful for the thin cape she drapes around me. I push my knees forward into the fabric so the cape doesn't tent over my lap. She fastens it in the back, her hands brushing the nape of my neck and making me shiver.

"You okay temperature-wise?" she asks. "I can turn on the space heater."

"I'm fine," I lie.

I'm burning up.

13

———————

SONYA

I like cutting Quinn's hair.

And it goes beyond the fact that I've missed styling. I don't cut hair much anymore, not since I started managing salons instead of working in them. I've missed the simple pleasures of *lather, rinse, repeat* and the rhythm and cadence of scissors in hair.

But touching Quinn is even better than that. It's about Quinn himself.

He's so obviously *grateful.*

The way he drowses over the massage of my fingers in the sink.

The expression of bliss on his face when I work his bedhead waves over, first with cream and then with the soft hot puff of the diffuser.

I get the feeling he's a little bit touch starved.

I don't do relationships. Take my word for it...I've tried. Call me married to science.

There's a whole story there, and I find myself...wanting to know it.

Maybe I spend more time than I need to on each step. Maybe I draw out the drying process longer than is strictly necessary. And maybe—when I turn him to face the mirror and hold up the hand mirror so he can see the back—I spend extra time on the finishing touches. The scrunching and patting and arranging.

He closes his eyes, which gives me carte blanche to admire his long lashes, straight nose, and chiseled cheekbones. And the pleasure on his face.

For a split second, I let myself ponder what it would feel like to push that pleasure over the line from innocent to something else.

Just because he's home-brewing shampoo for you and letting you cut his hair so he won't scare your customers away doesn't mean you can lose your mind, I chide myself.

Just because he looks like sin when he's lost in pleasure...

He opens his eyes, and I pretend to have been admiring my work. "Chris Evans called to ask for the name of your stylist," I tell him.

He scowls. "Chris Evans, huh? I'm hotter than Chris Evans. How about Chris Hemsworth?"

"And modest, too," I say.

"It's not bragging if it's the truth." The corner of his mouth tilts. So slightly it's almost imperceptible, but I log it with a sharp bloom of pleasure.

"It's still bragging, even if it's the truth."

"So you don't disagree."

Our eyes meet and hold.

I look away, busying myself sweeping the hair from the floor and into the path of the salon's stationary vacuum.

"Objectively, it's a good haircut," I say from that safe distance.

When I'm done, I ask, "You still want me to trim your beard?"

"If you don't mind."

"No, I'd be happy to."

In truth, there's a war going on inside me, between the part of me that wants to put my hands on Quinn's face and the part of me that knows I've already lost control of this situation.

I try to reduce Quinn's face to a series of lines, the way I do with any man whose beard I'm trimming. Top line—nice and straight, taking off only the clear strays.

Unlike some men's beards, Quinn's is uniformly thick. The hairs tickle my fingertips, and I force myself not to think about the way they would feel on other parts of my body.

I define the line behind his jaw, from his ear down, aware of how the skin back here is soft and lighter than his already pale facial skin. That it must be very sensitive to touch, that a kiss there would force a startled breath from his lungs.

My own breath is ragged and fast, and I wonder if he can tell. I wonder if this thing that's happening to me is happening to him, too, and why it's happening to me when I've only barely let myself like him.

"You like cutting hair?" he asks me.

I like cutting your *hair.* "Yeah."

"So you have a—what did you call it?—hair design license—and there are other certificates for you, too, right? On the wall in the last treatment room?"

"I'm also an esthetician and a manicurist."

"Wow," he said. "That's a lot of work."

"I did it a little at a time, after I came back to Rush Creek after...college."

"What do you like best?"

"Managing," I say, laughing.

"You have a knack for it."

I can't tell if he's teasing or serious, but either way, the heat under my skin blossoms and I have to work extra hard to keep my hand from shaking.

"What about you?" I ask him. "You must be eager to get back to work. Your real work."

"Yes."

"You love it? What you do?"

He's very still. Very quiet. I finish the back line and go to work under his chin, drawing an imaginary line across his Adam's apple, which bobs under my touch, a hard swallow. Maybe it's all in my mind and maybe it's not, but my body thinks it's real, everything from my belly button down molten and insistent.

"Yeah. I love the shit out of what I do. I love hypothesis and experimentation and precision and persistence. I love lab work and science-minded people. And the drug that's in trial now is a big breakthrough. It's going to help a lot of people."

It's the first time I've heard him talk like that, with real joy and enthusiasm, and it makes me realize how hard it is for him, being here, away from what he loves.

He's a standup guy, to do this for his sister. For his brothers. For me.

He's a good man.

I stop, stepping back to admire my work, to admire him, and then I'm sorry I did—because holy shit. With his hair drying in soft curls and his beard better defined, he already looks like a man striding out of the mountain mist in a truck commercial. And I have to admit to myself that I might have a mountain-man kink.

"What?" he asks. "Did you screw up? Did you leave a huge bald patch?"

I *think* he's teasing, but it's so hard to tell. "Is that why you don't get your hair cut more often? Scared we'll screw it up?"

He fidgets with the fabric of the cape, twisting it in one big but surprisingly nimble hand. "I don't like being touched," he admits.

"Could have fooled me," I say. "You looked blissed out."

"You're different," he says, eyes down.

I have absolutely no idea what to do with that or the shock of pleasure it sends through me, so I do nothing, letting it hang there until it drifts off like smoke.

I trim his mustache next, revealing the soft lushness of his lips, which open in response to the accidental touch of my fingers. I hear the breath slip out of his mouth, not the hard huff of need I'd imagined earlier but a soft, surprised sound, and all I can think about is setting the trimmers down and leaning in to touch my mouth to his, testing whether he's as soft as he looks. Whether he'd let me kiss him, whether he'd open to me, whether he'd kiss back, whether—as I suspect—he'd take control in an instant, his hands wrapped around the back of my head to hold me down to him.

My face has drifted closer to his, and I pull back to a

safer distance, watching his eyes close, with relief or disappointment or maybe neither of those things—maybe nothing. Maybe he's just getting his beard and mustache trimmed.

And it's one thing to have a moment of weakness with my fingers in his hair and our faces this close, but I know I'd never act on it, not when we have to spend two months in the salon together, an unknown number of days in the cabin together. No way to get space if the kiss turned out to be a disaster. And I have promises to keep and people to take care of and don't need another distraction, especially the kind who doesn't do relationships. Or the kind who clearly needs to get out of Rush Creek as soon as he can.

Been there, done that, bought the T-shirt.

14

SONYA

"Any progress on the investigation?" Hanna leans back against the enormous pile of pillows on her bed and stares at me.

I shake my head. "They haven't found Maura or tracked down any of the product. The insurance company is hung up on the fact that the product might still be recoverable."

Hanna sighs. "Damn. Is the spa okay financially until that's sorted out?"

I nod. "Thanks to your brother."

"My...brother?"

"He's developing a brandable hair-care line for us. It's going to help close the gap until we can either recover the product or get the insurance funds."

"My brother Quinn?"

"Is that so surprising?" I ask her. "He's a chemist."

"I guess not," Hanna says, but she still looks puzzled. "Is he— Are you two—getting along? He can be...bristly."

For some reason, that makes me think of the clean edge of his beard against my fingers.

"We're fine," I say. "I cut his hair last night."

"Wait. You *what*?"

"I cut his hair?"

It comes out more as a question than a statement, possibly because I'm talking to my boss, possibly because she sounds so flabbergasted, possibly because I'm still wondering what the hell I was thinking laying hands on a guy I have to live and work with.

"I can't believe he agreed to that. He was a bear about getting his hair cut even as a kid. I don't think he had it cut once from when he was eight years old until my grandfather buzzed him at shotgun-point somewhere around age sixteen."

"He did *not!*" I say, although I wouldn't put it past Fox Hott. That guy had threatened to go after my ex-fiancé with his shotgun, and according to Hanna, he'd once pointed it at Easton, albeit through a thick door.

"Not literally," Hanna said. "But he pulled out every threat on earth, including that one." She laughs. "I think in the end it was a crush that did it, though. We never found out who it was, but we all figured when he finally knuckled under and agreed to the clippers that there had to be a girl."

I pause, taking that in. And I wonder, for a split second, why Quinn gave in this time.

Am I the girl in this scenario?

A fizz of possibility races through me—and then I cut it off, like a barrier descending at a parking lot.

"So, what, did you shave him clean? Give him a buzz cut?"

"No," I say. "I just neatened things up."

When I was done with him, I stood Quinn in front of a mirror and we both admired my handiwork. Hair shorn to thick bedhead waves, beard trimmed full and close. My handiwork exposed the cut glass of his cheekbones, the lushness of his mouth, the hard definition of his jaw. And it added up to smolder.

I had to look away because the smolder was a net I was caught in.

"Aren't you going to wax my eyebrows, like you threatened to?" he asked.

"I never threatened that."

"You did. When I first showed up."

"I. Thought. You. Were. Someone. Else!"

The corner of his mouth tugged upward. He was messing with me.

"So? Eyebrows?" he asked.

His eyebrows, just as they were, thick and straight and well defined, were hot AF—but I wasn't going to say that.

Instead I shrugged, not meeting his eyes in the mirror.

"They're fine," I said, like I'd barely noticed.

"What?" Hanna demands. "What's that expression on your face? You look like you found out there's going to be a Marvel/*Bridgerton* crossover event."

"Oh, wow," I say, stopped for a moment by the thought of the trouble Loki could cause in Regency England. And how much I'd enjoy watching Tom Hiddleston smolder a debutante into, possibly literally, ashes. "That would be a thing."

Hanna doesn't push the question, which is good because Quinn is her brother and she's my boss, and I have zero desire to tell her how close I came to falling on him like a college student on a free washer.

Hanna tips her head to one side. "I'm sorry about all this," she says. "My granddad, my brother. The fact that my ridiculous family is now your problem."

"Not only my problem. Jessa and Easton's problem, too."

One of Hanna's closest friends, Jessa, is a wedding planner, and she's helping Hanna and her husband, Easton, at Hott Springs Eternal while Hanna's out of commission. With me at the spa and Easton and Jessa overseeing wedding stuff, the resort is in good hands. We'll be fine until Hanna's back on her feet after her maternity leave.

"We've got this," I say. "You rest up and incubate that little one. Not too much longer, right?"

"Right," she says.

I'd been one breath away from telling her that Quinn and I are now roommates, too, but I decide not to. Not yet. Maybe after she has the baby, when she's completely out of the woods. In the meantime, Quinn and I can keep that fact to ourselves and work on finding him a new place to live.

This morning, Quinn was brewing something that looked like strawberry jelly but actually smelled pretty decent. He barely noted me as I maneuvered around him, fixing my cereal and taking it back into my room to eat it. When I said good morning, he grunted back.

I can't blame him. I think both of us want to put some distance between us after I nearly attacked his mouth last night.

Feet pound up the stairs. A beautiful man bursts into the room. That's not an uncommon occurrence at Hanna's house because Easton is one of the Wilder brothers, a small tight-knit crew of successful outdoor adventurers who are works of art in man form. However, this beautiful man is *not* one of Easton's brothers. As soon as I see him, I know he has to belong with Hanna and Quinn, even though—unlike Hanna—he's tall and lean and—unlike Quinn—he's aggressively clean shaven with a head of professionally styled hair.

"Hey, Shane," Hanna says. "This is Sonya Rossi, my spa manager; Sonya, my brother Shane. The actor."

Oh God, that's right. The movie star. Quinn isn't the only extremely successful Hott brother. In fact, they're all superstars in their own fields. Minor hometown heroes—the kind who never come home to be celebrated.

"Hi, Sonya," Shane says, but he's not looking at me. He kneels by his sister's bed. "How are you feeling?"

Hanna chuckles. "I'm fine, dude. I'm going to be fine. The baby's going to be fine. You guys all have to chill the fuck out."

He shakes his head. "You scared us."

Hanna rolls her eyes. "Yeah, well, you scare me all the time doing your own stunts and partying yourself into jail cells. Turnabout is fair play."

He laughs at that, shrugging it off.

"You heading back to LA today?" she asks him.

He shakes his head. "Sticking around a few days." He shrugs again. "Easton said you needed someone to start getting bids on the barn project?"

Hanna raises her eyebrows. "Really? Really and truly? My famous movie-star brother is going to *help out around the ranch*?"

"I was gonna take a look. I can probably at least figure out the big picture and get some contractors in to give us an estimate."

Hanna gives him a jaded look, one eye shut appraisingly. "Are you sure you're not staging image rehab? *Hollywood's most notorious party-boy actor adorably helps out his family back at the ranch?*"

"I would *never*," Shane says.

He looks sincere, but Hanna's scrutiny doesn't waver.

"Han?" comes a call from somewhere downstairs. "You up there?"

"Where the fuck else would I be?" Hanna calls back. "I'm not supposed to leave this bed."

More feet on the stairs.

"I should go?" I don't actually *want* to. I'm extremely curious about the rest of the Hott brothers, and it sounds, from the feet on the stairs, like I'm about to meet more of them.

Sure enough, two more ridiculously attractive men squeeze into the room. Shane's a bit smaller than Quinn, but these two are both built on the Quinn scale and well dressed, one in a pair of charcoal dress slacks, a white dress shirt, and a tie, and the other in brown dress slacks and a tan shirt with a gorgeous pattern of brown stripes. Both clean shaven, both sporting decent haircuts. Apparently aversion to scissors is not genetic in the Hott family.

The finance guy and the lawyer, I think.

"Preston," Hanna says, pointing to the one in the tie. "Rhys," she says, pointing to the other. "Sonya, my spa manager. Did you guys come over to say goodbye?"

Both men shift uncomfortably. "Um. Not exactly," Rhys says. "I postponed my flight."

Preston fidgets. "Me, too."

Hanna narrows her eyes. "For when?"

"For...a few days out. I thought I could take a quick look at the resort's legal setup," Rhys says.

Preston nods crisply. "And I thought I could have a look at its finances."

She squints at them, her brows drawing together. "What about Kali?" she asks Preston.

"She'll be fine," he says.

Something in his tone drags my gaze to his face, but he's blank.

"If you can use our help, we've got a couple of days to pitch in," he tells Hanna.

She looks from one of them to the other, and they waver under her scrutiny, dropping their gazes. She points an accusing finger. "Easton yelled at you guys, didn't he?"

The brothers exchange glances, looking, if possible, even more fidgety than before.

"Yeah," Rhys says.

Hanna sighs heavily and rolls her eyes. "I told him not to do that."

"Yeah, well, it apparently didn't sink in," Preston says dryly. "He cornered us in the hospital and—loose paraphrase—told us we were dickheads."

Rhys frowns. "That's not a loose paraphrase. It's an exact quote. He called us dickheads, and he's right, Han— we've been dickheads. This is on us." He points to her, lying in the bed. "We put you there."

"Don't be ridiculous."

"We left you here to deal with Granddad and this business by yourself—"

She gives him a sharp look. "Does this have anything to do with why you haven't mentioned contesting the will again?"

When he looks away without answering, she says, "It's my business. And I'm good at running it."

"Anyway," Preston says, "we thought that since you can't do a whole bunch right now—"

"Huge understatement," Rhys mutters.

"Since you're flat on your back—"

"Technically, propped up," Rhys murmurs. Like the lawyer he is.

Preston glares at him. "Shut up, man."

I can't tell whether the laser-eye standoff that ensues is real hostility or the product of brotherly love.

"*Anyway*," Preston says fiercely, "since you're in bed, we thought we'd take a couple days and try to pitch in however we can."

"Aw," says Hanna. "You guys!"

"Hey," someone says from the doorway. Another brother. A really, really big brother. And when I say big, I'm starting with a baseline of Quinn Hott, mad scientist–mountain man. This one is easily six-four and built to beat up Quinn in a toe-to-toe battle.

He's not as outright scruffy as Quinn was, but when our eyes meet, there's a sadness, a deep grief in them that stops me in my tracks. His jaw is tight and wears a day's scruff; his mouth is set, and the lines around it are deeper than they should be for his age.

He doesn't acknowledge me, but I'm assuming this is

Tucker. And...something bad has happened to this guy—something I don't know about, despite the fact that news streaks through Rush Creek at the speed of light.

"Let me guess," Hanna says to the newcomer, "you thought you'd take a look at the resort's security procedures?"

15

QUINN

"**Y**ou look like Kit Harington when he cut all his hair off," Hanna says as I plop down in the chair next to her bed. She's home now, propped up on pillows and looking a lot more like herself—with a big baby belly. "Not the super-short cut. The tousled one."

"I'm gonna take that as a compliment," I say.

She shrugs. "Whatever. I never liked *Game of Thrones.* You just missed your brothers."

"Which ones?"

"All four of them."

"Seriously? They're all still here?"

I can believe Shane and Tucker are—Shane's between projects and Tucker's been cagey about what's going on with his work. But the idea of Preston leaving behind both his wife, Kali, and his job is foreign. And Rhys, while not a workaholic, has an intense and successful family law practice—mostly divorces. It's not a career that lends itself to a flexible schedule.

"I heard Easton yelled at you guys," she says in lieu of an explanation. "Called you dickheads."

"Not me," I say. "I think maybe he felt like I was already taking enough shit from Granddad."

"Fair." She frowns. "What do you think Granddad planned for the rest of them? I mean, is everyone going to get a summons? Am I?"

"Nah," I say. "I think this is about getting us back to Rush Creek, and you were already here."

"It can't be *only* about that. It's not like it was an accident that he put the guy who doesn't feel like he's a people person on the front lines of social interaction, right?"

"Probably not," I admit.

"So, what, all the others are going to get some kind of weirdo assignment, too?"

I shrug. "Unless Rhys still wants to contest."

"Seems like he might have dropped that mission." Hanna tilts her head.

"You noticed that, huh?"

"I figured maybe Easton's 'dickhead' rant shut him down."

I don't mention my theory that Rhys might have struck his own superstitious bargain in the hospital rather than risk Hanna's or the baby's life. Hanna would just scoff.

"So what do you think Granddad has in store for the others? Like Preston has to lie on a beach all day to counteract his workaholic tendencies, and Shane has to..." She ponders it. "What's the opposite of being a party-boy actor?"

"He has to wear a paper bag over his head and never leave the house."

She snorts. "So, that?"

"I don't know…but I think maybe so."

She extends an arm, reaching for a huge cup with a straw in it; I grab it and hand it to her before she can exert herself. She rolls her eyes at me. "I can get my own *cup*," she says.

"Not while I'm around."

Another roll of her eyes. "You guys are the worst."

I consider whether she means it or not, decide she doesn't. "So what does Easton calling them dickheads have to do with them still being here?"

"They all decided they needed to 'pitch in' with the resort. So Preston's combing through the finances, Shane's researching how much it'll cost to renovate the second venue, Rhys is looking at legal and contracts, and Tucker's digging into security. What?" she demands in response to my expression.

"I wasn't expecting that."

Once upon a time, the idea of my brothers all working together on a family business wouldn't have seemed like any kind of big deal, but that was *before*.

"How long are they staying?" I ask.

"Preston and Rhys were making noise about staying a few days. Shane and Tucker seemed more open ended."

I try to gauge her feelings about this turn of events. Hanna and I were the last two Hott kids left in Rush Creek. She used to crawl into my bed sometimes so we'd both feel less alone. If any two people know what it's like to watch our brothers' backsides recede into the distance, it's us. Which means if any two people know not to hang hope on them, it's us.

"Don't worry," she says, as if she can read my mind. "I get it. They're leaving again. *You're* leaving again."

I don't correct her because she's right—I'm counting the days.

"How are you handling being away from work?"

I shrug.

"You *hate* it," she says, frowning. "God, Quinn, I'm so sorry—"

"No. Stop. Don't. I don't hate it."

And for better or for worse it's true. I don't hate being in the spa. I enjoy working on the shampoo project. And...

Well.

I look forward to being near Sonya, even though sometimes it's tough because she's so close and I won't—can't—touch.

"What?" Hanna asks.

"Nothing," I say.

She watches me for a minute, unreadable.

"So," she says, "how's it going at my spa?"

"Fine," I say, shrugging.

"*Really?*"

"It's not bad. I sit behind the desk. I make appointments and ring up loofahs and soap that smells like 'Paris in springtime' and 'dancing in the rain.'"

"Can soap *do* that?"

"It can claim to do that," I say.

"And you and Sonya? Getting along?"

"Yup."

Her eyes narrow. Shit. I played that one degree too cool. Hanna, for all her avowed trouble grokking social cues, can read me like a book. "She was just here, you know."

Oh *shit*. Did Sonya tell her we're accidentally cohabitating? If so, my evasion will *definitely* raise Hanna's interest level to nuclear levels. But if not, I don't want to be the one to spill the beans.

I settle on a noncommittal, "Yeah?"

"Mmm," she says. "I just think it's interesting. Twice in your life you've cut a lot of hair off all at once. Once was when you were in high school with a mad crush on Katie Previns. The second time was more than ten years later, while spending a lot of time around Sonya Rossi."

"I did *not* cut my hair in high school to impress Katie."

"But you *did* cut your hair to impress Sonya."

I close my eyes, willing myself not to think about the haircut, Sonya, or that long moment when she was standing close enough that I could have slid my hand into her hair and drawn her mouth down to mine.

I open them to find Hanna staring at me, open mouthed. "You *did*," she breathes.

I frown at her. "You're such a pain in my ass. I didn't do anything to *impress* her. I just didn't want my bad hair to make it hard for us to sell beauty products. Beauty is aspirational."

She narrows her eyes at me. "Are you quoting Sonya?"

"No," I say. "Lily. Sonya says that the spa is about letting people take care of themselves in whatever way feels best to them."

Her mouth quirks. "Does she?" She appraises me. "Interesting," she says again. "Maybe Granddad was onto something after all."

I'm now extra glad she doesn't know Sonya and I are

living together under one roof. I can only imagine what she'd have to say about that.

"Stop it," I warn her.

"Stop what?" she says innocently.

"Stop implying Granddad had some kind of master plan. He was just pissed off that none of us did what he wanted while he was alive. He's a grumpy asshole who wouldn't recognize a good idea if it bit him on the ass."

Hanna's mouth turns up. "Well," she says, "takes one to know one."

16

———————

SONYA

Monday morning Quinn is gone again when I wake up and sitting at the desk when Gus and I arrive. But he's not by himself. He's surrounded by my people—Reggie behind the desk, Lily draped over the front of it, Serenity leaning against the makeup shelf.

"Sonya!" Reggie says. She's gotten a new piercing, this one in her eyebrow, and she's wearing one of her many vividly colored outfits of outrageous tops, short skirts, fishnet stockings, and combat boots or Doc Martens. "We were admiring Quinn's new 'do." She reaches for Quinn's hair, but he ducks away. "You didn't *cheat* on us, did you, Quinn? Because this is definitely not my work, and I'm pretty sure it's not Mei's, either."

"It's not Mei's," she confirms, joining us.

"You got your hair cut, too!" I say, pointing to Mei's new highlighted short bob, hoping to deflect attention from Quinn. I'm not sure why it didn't occur to me that his shorn head and face would raise my staff's curiosity.

Reggie raises her eyebrows. "Yes, but I actually *did* that cut and color."

Quinn looks as uncomfortable as I've ever seen him, and I can't blame him. "It's not cheating if he went to his own hair stylist," Lily points out.

"He's from Boston," Reggie says. "So unless he flew across the country and back to get his hair cut, he didn't go to his own stylist. He went to someone in the area *who wasn't us.*"

"Reggie, lay off," Lily says. "He has a right to go anywhere he wants."

"Of course he does," Reggie says. "I just want to know who it was because I like to scope out the competition. Where'd you go, Quinn?"

Quinn's eyes meet mine. I wince.

"I did it," I say.

They all turn to look at me. Even Gus cocks his head upward.

"You?" Reggie demands. "You never do hair."

"I do. Sometimes."

She raises an eyebrow. It's true that I basically only cut and style when Reggie or Mei aren't available or when we have bigger bridal parties and need all hands on deck.

"What I want to know," Reggie says slowly, "is *when*? You still looked like Grizzly Adams on Saturday when I left," she tells Quinn. "And now you're hot as hell. *Survivorman* called—they want to know where their star is."

Red rises on Quinn's cheekbones.

The thing is, neither Quinn nor I has mentioned the

fact that we're cohabiting. And right now, it would be Big News. A snow plow crashing through the wall of a house.

"Last thing on Saturday," I lie. "We were the only two left here and I, uh—"

"I asked her to," Quinn says, so low his words are almost swallowed.

Everyone turns to look at him, then back at me. I can read the questions on their faces. I inwardly cringe.

"Can we leave Quinn alone?" I ask. "He has work to do."

"Yeah," he says, flipping the bird to the lawyer's camera. "Big brother is watching."

"What work?" Reggie wants to know.

"Work," I say. "And so do all of you."

Her eyebrows go up. I almost never play the boss card. I know I'm in for it.

Sure enough, ten minutes later, Reggie corners me in the bathroom as I'm washing my hands. "We give private haircuts after hours now?" she teases, sticking out a studded tongue.

I try for nonchalance. "He's a much better advertise-ment for our services now, don't you think?"

She gives me a squinty face that says she knows I'm full of it. "There's something going on between you and Quinn is what I think."

"You're wrong about that," I say, with relief that it's true. I'm also secretly relieved that Reggie is giving me crap. Her husband left her recently for his yoga instructor, and she's been a sad and subdued shadow of herself.

Her blue eyebrows touch her pink bangs. "You know," she says, tilting her head to one side, "you *are* allowed to have fun from time to time, Sonya. And right now? That boy looks like a *lot* of fun."

"He's not a boy."

"No," Reggie says wistfully. "He really, really, really isn't."

"You're sure you can close up?" I ask Quinn, pushing my key across the counter. Gus tucks his nose against my hip and waits patiently.

I'm leaving early to check on my dad, who lives in an apartment north of town. I look in on him once a week or so, and it's been more than that, with the upheaval of Quinn's arrival.

Quinn gives me a hard look as he takes the key from me. "I can turn off lights, set thermostats, and lock doors." He considers me. "You really don't like to let other people do stuff for you, do you?"

"No one likes to let other people do stuff for them."

"That's not true," he says.

"I don't think I'm *particularly* opposed to letting people do stuff for me."

"That's why you came in here Sunday afternoon and cleaned all the sink traps—on your day off."

"How do you know that?"

He sighs. "Because Lily told me that you do, every Sunday, and that you won't let her alternate with you."

"She shouldn't have told you that."

Lily wouldn't even know it, except she'd finally demanded to know why the sink traps were always already clean when she went to take care of them. *I don't know* didn't seem like the kind of answer that would satisfy her.

Quinn's eyebrows go up. "Well, she did."

I slide my hand off the counter. "Bye, Quinn."

There's a long pause before he says, "Bye, Sonya."

I'm almost to the door before he calls out, "See you at home."

I give him a dark look over my shoulder, and I swear, the corner of his mouth almost hits actual-smile heights.

Gus and I take a quick walk around the spa grounds, then drive to my dad's apartment, a one-bedroom in a bland brick building not too far from Rush Creek's main street. We climb the concrete stairs, with their iron railing, to the fourth floor.

"Sunny!" my dad says, throwing the door open and grabbing me in a big hug. He spins me around.

"Hey, Dad," I say, hugging him back. When I was a kid, his hugs were solid and reassuring, a promise that he'd take care of me and Mom and that everything would be okay. Now when I hug him, I think about the fact that for as long as I can remember, I've been the one taking care of him. "How's it going?"

"Good, good!" he says, which is what he always says. He's seventy-two, retired Navy. Balding, heavyset, with a gray mustache. "Come on in. Tell me all the things!"

While Gus settles at my feet on the kitchen floor, my dad brews me tea. He keeps a bag of Pepperidge Farm Milano cookies, just for me. We sit at the kitchen table, and he makes me tell him everything that's going on at work. He laughs when he hears about Quinn, laughs harder when I tell him about Quinn showing up at the cabin, ready to move in. I don't tell him about the unpaused episode of *Sex Education*, but I do tell him about Quinn's chemistry experiments in the kitchen. When I'm done with my stories, he tells me what's been going on for him. He's learning how to swim at the Rush Creek Rec Center. He signed up for some kind of foraging course with Wilder Adventures, the outfit run by Easton's family.

"And I met someone," he says without pausing his narrative rhythm, which means I don't see it coming and nearly choke on my tea.

"You—*met...someone?*"

"A very nice woman. At the pool. She swims every day at eight a.m., and we got to talking."

I try not to picture my dad, his big belly hanging over the waistband of his bathing suit, chatting up a woman in *her* bathing suit.

"We've been out a few times. I want you to meet her."

"That's—great," I say, meaning it but also worried. My dad tends to do best when his life is calm. Stable. He has a gambling addiction, and he's struggled to keep it under control ever since my mom died. He's been doing pretty well lately—as far as I know—but change tends to throw him off. And a romantic life is a *big* change for a guy who's been single for the last fifteen years.

My dad—son of an Irish dad and an Italian mom, both lapsed Catholics—would have loved a big family with a whole bunch of kids, but that wasn't how things worked out. After me, my mom's cancer got diagnosed, she had a hysterectomy, and they felt like things were too uncertain for adoption or surrogacy. She went into remission, and they were just glad to have more time together, the three of us as a family...until the cancer came back and we lost my mom.

It's been just my dad and me since then, except for the years I was at college...

"Be careful," I say.

He knows what I mean.

"Of course," he says. "You don't have to worry about me. I made a lot of mistakes. But now I'm on a better path."

"I know you are, Dad," I say, hugging him.

"Speaking of that." He puts his mug down, and there's a cautiousness in his voice. "I'd like to pay you back some of the money you spent getting me back on track."

"Dad. We've been over this. We're family. You don't owe me anything."

"I've been doing a little work. Writing content for blogs and other sites. About addiction."

He's startled me. "Yeah?"

"Yeah. It's not a lot of money, but I've put it all aside for you."

"You didn't need to do that. You should use it to fix up the house. Replace Moby."

Moby is the name he gave the giant grape-colored beanbag that he sits in when he watches TV. Someone left it in the heap of free stuff at the transfer station, and he upcycled it. But it's not comfortable, especially for an older guy. He should be sitting in an armchair. A recliner, maybe.

He shakes his head. "That money's yours."

"I don't want it," I say.

"Stubborn," he says. Fondly. "Like your mom."

But he doesn't fight me further. Instead, he pushes the

cookies back to me. I take one more and roll the bag closed. "How's the fridge?" I ask him.

"Oh, you know," he says. "Not too bad."

Not too bad, in this case, translates to *nearly empty*—a package of ham I sniff and toss, the butt end of a loaf of bread, limp lettuce, and not quite enough milk for a bowl of cereal in the morning—if there were any cereal in the pantry, which there isn't.

"I'm gonna grab you some groceries," I tell him.

"You don't have to do that," he says. "I'll get to it tomorrow."

"You don't have anything for breakfast."

He shrugs. "There's toast. And I think there's an egg."

"There isn't," I say.

"Peanut butter."

"Dad," I say, "that's not breakfast. Let me get the groceries."

He gives me a look. "You know I don't need you to do that."

"And you know I don't mind."

He sighs. "You're a good kid, Sunny."

"Good genes," I say as I grab my purse and pat my thigh to get Gus up from the floor.

"I'm going to assume you mean your mother," he calls after me.

17

SONYA

By the time I get home, I'm so tired that all I can think about is feeding and walking Gus, getting into my PJs, and falling into bed. Except my stomach is empty and gnawing, and *damn*, I forgot to get myself something for dinner.

Not even one lousy frozen dinner to get me through tonight. And I'm so tired that calling for takeout and picking it up sounds like running a triathlon. Because Rush Creek is out of the way, the rideshare food drop services costs a fortune, and the one guy who delivers locally is off tonight.

On the chance that I've forgotten about a box of pasta and a jar of spaghetti sauce in my cupboards, I pull in next to the cabin and trudge up to the front door. The lights are on inside, and I expect to be greeted with the unpleasant odors of science.

But instead, it's quiet as I approach the front door, and when I open it, Gus and I step into a cloud of food scents so delectable I almost trip over myself. He whines and stretches his nose into the deliciousness, then bolts into the kitchen.

"What…?"

Gus is already face down in his full food bowl, which Quinn must have set out for him. And Quinn is, indeed, stirring something. But whatever's on the stove isn't shampoo or conditioner or face cream.

"What *is* that?"

"Beef stew," he says.

"It smells *amazing*."

"Good Maillard reaction when I browned the beef cubes," he says offhandedly, opening a spice bottle that I definitely didn't own before today and tossing some in without measuring.

"Good *what*?"

He stirs the contents of the pot. "The chemical reaction that happens when you expose meat to high temperatures. Named after the French chemist who discovered it in 1912. It's a non-enzymatic reaction," he adds.

I snort. "Thanks for the clarification."

The corners of his mouth turn up, and I admire the neat trim of his beard and mustache, the slight curve of his lips. "As opposed to what happens to apples or avocados after you cut them," he says. "You know how they turn brown? That's an enzymatic reaction. But this is similar to what happens when you caramelize onions. Pyrolysis."

"I'm not sure I've ever caramelized onions," I admit.

His eyebrows go up. "That's a shame," he says. "They're excellent on barbecue chicken pizza."

"I usually order my barbecue pizza from Royal Pizza."

"That's where we used to get it when we were kids."

"Speaking of kids, I met your brothers on Sunday. At Hanna's place. They're quite a crew."

"They are that," he says, rolling his eyes.

"Tell me about them."

I'm not sure what makes me this bold. Up to this point, Quinn hasn't talked much about himself—or anything—but I'm starting to wonder if that's by choice or if he just isn't used to doing it.

A guy who'd brew shampoo to help you save your surrogate mom's job and cook you dinner when you're too tired to do it yourself isn't as much "not a people person" as he claims. But for some reason, he thinks of himself that way.

And I guess I want to understand why.

He scowls. "You met them. You don't need me to tell you about them."

I ignore the scowl. I get it now—how much those scowls are a defense. "I want you to. I got my own impressions, but I'm curious about yours."

He hesitates, and I prepare myself for the walls to go up, but then the scowl loosens a bit. "Uh. Well. Shane and I are pretty much opposites. He's Mr. Sunshine, always up, like you. And he teases a lot."

"Whereas you're grumpy and always serious."

"Always," he says. But he gives me a sideways glance that makes me think that maybe, just maybe, he's teasing. "Rhys and I are more alike."

"He's the divorce attorney?"

"Yeah. Busy. Serious. Cynical."

"I would guess being a divorce attorney would do that to you."

"Or it's the other way around," he says. "He became cynical first—because he saw marriages fall apart in our childhood—and becoming a divorce lawyer just made sense."

I open my mouth to ask more, but he's already moved on, slamming the door shut on that line of inquiry. "And Tucker—I'm in my head, and he's—physical. Tough, played football. A man's man." He shakes his head. "We were so close in age and so different. We had to find our own ways, so I think that's why we weren't closer."

"What about Preston?"

His face goes dark, then blank, and I'm sure he's going to clam up, refuse to say anything about his oldest brother. But then he says, "He was always supportive of me."

It's not at all what I was expecting.

And I'm not expecting him to keep talking, either, like a dam's come down. "My granddad, he was the opposite of cerebral. You can't imagine a man less in his head or less self-aware. And he couldn't deal with my *braininess*"—he says it with the blunt force of a man who's had the word used as a weapon against him—"but Preston could. He told me I'd be a great scientist one day."

"And you are," I say.

He blushes and waves it off.

"Anyway, enough about all that," he says gruffly, and I can tell show-and-tell time's over. "What bowls should we use?"

I take down two of my favorite bowls, hand-thrown by a local artisan, glazed blue with swirls of vivid green, and he ladles stew into them.

He hands me the bowl as Gus finishes licking the last detectable crumb from his bowl.

"I'll take Gus out," Quinn says. "You start."

Out of nowhere, my eyes fill with tears. I swipe them back with my free hand, surprised at myself. I'm not an easy crier.

"Sonya."

"No, it's nothing." I wave him off

"It's not nothing," he growls. "What's wrong?"

"It's just—this is nice."

And I don't let people do nice things for me very often. Somehow, he crept past my defenses.

He takes the bowl out of my hands and sets it on the table. "Come here." He holds his arms open.

I hesitate.

He steps forward and wraps me up.

I would have expected him to be one of those stiff huggers, but he's not; he's a bear hugger. His arms are strong and fierce, his body hard and muscular, and with my face pressed into the softness of yet another ridiculous T-shirt, the smell of his soap and skin filling my senses, I feel instantly better.

I want to stay right there for a long time. Much longer than is socially appropriate. And that's what makes me pull away: I haven't wanted to be held in a long time, and I don't want to let myself get used to the feeling. Because as soon as he fulfills the terms of the will, Quinn is taking off. Whatever this is between us—and I wouldn't know how to start labeling it—will vaporize.

I step back.

"I was so tired and hungry," I tell him, "and went

grocery shopping for my dad, and I forgot to get anything for me, and then this was here, like magic..."

And that kind of magic is scarce in my life. But I don't say it. I have a strict no-whining policy. That kind of magic is scarce in lots of people's lives. Bella's, for example.

"Sit," he says. "Eat."

So I do, while he leashes Gus up and they head out.

And God, it's good. The beef is tender, the stew rich and fragrant, as homey and comforting as Quinn's hug. I don't know if it's an enzymatic or non-enzymatic reaction, but I *love* it.

They come back through the front door. Gus lies down at my feet, and Quinn sits down across from me.

"Quinn, this is amazing." I take another bite, moaning my appreciation.

His eyes settle on me, dark and intent. I may not have seen that look from a man for a while, but I know it—it's like the pull of the moon on the tides, a tug of need between my legs.

He looks away. "Thanks," he says, shrugging.

"No, really."

"Chemistry." He shrugs again. "It's my thing."

The word *chemistry* makes me think of how good his body felt pressed against mine, the sea surge of my blood and tingle of nerves. My molecules recognizing his.

If it's only pheromones and hormones, all the more reason not to let it make me reckless and stupid.

"So. You grocery shop for your dad?" he asks.

Grateful for the distraction, I tell him, "When I can. He's been on his own since my mom passed, and I try to help out."

"In lieu of grocery shopping for yourself," he says, raising an eyebrow.

"I just forgot today."

"Do you do that a lot? Forget to buy food?"

"Occasionally. I guess. Doesn't everyone?"

"I've never forgotten to eat in my life," he says. "You take care of a lot of people, don't you." He scowls, but it's not a scowl *at* me. It's more a scowl *with* me. It sends a small shiver of warmth into my low belly.

Arms crossed, eyebrow raised, he studies me. "Lily says almost everyone at the salon right now used to work at the salon your mom owned when you were a kid. That you've been rehiring them all."

I turn away from his scrutiny. "Lily talks too much."

His lips quirk, but his voice softens. "We don't have to talk about it if you don't want to. I just—think it's pretty cool, you making sure they all have jobs."

"Bella's the last one," I say. I'm not sure why I let the words slide out. Maybe it's because he cooked for me. Or because he hugged me. Or maybe it's the way he's got his head cocked, like he'll be a good listener.

"Who's Bella?"

"She was the receptionist at my mom's salon, part of my mom's A-team. I would have hired her first, but she actually had a great assistant manager job at a salon in Bend...and then that place closed, but by then I'd hired someone else. I've been trying to get the budget to hire her ever since."

And then I find myself telling him about Bella—how she's raising her daughter's kids because her daughter struggles with addiction, how her mom's dementia is getting worse, how Bella keeps getting fired from shitty jobs because she has to pick a sick kid up from school or keep her mom from wandering.

He's a good listener. An amazing listener. The kind who doesn't talk at all, just keeps his eyes on my face, like he's trying to read what I'm not saying.

When I'm done, he says, quietly, "So Bella's the one you want to hire. The one you're selling all the product for."

I nod.

"We'll do it," he says.

There's something about that *we* that's both comforting and a little terrifying. I'm used to *we*—of course I am. I have coworkers and friends and my dad. But usually *I'm* the one saying *we*, and when I say it, I mean *mostly me*.

I'm quiet too long, and worry creases his forehead. I might have mistaken it for another scowl a few days ago, but I'm starting to understand him better.

"I haven't fucked it up yet, have I?" he asks wryly.

I can't help myself. "Not *yet*," I say, and he shakes his head and rolls his eyes at me.

"You're a mean boss," he says, but he's smiling at me. *Smiling!*

I have trouble looking at him straight on. With that smile, with the shorter hair and the neatly trimmed beard, he's like gazing into the sun.

Maybe the Bible story of Samson and Delilah had it backward. That story goes, when he let her cut his hair, she took his power.

But I think when she cut his hair, she was the one who lost her will to resist...and maybe her way, too.

18

QUINN

Great idea, Quinn. Cook for her.

I did it because she told me she was bad at it, because it was clear she rarely—if ever— enjoyed a homecooked meal. And because it's becoming clear to me that she can't let anyone help her and cooking for her seemed like a way to make her life easier—one that she might be able to accept.

It worked...except that I completely underestimated how good it would feel to feed her.

Her moan. Her hums of delight. I'm not sure she knows she's making them, but I do—and my body definitely does.

It's delicious torture.

It almost makes me forget the news I've been saving up for her, but not quite.

"I've got some bad news and some good news," I tell her.

"Uh-oh," she says.

"I'd like to think the good news outweighs the bad."

"Ohhhkay."

"The product shipment is on back-order for another two months."

"*Noooooooooooo!*" she cries.

"Okay, but wait right there." I hurry back to my bedroom and collect the two takeout containers sitting on my dresser. I come back and set them on the table in front of her.

"Hott Spot's own branded hair care," I tell her proudly. "I've been doing lab tests on them. Efficacy, substantivity, and moisture content."

She tilts her head. "Okay, wait, don't tell me, we learned this in my stylist program—how well the shampoo works, how well the conditioner sticks, and how much moisture the hair absorbs from the product?"

"Yup."

"You coulda just said that," she teases.

"I'm a chemist," I say. "We like weird, long, Latinate words."

She bites back a smile, teeth denting the softness of her plush lower lip in a way that definitely doesn't calm my body down.

Quinn, I chastise myself. *Eyes on the prize.* And in this case, the prize is helping Sonya's business and saving Hanna's. Lust is a distraction, the way it basically always is.

I push the two containers across the table to her.

She squints at them. "You're gonna have to work on packaging."

I shrug. "Who cares about packaging if it's a good product?"

Her eyes get huge. "Who cares about—*who cares about*

packaging?" she sputters. "Packaging is *everything*. Packaging is what sells the product."

"Isn't what sells the product whether it works or not?"

"Research shows," she says, "that consumers choose beauty and self-care products based on packaging the first time out. They come *back* because the product works for them."

"I'm not convinced," I say.

"Get convinced!"

I laugh.

She stares at me, eyes wide. "Are you *laughing*?"

"Yes. You're very bossy."

"I'm your *boss*!" She tilts her head. "Stop laughing!"

But she doesn't look like she means it. She's laughing, too. It feels good to laugh with her. I can't remember the last time I laughed.

I tap the top of one of my containers. "Don't look now, but your bathroom sink cabinet is now *filled* with competitor product. I had to compare."

Her grin gets bigger. "Did you wash your hair with all of them?"

"No. Did you know there are hair swatch sets you can do it on?"

"Yup. We use them to test color."

"I used a lot of those. The kitchen trash looks like a serial killer lives here."

"*Maybe she does...*" she says in what I think is supposed to be a serial-killer voice.

I roll my eyes at her.

"How'd it go? The testing?"

I try to hold back my grin but can't. "I think we've got a

good thing. But I need someone besides me to try the shampoo and conditioner."

"You mean *me*?"

"I mean you. I tried both products earlier. When I got home."

"And?"

"You be the judge." I get up from my seat, round the table, and crouch next to her, tilting my head her way.

But as soon as I do it, I realize what I've done.

I've invited her to touch me again.

Her fingers tangle in my hair, stirring the strands, stroking my scalp. My eyes drift closed.

Sonya lets out a sigh, and it makes me instantly hard.

I open my eyes and find her looking down at me with a hungry expression in her eyes. And the temptation to lunge up and kiss that expression off her face—to feed that hunger the way I fed her other hunger earlier—is almost overwhelming.

She licks her lips, which doesn't help.

"Your waves kept their body... It's soft, and it's not greasy at all," she says. "No obvious residue. And doesn't feel dry."

I smile wryly. "Ah. The words of praise every man longs to hear."

The corner of her mouth turns up. "Man, or scientist? I thought I was assessing the efficacy, moisture content, and what's the other one?"

"Substantivity."

"Okay. Well. On the science front you pass with flying colors."

And the other?

"And you do have very nice hair." She blushes. She's

wearing another blouse open to the second button, and the pink sweeps across the sweet upper curves of her breasts, taking all the blood out of my head.

"It feels good when you touch it." My voice is low and rough.

Her eyes flare dark. For a long moment, she just looks at me. Then she reaches out. Runs her fingers through my hair again, soft as a breeze, her gaze never leaving me.

"Sonya," I groan. I reach up, put my hands on both sides of her face, and pull her down until her mouth touches mine.

Her lips are soft, and she opens without hesitation, her hands sinking deeper into my hair, clutching at the back of my head. "Oh God," she whimpers, and that's it for me. I'm lost and desperate, my tongue sinking into the silk of her mouth, finding hers, trying to give both of us as much pleasure as I can before one of us comes to our senses. My hand slips to the hem of her blouse, then under. She moans at the touch, and my groan answers, like it has a life of its own.

I'm not sure which of us pulls back first, only that we stare at each for a split second before we both turn away.

"We work together," she says, not meeting my eyes. "I work for your sister, you work for me. And you don't do relationships."

"Yeah," I say because everything she's said is true. I want so badly to kiss her again, to plunder her mouth and touch her everywhere she'll let me, but it can't lead anywhere good—for either of us. "Plus I'm headed back to Boston in a month."

She takes a deep breath. "Okay," she says. "So. As a scientist, you'd concur, right? Bad idea."

"Bad idea," I agree.

The moment stretches out, the way awkward ones always do. Finally she reaches for the shampoo and conditioner.

"You want me to try these?" she asks.

"Oh. Yeah. That would be great."

She takes one in each hand and drifts away, toward the bathroom. After a few minutes, I hear the shower running. I try not to think about it: Sonya slowly stripping out of her clothes, unhooking her bra, sliding her panties down. Sonya stepping under the spray, the water streaming through her hair, droplets rolling over her curves. Pink rising on her skin, pleasure blooming on her face.

The smell of vanilla drifts toward me, and even though I know the way I feel is just a chemical cascade—scent, association, biological response—it doesn't keep me from getting hard.

As a scientist, you'd concur, right? she said. *Bad idea.*

I do concur. But there was something I could have said back to her—but didn't.

As a man, though: I want to fuck you until you cry out my name.

19
———————
SONYA

One of my favorite things to do in Rush Creek on my day off is the farmers market. And this Sunday, I need a good distraction.

I can't stop thinking about that kiss, even though it was more than a week ago. His groan, my name on his lips, the long, sweet moment before he tugged my mouth to his. How confident he was, with his hands on the side of my face and his tongue dipping, seeking, giving pleasure.

I thought about it in the shower, surrounded by the delicious smell of the shampoo and conditioner that Quinn had home-brewed to help me solve a problem that shouldn't have mattered to him at all.

I thought about it while I was drying myself off, my body still buzzing with excitement and need, while I was blowing my hair dry (shiny, glossy, frizz free), and while I was wrapping myself in a thick terry robe with a baggy hood.

I thought about it while I was telling Quinn that his shampoo and conditioner were pretty fucking great, and while he was wearing a small, pleased smile that he couldn't hold back, him and Gus sitting on the sofa side by side, his hand moving firmly back and forth along Gus's back while Gus melted into a pool of satisfied pooch.

I thought about it in bed afterward when I couldn't sleep.

I slid my hand between my legs and circled my fingers over myself until I cried out, silently.

His name.

Bad idea.

I'd been so disappointed when he agreed with me, even though I shouldn't have been. I should have been relieved because his honesty and good sense had saved me from another error in judgment.

Still, I've thought about it all week, as Quinn and I have managed to mostly avoid spending time together. I'm sure he would have been out of the cabin if he could have been, but there are still no other openings. Instead, he's managed to arrange his schedule so we aren't home together much— and for my part, I've left him alone at the front desk as much as I can.

Gus and I head into town, my car crawling along Rush Creek's pretty main street behind the other farmers market traffic. It gives me time to soak up the Sunday-morning atmosphere: pairs and groups of women with shopping bags, a few clumps of wedding attendants still hungover from last night's celebrations. Some of them might even be from the wedding Hott Springs Eternal hosted last night. We pulled it off in style, and I don't think anyone even noticed the hoops we jumped through to make sure Hanna wasn't missed.

Luckily, for the most part, Hott Spot shone, without too much drama.

I find a lucky parking space in front of Rush Creek Bakery, wave to Nan through the window, and amble with Gus to the town green. Right on the edge of the green, near the entrance to the market, there's a makeshift stage. Four small dogs of varying breeds, doing a coordinated dance to "I Will Survive" as their *owner? handler? dance teacher?* issues instructions. They turn in circles, nod their heads, and prance on their hind legs, their fancy hairdos bobbing.

I clasp my hand to my mouth, giggling. They're adorable. And hilarious. And *ridiculous.*

Pretty sure Gus agrees. He has his head tilted to one side like he's trying to decide what to make of them.

"Sunny!" a voice says.

It's my dad, reaching down to greet Gus, who licks his hand enthusiastically.

"Dad, what are you doing here?"

To my surprise, he blushes. "I'm here to support Wendy."

"Wendy?" I ask.

He gestures to a woman standing behind the performers—the doggie dance teacher. She's five-two, max, with a lot of very yellow, almost certainly bottle-dyed hair, big blue eyes, and a ruffly dress.

"That's the woman I've been seeing," he says. "She has a YouTube channel and traveling show," he adds proudly. "She's just doing the farmers market today as a community service."

"It's certainly that," I say. "They made me smile."

Wendy's charges have finished their current dance, and

she deftly leashes them and turns them over to a middle-school-aged handler. "Intermission!" she calls to the gathering audience—my dad and I were definitely not the only ones attracted to the spectacle.

Then she hurries over to us and throws her arms around my dad.

His face lights up.

"You're amazing!" he tells her.

"You think so?" She beams at him.

"Absolutely."

I try to suss out her age. Over fifty, for sure, but I'd bet she's fifteen years younger than my dad. In good news, I don't have to worry that she's a gold digger. There's no gold left to dig. Except the money he's "set aside for me."

"Sonya, this is Wendy; Wendy, this is my daughter, Sonya."

"Such a pleasure!" Wendy says, turning the full force of her smile on me. "I've heard *so* much about you."

Weird, I think, *because my dad didn't mention you until a few days ago.* But I say, "You, too!" because I can tell, from the expression on my dad's face, that that's what he needs.

Still, I wonder why it took him so long to tell me about Wendy. I can tell they're more serious than my dad's "we've been out a few times" would indicate. They link arms and smile at each other, Wendy's chin tipped all the way up so she can look into my dad's eyes, my solemn dad unable to keep the big dumb grin off his face.

It's really cute.

"Are you just browsing?" Wendy asks me.

"Looking for a gift for a coworker who has a birthday gathering tonight."

"If you don't find something you like here, you should check out Five Rivers Arts and Crafts in town," my dad says.

"Yes!" Wendy exclaims. "Your father got me this adorable hat there for my birthday last week."

She produces, from a large pocket, a black bowler-style quilted hat with a fat red fabric rose sticking out from the front and settles it on her head, slightly askew.

"It's—lovely."

I don't look at my dad, who has never been much of a gift giver. When my mom was alive, she used to gripe in a loving way about my dad's habit of forgetting anniversaries, Valentine's Day, and Mother's Day. And since my mom died, my birthday present every year has been the same thing: dinner out and a gift certificate to Rush to Read Books. And don't get me wrong: I *love* my yearly gift from my dad. But felt hats with roses on them are definitely outside my dad's comfort zone. As is shopping. Period.

Huh.

"I have to get back up there!" Wendy says, and she gives my dad a big kiss on his wrinkled cheek. He relinquishes her hand unwillingly, like they're a slow-mo movie montage of saying goodbye.

A moment later, she's back onstage, the dogs are unleashed and lined up in their places, and Walk the Moon's "Shut Up and Dance" spills out from the sound system. My dad's full attention is back on the stage.

"Oh, wow," says a familiar voice behind me. "That's— something. Gus, are you feeling *jealous*?"

I turn to find Quinn, crouching to scritch a blissed-out Gus behind his hair tuft and ears. Quinn's wearing a T-shirt that says, *I tell bad chemistry jokes because all the good ones argon*, with argon in its periodic-table square. Like all his T-shirts, this one is snug across his shoulders, biceps, and chest. My mouth goes dry.

He shifts from one foot to another, eyes on Gus; he's still, ostensibly, waiting for my dog's answer to the question of whether he's jealous of the dogs on stage.

I wonder if he's thinking about the kiss, too.

"Hey," I manage, "I can't speak for Gus, but I'm feeling pretty jealous. I need to get myself a few more dogs and work something up." In fact, the only thing I'm jealous of here is Quinn's hands on my dog instead of on me—but I don't say that.

"I imagine 'Who Let the Dogs Out' shows up here at some point?" He sends Gus into a frenzy of joy with under-chin scritches.

I laugh. "It would have to, right?" I tilt my head, examining him. "What are you doing here?" The Rush Creek farmers market is an unlikely destination for an introvert on his day off.

To my surprise, a faint red streak rises in his cheeks as he stands. "I'm, um, looking for inspiration for packaging," he says.

I press my lips together against a smile. "Wait. Say that again."

"I figured no one knows beauty-product sales better than you do, and if you say packaging sells it...well, then, packaging sells it."

Our eyes meet; he's almost-smiling at me again. I lose a few brain cells to lust.

"Tell you what," I say, "we can look around together for

inspiration, and I know someone who can design the packaging. You work on production and testing."

"On it. One of my lab staff has a friend who does skincare production and testing."

"Who's this?" my father demands.

I shift my attention to discover my dad staring at Quinn, eyebrows up. "This is Quinn. He's working at the salon's reception desk for a bit."

"Ah," says my dad, obviously disappointed that Quinn's not a romantic interest.

Join the club, Dad.

Wait. No.

That's not a thing I want.

More to the point, it's not a thing I can *have*.

"Thomas Rossi," my dad says because I've lost the thread and failed to complete the other half of my intros.

"Nice to meet you, Mr. Rossi," Quinn says and shakes my dad's hand.

Wendy's assistant comes running over. "Mr. Rossi," she says, "I have to take a bathroom break. Can you hold Timber's and Pal's leashes for a minute until Ms Gold is ready for them?"

"Of course," my dad says. "Nice to meet you, Quinn. Good to see you, honey." He hesitates a moment. "I'm so glad you got to meet Wendy."

"Me, too," I say.

Quinn gestures at the market. "Shall we?"

"Sure."

We walk side by side, close enough in the crowd that our bodies touch from time to time. His arm is warm. The side of his body is warm. Everything in my own body heats up to match.

You were right not to let anything else happen, Sonya. It was a good judgment call.

Bad idea.

We stroll up an aisle. There are quite a few booths with handmade soaps, lotions, and creams. One booth has all kinds of scented bar soaps, each wrapped completely differently—in papers, grasses, fabrics, ribbons. They're beautiful and distinctive, and I want to touch them all—take in their smells and textures.

"Pretty, right?" I say.

He shrugs. "To me, it's what's on the inside that matters."

"But not everyone makes decisions that way."

"They should."

He frowns at the soaps. "You know what?" he says, turning his body so the low murmur of his words is audible only to me. Something in my belly purrs to life at the confidential tone, the incline of his body. I fantasize that the next words out of his mouth will be an invitation:

I can't be this close to you and not think about kissing you.

The whole time you were in the shower, I was picturing you.

Every night this week, I've been dreaming about you.

"We should be selling her soaps," Quinn says, knocking me and my ridiculous thoughts right on their asses.

"You know what?" I say—because what the hell else *can* I say? "You're totally right."

I ask the vendor if she does any retail or if she'd be willing to sell her soaps on consignment through us, and she lights up. We exchange info with her, take some photos, and move on.

We stop at another booth to admire bottles of hand cream and tubes of lotion that are simple but lovely— shades of gray, easy-to-read script. We ask the creator if she's interested in selling through us, too, and she bounces up and down with excitement.

Then we come to another booth, jars that look sourced from the recycling bin, labels ugly, too-busy bright colors that war with each other, and as if by unspoken agreement, we pass by without stopping.

As soon as we're past, Quinn says, "Okay, you were right. Packaging matters."

"I know," I say.

We both laugh.

God. Quinn's laugh. Rich and low and husky as if from disuse. And *for me*.

"Quinn Hott at a farmers market," a voice says behind us. "That's a sight I never thought I'd see."

20

QUINN

I turn around to find Shane behind me, his face the picture of amusement.

Shit.

The last thing I need, with Sonya at my side and the memory of her kiss still on fire in my brain, is brotherly love. And Shane is the brother who definitely feels free to give me the hardest time.

"You guys are *still* in Rush Creek?" I demand.

Shane shrugs. "I'm between roles." He aims a thumb behind him. "I heard the taco truck hangs out at the farmers market on Sundays, so I decided to check it out. What are *you* doing here?"

I shoot Sonya a quick look. "I heard the same rumor—great tacos."

Her eyebrows go up, but she doesn't out me.

If I'd thought there was the slightest chance that kissing Sonya would put to bed my physical hunger for her, I was dead wrong. If anything, the spark is more powerful than before.

But she made it clear that she thinks anything between us is a bad idea—and, worse, she's definitely right. Every word out of her mouth made perfect sense to me. I don't belong in Rush Creek. I don't do relationships. She doesn't do out-of-towners or casual.

We're a hard nope.

And I've been a hard yep in bed every night this week, trying to rub the lure of that kiss out of my brain. You can guess how successful I've been at that.

"Hey, Sonya," Shane says.

She beams. "I wasn't sure if you'd remember meeting me! We were all distracted that day with Hanna's health."

"Of course!" my brother says, giving her his million-dollar smile. "You're very memorable."

She blushes, the way she did when I kissed her, and I think about murder. Arsenic or cyanide in his food. Suffocation by pillow in his sleep. Strangulation with the silver bolo tie he definitely bought at this farmers market and which looks good on him because he's also somehow acquired Wranglers and a thick-buckled belt and a pair of cowboy boots since setting foot back in our hometown. And of course because he's an actor, he can pull it off.

I'd look like such a poser.

"Well, thanks," she says, giving him a kinda-sideways, under-the-eyelashes flirty smile. And he smiles right back, sunshine to her sunshine.

Which is what she deserves. Sonya *should* have the sun shining on her twenty-four seven. It just shouldn't be coming out of my brother's ass.

"How are you both feeling about being back in Rush Creek?" Sonya asks Shane and me.

"It's so different than when we were growing up," Shane says.

He's right. The basics are pretty much the same—Old West–style low-slung gas lights, rain barrels stuffed with flowers, wagon wheels as decorating elements. But the focus has shifted. The old tack shop—which at one point in the past was actually owned by my dad's dad—is half the size it was when I was growing up. The outdoor store sells bikinis and straw hats along with camping gear these days. You can see the difference even at the farmers market. Yes, you can still buy a pair of hand-tooled cowboy boots or a belt by Native American artisans...but you can also find wedding favors, spa treats, and homemade chocolates.

It's all because of the hot springs. When the springs popped to the surface, shortly after the rodeo left town, spas and weddings became the town's money maker. And more recently, my grandfather and Hanna built the Hott Springs Eternal empire, including Hott Spot.

"How do you feel about the changes?" Sonya asks.

I shrug. "Hanna wouldn't have a business without them. You wouldn't have a job. I can celebrate the new Rush Creek for those reasons. And I mean, I'm leaving. I don't have to love it or hate it, you know?"

Something flickers behind Sonya's expression, before it goes blank. "True," she says.

"I'd forgotten how great it is here," Shane says. "Everyone's so friendly. I've already gotten invited to a couple of parties and barbecues." He sighs. "Of course, it's mostly because people want me on their Instagram feeds, but who cares if the food and drink and company are good?" He beams at Sonya. "Hey—if you're looking for something to do Saturday night, I got invited to a book signing at Rush to Read Books. If you're not busy, you should come, too."

Sonya's cheeks get even pinker. "Oh, wow. Thank you. That sounds fun."

"Here," he says. "Let me give you my number, and you can text me if you decide to go."

Sonya extends her phone. I'm not even sure she knows what she's doing, that's how powerful Shane's effect on women is. She holds it out, her expression faintly dazed, and he types his number in, texts himself, and hands it back to her.

I watch, awed and still murderous. Death by nail gun, maybe.

"Sunny!"

Sonya's father is beckoning to her from a few yards away.

"Will you excuse me?" she says. "I'll be right back. That's my dad."

As she walks away, Shane turns toward me, beaming. "She's something," he says. "I like her."

"No," I say. "No way. Shane. No."

"What?" he asks.

"She deserves better than a guy who's photographed every night with his arm around a different woman."

A shadow crosses my brother's face. But then he shrugs. "Probably true," he says ruefully. "But I like her. I'm going to try to spend time with her."

I scowl.

Shane's expression changes to sly amusement. "Quinn Hott. Do you have a thing for your boss?"

"She's not my boss."

"Mmm," he says. "Granddad begs to differ."

"Your time is coming," I growl.

Shane's eyebrows go up. "Maybe. You don't have any evidence of that."

"The fact that Granddad wouldn't miss an opportunity to laugh at any of us from beyond the grave isn't evidence enough?"

"So you're convinced he's gunning for all of us."

This makes me picture our grandfather with his shotgun slung across his body, hands extended zombie-style, brain lust written on his face. I bite back a smile. "Yeah," I say. "I do."

"I saw you laughing with her earlier," Shane says, tilting his head to indicate Sonya.

Since I can't deny that, I scowl.

"The great Quinn Hott—*laughing*."

"I laugh."

"When, fifteen years ago?"

"Fuck you," I say mildly. Though, in fairness, that might have been the last time Shane heard me laugh, and even back then, it wasn't a common occurrence.

"You should bring her," he says. "Sonya. To the book signing."

I scowl harder.

"If you like her, you should ask her out."

"She's my boss."

"You said she wasn't."

I roll my eyes. Shane makes me feel like I'm twelve again, and not in a good way. "For the purposes of employment, she's not. For the purposes of dating, she is."

"I don't think you get to have it both ways," Shane muses.

"Besides," I say, "she's not my type."

"True," Shane says. "She's beautiful and friendly and smart enough to manage a business. None of those things are remotely appealing to you."

It's funny, but I don't think he knows how true those words are. Not that those things aren't appealing—they are—but they're pale versions of what I like about Sonya. She's beautiful, yeah, but it's not because she's as symmetrically pretty as the model on the cover of any magazine. It's because when she's in motion, busy, bustling, teasing and chatting, her beauty shines through, like there really is sunshine inside of her. And saying she's friendly—that's damning with faint praise. She's loyal enough that she orients her work around making sure the people she cares about are safe and supported. And as for smart? Fuck that. Anyone can manage a business, but only a few people can do it the way Sonya does, protecting what matters without losing her cool, her sense of humor, or her warmth toward the people around her. Look at how well she handled the setback my presence dealt to her plans.

And none of that even touches on the intense chemical reaction my body undergoes every time hers is near.

Shane is staring at me. "My dude," he says, "you are full of the utmost shit."

"I don't know what you're talking about."

"'She's not my type,'" he mocks. "She's so completely your type. You're totally into her."

Two different species.

"I'm not," I insist.

I don't know why, exactly, I argue with him. Maybe habit. Back when we were kids, Shane was the brother who knew how to get under my skin, and he apparently still does.

Or maybe I argue because of an uneasy sense that he's too close to the truth.

"Okay," he says, throwing up his hands. "So, then, you won't mind if I stop by the salon later this week and do my best to talk her into coming to that book signing with me?"

He gives me a sly, knowing look that throws fuel on the fire of my stubbornness

"Nope." I do my own Hott-brother shrug, like I couldn't care less what Shane does with his free time—including Sonya. "Have at it."

"**H**ey."

Quinn's voice, from the bedroom hallway, is low and husky, raspy with sleep.

I'm sitting on the couch with a sewing project in my lap, watching TV on the lowest volume. It's several nights after the farmers market visit.

"Oh, sorry, did I wake you?"

"I don't think so. I just couldn't sleep." He settles onto the couch next to me, and I boost the volume up a couple of notches.

"I couldn't, either," I confess, though I don't tell him why—that I'm still having trouble putting our kiss out of my head.

"What happened to *Sex Education*?" he asks.

"I watched the rest of it on my tablet. Figured it might be less...awkward."

"Ahhh," he says. "Makes sense. It's a tough show to watch when you have a houseguest."

"Roommate," I correct.

"Are we roommates?" he asks. "I guess we are." He seems to like that and leans back, satisfied. "I've never had a roommate before. So what are we watching?"

"You've never had a roommate before?"

"Nope," he says. "Always lived alone."

"Do you live in, like, some penthouse in Boston?"

Color rises in his cheeks.

"You do!"

"I do okay," he says.

"Are all the Hott brothers filthy rich?"

He thinks about that a moment. "Yeah," he says, "I guess we are." The corner of his mouth turns up. "Filthy rich and really fucking good at what we do."

That shouldn't be hot, but it is. I have to turn away for a second to cover the flush that rises in my face.

"The show's called *Chemical Reaction*," I tell him.

"Chemical...?"

"She's a chemist. He's her next-door neighbor who she hates. She makes a love potion, and he accidentally drinks it."

His eyes almost bug out of his head. "She's a *chemist*?"

"It's a Screenflix limited series, you know, like *The Queen's Gambit* or *Unorthodox*. A story in eight episodes. I'm on episode three already, so you're coming in mid-story."

"You *really* can't sleep."

"I have to drive to Portland tomorrow for a professional-development thing. I get nervous, and then I can't fall asleep." Not the whole truth, but most of it. "And there's no point in fighting it. I'll get sleepy at some point."

"Okay," he says. His eyes travel over me. "Are you going to share the blanket?"

I have my mother's quilt over my legs. I turn it longways and lift a section over him. He scoots closer, setting off the invisible detection system that knows when someone you like gets in your personal space. Hairs on end, nerves alive, body heating.

You could kiss me again.

We could see where it goes.

And goes, and goes, and goes—

I'm hot all over.

"You know," he says, "I'm not a good person to watch science shows with."

"I'm not surprised," I say drily. "I assume it's like watching doctor shows with doctors or lawyer shows with lawyers."

"Or salon shows with hair stylists."

"Ha. Yes."

I pick up my sewing.

"Are you making another bag?"

"No...I quit that. It was too hard to do without a sewing machine. I'm stitching an appliqué onto these jeans."

"You don't have a sewing machine?"

"No. I sold mine. Okay if I start?" I hold the remote aloft.

"Sure."

We watch for several minutes before he makes a small noise of frustration. I pause. "Yes?"

"That experiment?" He points to the screen. "Would have taken days."

"Suspend disbelief," I tell him and restart.

But a minute later, he crosses his arms and groans.

I hit Pause again. "Are we going to have to stop every

time she does something that couldn't actually happen in real life?"

"Yes," he says.

"And are you going to have to tell me exactly why it can't?"

"We all have to have hobbies," he says. "You've got sewing, and I've got deconstructing…" He points to the screen. "Bad TV."

"There's nothing bad about my TV!"

"Except the science," he says.

"Okay, except the science. What do you actually do for fun, smarty pants? Besides rip other people's media choices? And make shampoo," I add, wanting to be fair.

"Speaking of which, how's the package design coming?"

Pretty sure he's changed the subject on purpose, but I'm excited enough about the package design not to care.

"You want to see our options?" I ask.

"Yes!"

I reach for my laptop on the side table. There are two designs, both simple and classy, one with an organic pattern of pebbles and leaves, the other whimsical, a white background with bold black polka dots—and one bright pink one. A single hot spot for Hott Spot.

"I like this one," he says, pointing to the pink spot. "It's eye catching."

"Agreed," I say. "And it's fun. But in a way that still feels high end."

"How fast can your designer get them printed?"

"She says less than two weeks once we make a decision."

"Oh, wow." He examines the laptop again, smiling at

what he sees.

"So what about production and testing?" I ask him.

"In full swing."

I raise my eyebrows. "Was there money exchanged?"

"I made arrangements for you to compensate them when revenue comes in for the product. They owed me a couple of favors."

"You shouldn't have called in favors on my behalf—"

"It was my idea to brew our own," he says. "It wouldn't be fair for me to ask you to lay out money for that." He frowns. "You wanted to know what I do for fun."

"You're a master of changing the subject when you don't want to talk about something, aren't you?" I demand.

He ignores me. "I work out."

Oh. That explains a lot. I try not to let my eyes skate over his corded forearms.

"I play board games. And lately I've gotten into escape rooms."

"Wait," I say, "aren't those both things you do with *people*?"

"Uh, yeah?"

I smile because I can't help myself. "I know a secret about you, Quinn Hott."

He frowns, which only makes me smile harder, which only makes him frown more. "Yeah, what's that?"

"That you're way more of a people person than you want to admit."

"I did those things with people from work."

"You mean *friends*," I say. "I rest my case."

"Put the show back on," he says, sulkily, but after I do, I sneak a look in his direction, and he's smiling.

22

———————

QUINN

"**Q**uinn?"

Sonya was supposed to leave a few minutes ago for her Portland training thing, but she's standing in the doorway with a pained expression.

"Car won't start," she says, biting her lip. "I think it's the starter. It's not the battery because I'm getting lights and chimes."

"Want me to take a look?"

"Do you know cars?"

"I worked a couple of summers at Rush Creek Auto. I was supposed to be in the office, but I got dragged into helping out from time to time in the garage, and it turned out I had a knack."

I follow her outside and slide behind the wheel. As soon as I turn the key—yes, the car's that old—and hear the clicking, I can tell that her diagnosis is likely right. "Could be the starter," I confirm. "Or the alternator."

She closes her eyes. "How much is that going to cost?"

"Could be as little as a couple hundred."

She scrunches her face even more. "Or?"

"Not more than a thousand, for sure," I say quietly. "Probably low hundreds. Seriously."

She buries her face in her hands.

"Hey," I say, reaching out the window to touch her arm. She looks like she's on the brink of tears, and my heart clenches. "Would a loan help?"

"Absolutely not." She gives me a fierce look. But her chin is down, her shoulders slumped, the way she was that day in the office when she discovered she couldn't get the custom-branded product. Defeated. I hate seeing her that way.

"I could talk to Hanna—"

"No!" she cries. "Don't you *dare*."

She turns to me, and there's panic on her face. Not because of the car, I don't think. She's genuinely freaking out that I might talk to Hanna about her salary.

"What is it?" I ask.

She shakes her head.

"Sonya. What. Is. It?"

She closes her eyes. Then she opens them and squares her shoulders. "I haven't been taking my whole salary."

"You've—*what?*"

"I gave up a chunk of my salary as part of the plan to hire Bella back."

"I don't understand. Why would you—"

She crosses her arms, and her face sets into a stubborn expression I'm getting to know well. "Because—she's the last one."

"The last—the last *what*?"

She swallows. "The last employee of my mom's old salon."

"Right." She mentioned that the night I cooked for her —the night we kissed. There's something here I can't see. Something that doesn't make sense. "Why is it so important to you?"

She turns away.

"Sonya."

"After my mom died, the salon was all I had."

"Your dad?"

"My dad was a mess. I stopped going home after school because all he did was sit in front of the TV. It was like he'd disappeared into his grief. So I started going to the salon after school. People there talked about my mom, how great she was. They reminisced about her. They gave me tasks to do, introduced me to the people who came in. They taught me how to cut hair, paint nails, run the salon. They were my friends and my family. Reggie, Serenity, Lily. But especially Bella. She was like a mom to me. I survived because of them. Because of her."

It's like now that she's started telling the story, she can't stop, and I wonder if she's ever told it before. If anyone knows what she's still carrying around from that time.

If her dad knows.

"I wanted to stay there and run the salon with them, but Bella talked me into going to college. She wanted me to get a business degree because she hadn't and she'd always regretted it. So I went. And I threw myself into college totally. I was so relieved not to have my dad be my problem anymore. I met a guy who was a few years ahead of me, we got involved... He was working for the college admissions department, living off campus. We were going to get married after I graduated. But right after I started senior year…my dad… He was drinking, he was gambling. And he gambled it all away. The house we lived in. The salon. He lost it all.

"I took a leave from college and scraped him off the floor, put as much of our lives back together as I could. The salon was gone. I found him a place to live, worked a bunch of jobs I didn't love…until I heard Hanna was opening this place. I came to her and made a case for why I was the best person for the position, and she gave me the job—and basically carte blanche to run it how I wanted."

I rake my fingers through my hair. "She doesn't know you're not paying yourself."

Sonya doesn't answer.

"She'd be furious if she knew," I say—but of course that's the point. That's exactly why Sonya hasn't told her.

"She'd try to find the money somewhere else," she says. "And I don't want that. I don't want her to take it away from her business. This isn't about her. These are my people, and it's my job to take care of them. And it's not the end of the world. I walk to work. I can take the resort shuttle to town when I need to go. And I'll have enough to repair the car in a couple months. With the product we've developed, I'm pretty sure I'll be able to hire Bella and still be able to pay myself my full salary again by the end of the year."

Her loyalty…floors me. The idea that there's someone in this world who feels that way about the people they work with, who would quietly, behind the scenes, fight for them—

She's amazing.

But it's too big a sacrifice. She shouldn't be out here in tears next to her car. She shouldn't have to be.

"That's—what you're doing—it's brave and kind. But also...you know it's not your fault, right?" I say. "Your going to college didn't make your dad lose the salon, and it didn't make them lose their jobs."

She bites her lip, and tears well in her eyes. She nods. "I do know it, but sometimes—"

She doesn't finish, but she doesn't have to. "I get it," I say quietly. "You can *know* a thing and not *know* it." And then because I want her smiling again, "If you, um, *know* what I mean."

She laughs. It's shaky, but it turns into a real smile, a small, confident curve that I want to set my mouth to.

I'm not going to stop wanting her, I realize with a jolt. It's scary and also, oddly, reassuring.

"How's he doing now?" I ask. "With the gambling and drinking?"

"Holding steady with recovery. He's had a few relapses, but nothing in the last couple of years."

"That's why you check on him all the time?"

She nods. "Yeah. I need to do that actually. I've gotten distracted these last two weeks by our project."

"And you haven't been back to college?"

She shakes her head.

"What happened to him?" I ask. "The guy you were going to marry? After you came back?"

"Doesn't matter," she says.

"I bet it does," I say quietly.

Her eyes come up to meet mine. "He didn't want to, but he agreed to come back here with me. He hated it here from minute one. The town was too small, he didn't like that everyone was up in our business—his words. We lasted a few months, and then he gave me an ultimatum: him or Rush Creek. I told him I couldn't leave. That I belonged here. That I'd left once, but I wouldn't leave again." She sighs. "He broke off the engagement a few days after that. He said he'd realized he couldn't be stuck here for the rest of his life."

My chest tightens because I know exactly how that feels. *I thought I could do this, but...*

...I just don't love you enough.

The words don't have to be spoken; they're there anyway.

I know Sonya means what she says about Rush Creek. She won't leave. Not ever. The ties that bind her here are deep and real, and she's not the kind of person who would let herself walk away from them twice.

No one who understood anything about her would ever ask her to walk away from them again.

It chafes me that there was a guy who could have showed her that, and he chose not to.

I hope I never run into him because I'll tell him exactly what I think of him.

23

SONYA

A week or so after the car fiasco, Bella picks me up for a girls' night out at Oscar's Saloon and Grill.

"What's up with your car anyway?" she asks as she maneuvers the car gracefully into a spot in front of Oscar's.

"Long story," I say, waving a hand in front of me. "Needs to go into the shop, shop couldn't take it right away."

I've never wanted Bella to know the details behind the plan to rehire her. I don't want her to feel like a burden to me or the spa...because she sure as hell never made me feel like a burden to her. Not once in all the days, weeks, and months I did my homework at an empty station or at the salon's front desk; not once in all the times she told me there was extra dinner and I should come home with her to grab some; not once when I showed up at her house unannounced to cry on her shoulder.

No—I'll tell her the story someday far in the future when we can both laugh about it, after I've paid myself back, after the investigation's over and the spa's recovered the lost income, when Quinn's product is a big hit and Bella's selling the shit out of it with her funny newsletters and her charming front-desk manner.

"It's a haul to town, though," Bella says, turning off the ignition and reaching for her handbag.

"The resort shuttle goes in three times a day." Though that reminds me: I still owe my dad a grocery restock. That might require hiring Rush Creek's single rideshare driver.

Bella pauses, purse suspended. "The shuttle's no fun with groceries, though, right?" she asks, eyebrow up.

I shrug. Quinn's been buying our groceries lately; I tried to convince him he doesn't need to do that, but he said that my refrigerator was like the Gobi Desert and that for his own peace and well-being, he needed to remedy that.

I don't tell Bella that, though. I still haven't told anyone that Quinn and I are living together in addition to working together. Not even Hanna knows. I wouldn't say that we're deliberately keeping it a secret, just not...broadcasting it. We rarely leave at the same time, and when we finish our days simultaneously, by unspoken agreement, we stagger our departures. To make sure it doesn't become a source of drama.

I steal a glance at Bella, but she's already slipping out of the car, hurrying toward the bar. I exhale hard and push my own door open.

Oscar's is a Rush Creek institution with real live saloon doors, animal heads over the bar, and a gorgeous mural of Rush Creek's cowboy days on the back wall. It's crowded, being a Friday, with familiar Rush Creek locals and a slew of tourists. There's even a bachelorette party in progress, the women in T-shirts that read, *Most Likely to Get Hitched,*

Most Likely to Get Us All Arrested, Most Likely to Dance on a Table, and so on. Oscar's eclectic music blend is in full force, Tim McGraw giving way to Pearl Jam as we head toward our friends waving wildly to us from their big booth.

We join Reggie, Serenity, Lily, Mei, and Catalina, who hug us like long-lost family, even though we just saw each other. I slide in next to Lily.

The other women have already stocked our table with plates of wings, potato skins, and cracklings, and everyone's got a drink in front of them. Jill Cooper, who's been serving at Oscar's as long as I can remember, asks Bella and me what we want and shows us photos of her new baby, Malcolm, a fat-faced cherub in the most adorable baby-blue seersucker suit for his christening.

A few minutes later, Bella and I have our drinks in hand and are digging into the wings, going through napkins like there's no tomorrow.

"The hottie at the front desk's working out well, huh?" Catalina asks.

"The hottie at the front desk?" Bella asks.

"She doesn't know?" Reggie asks me.

"Nope," I say.

"You will not *believe* this," Reggie tells her. "You know the Hott brothers?"

"Hanna's brothers—sure, of course," Bella says.

"One of them is working at the front desk of the spa. It's a clause in his granddad's will. He has to work there for two months."

Bella raises her eyebrows. "Am I going to get to overlap with this hottie?"

"Unfortunately, no," I say. "He'll be gone right when you

come on board." I cross my fingers under the table, insurance for our shampoo-and-conditioner plan.

"You should come see him, though," Reggie says. "He's worth a trip."

"He's not a tourist attraction!" I yip.

"He kinda is," Serenity and Lily say at the same time. "The senior set *loves* him," Serenity adds.

It's true. Quinn has turned out to be oddly successful at the front desk, like a grumpy-scientist therapist. He has this gruff banter thing he does with the older women, and it's absolutely clear they adore him, swatting his compliments away and blushing. Brides, too—they stop by the desk and want him to weigh in on photographs of updos or veils or the favors they're DIY-ing off Pinterest. They love his bluntness, even when he says, *I don't like any of those.*

He's selling more product than our criminal ex-receptionist claimed to.

"He knows every single product SKU by heart," Lily says. "It's a little scary. And he knows what they all do. And he can pretty much always talk someone into buying, even when what he's saying is the exact opposite of what I'd say. Like, yesterday I heard him tell someone that the scarf she was wearing looked absurd on her, and two minutes later, she'd bought three T-shirts."

"It's sex pheromones," Reggie says. "They can't help themselves. They have to please him."

Sex pheromones. That's probably why I still want to climb Quinn like a tree, despite knowing that at best it would be a temporary itch-scratching thing.

Mei turns to me. "Rumor has it that you two are shacked up together."

I wince. So much for my staff not knowing.

"Seems like the kind of thing you might have mentioned sooner?" Lily says, eyebrow raised.

"I—it's not—"

"It's not what?" Serenity asks innocently.

"'Shacked up' makes it sound like we're—"

"Fucking like bunnies?" Reggie supplies.

I roll my eyes at her. "Yes."

"Are you?"

"Jesus! No! His granddad's will says he has to live in ranch housing, and I had the only available room."

"*Suuuuuure* you did," she says. "You have the only available vagina, too?"

"Reggie!" I cry. But I can't help laughing, either.

She crosses her arms. "Look us in the eye and tell us nothing is going on between you two."

"Nothing's—"

I falter.

"Ha!" Reggie says.

"Nothing's going on between us," I say, finding my solid ground again. "There might have been a moment—"

They all fall elbows-first on the table, leaning in for details.

"It was just a kiss."

"It's never just a kiss!" Lily says.

"Well, this was. My defenses were down. He'd cooked for me—"

"He *cooked* for you?" they all demand at once.

"We're roommates," I point out.

"It's still nice!" Mei says

It *was* nice. It was very nice. As was the kiss. And the

conversation. And the way he sat up with me the other night when I couldn't sleep. And advised me about the car. He's put dinner on the table half the nights this week, and yesterday, he cleaned the bathroom. He's a good roommate.

A. Good. Roommate.

I decide now would be a terrible time to tell them that Quinn's movie-star-gorgeous brother asked me to a book-signing...and that I turned him down when he finally texted me to check on whether I was up for it. Knowing that I declined that date will only reinforce their naughty ideas about what's going on between me and Quinn.

They're all staring at me, big eyed. "Anyway," I say, "we agreed nothing else would happen. He doesn't do relation-ships, and he's leaving town—"

"Who needs relationships?" Reggie demands. "Just get some of that beard between your thighs."

Serenity's mouth falls open. "Reggie!"

"What?" Reggie cries. "Tell me you don't fantasize about that beard when you're by yourself at night."

"I don't fantasize about that beard when I'm by myself at night!" Serenity says.

Reggie stares at me. "*Sooooooonya,*" she sings.

I bury my face in my hands. Because I've definitely been fantasizing about that beard when I'm in bed at night. The soft buzz of it on my face when he kissed me. And all the other places I'd like to experience it.

I look up to find them all watching me with amused smiles.

"Well," Reggie says brightly, "when you finally break and accept the inevitable, I want to hear *all* the details."

We stay at Oscar's so long that Jill apologetically tells us we need to settle up and brings the mini point-of-sale terminal to the table. "You don't have to go!" she says. "You can stay as long as you want. I just need to close out."

We hand over our cards, and she swipes them. It all goes smoothly till she gets to Bella's.

"I'm sorry," Jill says, wincing. "It's—not going through."

Reggie and I exchange a quick look, while Bella's face flames and she digs for another one.

"Put it on mine," Reggie says—she's next in the stack. "I owe you."

"For *what*?"

"You paid for my drinks that night when we went to dinner in Bend."

"That was because you'd just gotten a job at Hott Spot and we were celebrating."

"Well," Reggie says, "you've just gotten a job at Hott Spot, and we're celebrating."

I love Reggie.

"Thank you," Bella says, easing the second card back into its slot in her wallet. The red in her face has subsided, and I know the gratitude in her voice isn't only for the drinks.

I thread my arm around her shoulders, tug her close, and hug her. I'm feeling grateful, too. To Reggie, who managed that moment with so much grace. To Bella, who has always been there for me.

And to Quinn, who's home right now having a last-minute conversation with his production and testing buddies about a small issue that arose on the assembly line.

Because after he told me the other night that he'd set things up so we wouldn't have to pay till the product started to sell—after he told me that he'd called in a favor on my behalf—I started thinking more about this whole thing.

I'd told myself he was doing this for Hanna or for the spa...

But I'm slowly realizing that the product isn't essential to the spa's survival or even to Hanna's holding onto the land and her business.

The only person Quinn's big chemistry experiment benefits is Bella.

Meaning he's doing it for me.

24

QUINN

"Assuming they don't catch anything in testing, they can get us a hundred of each for the official launch in two weeks," I tell Sonya. "Do you think that'll work?"

"Perfect."

It's Saturday, so she's spent most of the day doing bridal hair and overseeing other beauty-related tasks for a Hott Springs Eternal wedding. Now we're both behind the desk as she does a piece of final paperwork for the wedding, her hip bumping the arm of my chair, her hand brushing my shoulder and setting me on fire. There's a strand of hair that's come lose from her messy bun, and she keeps pushing it out of her face. I want to tuck it behind her ear. Brush my thumb over her cheek. I want to kiss her until we both burst into flames.

She looks exhausted but upbeat, and I think about how she is when people don't see her. At night, when the wear of the day shows on her face, when no one else is around. She's almost cried a few times at basic human kindness. A meal cooked for her. Someone bothering to check how she's doing. Giving her a second opinion on the state of her car.

I've noticed that if she doesn't see something as *help*, she'll often let it happen. That's how I managed to become the grocery shopper, by telling her I couldn't hack an empty fridge. If I'd asked her if she wanted me to do a grocery run for her, I can guarantee the answer would have been no.

She still hasn't done anything about repairing her car, more than a week after it wouldn't start. She's been walking to work and taking the resort shuttle into town. Whenever I catch wind that she's doing that, I offer her a ride, and sometimes she takes me up on it—but mostly she doesn't.

I'll just have to "need" to go into town more frequently. If I'm already headed there, it won't count in her mind as accepting help.

She pushes a strand of hair behind her ear. "I think the packaging for the products has already shipped? Here, let me look." In the early days, she would have made me get out of my seat or gestured to me to roll myself out of the way; now she just bumps her body in front of mine and navigates to her email.

She's so close, I could palm her hips and draw her down onto my lap. *Rest for a sec,* I want to say. Of course, my body anticipates what would happen next, coming to life, my cock heavy, on its way to hard. I want to show her: *This is what you do to me, Sonya.*

And this *is what I want to do to you,* I'd say, pressing up against her—

"Yes!" she says.

It takes a moment for my brain to catch up.

"We have a tracking number and everything." She clicks a link and opens the final design. It looks great. "It took us a while to find a font that was cute, classy, and legible all at the same time," she says, laughing. "But I'm really pleased. What do you think?"

She's right. They've managed to find the rare script font that complements the design with the single standout pink dot.

"It kicks ass," I say. "You did an amazing job."

You're amazing.

It's like I've spoken it out loud, the way her eyes find mine and stay there, searching. Then she looks away—and steps away.

"Oh—" she says. "Also. I put an appointment on the books for your brother."

My mouth falls open. "Shane?"

"Yeah."

I scowl so deeply it hurts.

She raises an eyebrow. "Is that a problem?"

"Of course not," I lie.

"Good," she says with a lift of one shoulder. "He should be in any minute. You can send him back to me."

"To *you*?"

Sonya rarely actually does any services, and every hair on my body rises in suspicion. "Serenity went home early and Reggie and Catalina were both already scheduled, so I'm it for estheticians."

How, exactly, did Shane suss out that if he came in now, Sonya would be the only one available? What's his game? And *how can I stop it?*

He has clearly inherited all my grandfather's mischief genes.

Sonya turned down Shane's offer of a date to the book-signing...which I know only because he texted me to tell me, as if he thought it might matter to me one way or the other.

I hated to admit to myself how much it did.

"When he comes in, tell him I'm in treatment room two," she says and slips out.

She's barely disappeared when Shane steps through the salon's front door. "Hey, Quinn!" he calls.

I glare at him. "You could fly your hair stylist here from LA. You don't need to come here."

A smirk forms at the corner of his mouth, but he presses it flat. "That would be wasteful," he says, deadpan. "Bad for the environment. Entitled. Besides, I want to support your place of business."

"You are *full of shit*," I tell him.

"Who, me?" he asks, all innocence.

"I should've let you eat that jack-o'-lantern mushroom," I say.

I'm talking about the time that Shane thought he'd harvested chanterelles...but had found their toxic cousin instead.

He's never actually thanked me, and I've never been sure I made the right decision.

"You would have deprived the world of an excellent actor," he says.

"A mediocre actor," I correct. Unfairly. I've seen all Shane's movies, and even if some of the movies themselves are travesties, he's clearly talented.

"Don't be ridiculous," he says. "I'm great." But he's laughing. "Whatever. It doesn't even matter. Hollywood doesn't care whether I'm good or not. It only cares that I'm hot. Speaking of which...my appointment." He raises an eyebrow my direction. "Getting some 'scaping done," he says.

"Do you mean *manscaping*?"

There's no way I'm going to sit at this desk while Sonya waxes my brother's...anything.

Shane's eyes travel over my outraged expression; his grin gets even bigger. "That's right, Quinn. Manscaping. You should try it. Makes you look bigger. Not that I need the help, but you might."

"You—"

My eyes flick to Weggers's camera; I have the sudden, unpleasant thought that he's watching and has read my lips through this whole exchange. I'm sorely tempted to throw something over the camera—but I've made it too far to give Weggers the satisfaction of making me forfeit.

Lily steps out from the back, bag over her shoulder. Her eyes get huge at the sight of Shane. "You're Shane Hott! Shane fucking Hott. Oh my God, Shane Hott! Will you sign my right breast? And my left breast? And my ass?"

"Happily," Shane says, managing to smolder and twinkle at the same time. He's always been good at that shit, even when we were kids.

"Seriously," Lily says, fishing in her bag. "What can I get you to sign? I don't want some torn sheet of paper."

"Toilet paper," I mutter.

He glares at me. "I'll get you a signed photo," he tells her. "I'll bring it in tomorrow."

"To Lily?" she asks, eyes huge.

"To Lily," he affirms.

"Oh my *God.*"

"Shane," Sonya says, appearing, beaming at him. "You ready?"

"Always ready," he purrs. "Bye, Lily. It's been a pleasure, and I'll make sure I get you that photo. Good to see you, Quinn!" He gives me an impish smile and follows Sonya into the hallway before I can do something caveman-ish. Like wrestle him to the ground, bind him with rope, and leave him for coyotes—which is my natural impulse.

"No," I growl.

"No what?" Lily asks.

"Just *no*," I say.

"You're so lucky," she says. "Shane Hott is your *family.*"

And she hoists her bag higher and heads out.

I watch her go, then rake a hand through my hair.

Right now, imagining my pain-in-the-ass brother peeling off his clothes in Sonya's treatment room, I feel anything but lucky.

25

SONYA

"So, yeah, get yourself a jade roller," I tell Shane as I walk him back toward the front of the spa, his appointment finished. "It helps so much with the redness afterward, especially if you put it in the freezer. And it's a luxury in the summer."

"I can only imagine—"

He stops like he's walked into a wall. A woman has stepped out of one of the other treatment rooms, Catalina right behind her. She's one of our regulars, tall and slim in a fitted pale pink T-shirt and skinny jeans. She's beautiful, too: long honey-blond hair, high cheekbones, a mouth that's naturally a bit wry, that makes you feel like she's laughing at herself. Her head's down, but she lifts it when she sees that there are other people in the hallway. I smile at her, and she gives me a radiant smile back.

"Hey, Ivy." I don't know her well because she's only been in the spa a few times. Ivy Scofield is better known as famous actress Eva Scott, but she's been living as Ivy here. Rumor has it that she thinks no one knows who she really is, which is hilarious. We all know. We're just—except probably for Nan at the bakery—too polite to say so.

Ivy and Catalina step into another treatment room.

"Who was that?" Shane asks.

He's pitched his voice to be deliberately nonchalant, but he looks like he's been smacked in the stomach. He's definitely not the only man to have felt that way—Ivy's straight-up gorgeous.

"Ivy," I tell him, equally nonchalant, because if Shane hasn't realized yet who she is, I'm not going to help him figure it out. I know Ivy must have her reasons to lie low, and I'm sure the last thing she wants is a fuckboy Hollywood actor chasing after her.

I try to imagine what will happen if Shane decides he wants to pursue her. I'm betting she'll run the other way as fast as she can. And I suspect Shane Hott is *not* used to not getting what—or whom—he wants.

Shane shakes himself a bit and recovers, and we continue toward the front, where Quinn is sitting behind the front desk, poring over something on the computer screen. He looks up when we come in and scowls again.

"Here, I'll ring him up," I tell Quinn. "Can you grab him a jade roller? I used one on him, and he really liked it. Feels great, doesn't it?" I ask Shane.

"*So* good," he says.

Quinn's scowl deepens so much I worry about premature wrinkles for him. He's in a particularly grumpy mood today. He scoots out of the way, fetching the jade roller I asked for and dropping it onto the counter harder than is strictly necessary. I glare at him. It's been a while since I've seen him this out of sorts.

"That'll be thirty-five dollars for the service and thirty-two for the roller," I tell Shane, turning the screen around to show him the total. I cast my eyes down. In general, I try not to watch when people put their tips in; after all, that kind of stuff is personal, and I don't judge.

"Jesus, Shane," Quinn says, and I have to look…

Thirty-five percent on the total, including the roller, which is about as high as you can tip without making it look like some kind of illicit act took place in the back room.

"Thank you," I tell Shane.

"Thank *you*," he says.

"Do you want to make another appointment?"

"I'm not sure how much longer I'll be in town, so I think I'll hold off."

"Sounds good," I say. "Thanks for coming in."

"Oh," Shane says, "the pleasure was *all mine*."

But he's not looking at me. He's eyeing his brother sideways.

That's when I get it—Shane is winding Quinn up. I look from brother to brother, Shane with a smirk on his face, Quinn refusing to look at Shane at all. *Ohhhkay*. Probably time for me to make my exit.

I'm in the hallway, headed toward my office to shut things down, when I hear Quinn say, "Fuck you, Shane."

I pause. If there's something going on out there, it's my job as a manager to know.

And also, I'm wildly curious.

"You know I'm just messing with you, right? I was getting my eyebrows done. She used the jade roller on my *eyebrows*."

"You're a monster," Quinn growls.

"You might want to consider why it makes you so angry," Shane says.

I freeze, my heart pounding.

"You might want to leave before I ruin your pretty-boy face."

"Love you, too, bro," Shane says airily, and after a moment, I hear the jingle of the door.

I poke my head back out. "What was that about?"

Quinn glowers. "Nothing."

"What did you think I was using the jade roller on?" I ask him.

He stares at me.

"Quinn?"

He folds his arms and stares at an invisible point on the ceiling.

"*Quiiiiiinnnn...*"

Finally, he closes his eyes and says, through a clenched jaw: "He told me he was here for manscaping."

"Oh, wow," I say, breathless. "Why would he do that?" My heart is going a million miles an hour—but I don't want to make any assumptions, either.

Quinn rubs a hand over his face. Then he raises his head. Looks me straight on. His eyes are dark and intense.

"It's possible he might have been trying to make me jealous," he admits.

I can't look away. Not from the frustration or the hunger in his gaze. My low belly lights up, a rush of liquid heat.

"And..." I bite my lip. "Did it *work*?"

My face is flushed. I don't know whether he'll answer

me or not, whether he'll be honest...or even what I want to hear from him.

He stalks toward me. My heart rate kicks up, heat flooding me. He crowds my space, his eyes never leaving mine.

I can't breathe.

He cups his big hand behind my head and kisses me.

His mouth slants over mine, and I don't need another invitation; I open to him, done holding back, done with excuses and reasons.

In fact, I'm done with everything right now except Quinn.

His hand behind my head is confident and strong. His lips are as soft and generous as I remember. He groans into my mouth, and I whimper into his, and then our hands are everywhere. Mine clutch at his hair, his beard, his shoulders—Oh God! I finally have permission to touch the gloriousness that is Quinn's body. The solidness of his thick biceps, the satisfying hardness of his pecs. I slide a hand down his chest, over a field of ridges that sends a wave of lust into my own low belly. He grunts at the feel, grabs my hand just before I reach my goal, kisses me harder. We're devouring each other now.

He lifts his head, breaking the kiss, and I grab his hair, which makes him laugh. A rich, warm, husky, all-in Quinn laugh, which is maybe even better than kissing.

"Quinn—" I beg.

"I'm not going anywhere," he says. "I want this, too. I just—" He takes a small step back, his hands still on my arms. He gestures to the lawyer's camera. "This is maybe not the best place for me to do what I want to do to you.

What I *really* want to do to you. Maybe we could—take this someplace else."

I nod, feeling a little frantic, still worried that he's going to change his mind. "I know I said—"

"We both said a *lot* of things," Quinn says. He brushes my hair off my forehead, tilts my head back, looks down at me with an expression on his face that makes my legs feel watery.

"I just really—"

But before I can get the words out, the spa phone starts ringing. We look at each other and laugh.

"You'd better get that," he says.

Grudgingly, I move away from him, cross to the desk, pick up the phone. "Hello?"

"Hey, Sonya, this is Easton. Is Quinn there? We're at the hospital, and—Hanna had the baby!"

26

––––––––

QUINN

In the car on the way to the hospital, my body and mind are a mess.

I'm still full of the taste and sensation of Sonya's mouth. I'm awash in craving and need. I'm on overdrive.

I kissed her. She let me. She *wanted me to.*

God, I want more. So much more.

Somewhere on the ride to the hospital, though, my head clears enough that I realize something else amazing:

I'm about to meet a brand-new person, for the first time.

Holy *shit*.

It's a lot for my brain, all at once.

I'm grateful that Sonya doesn't try to make conversation. She doesn't ask questions, she doesn't seem to need to pin down what just happened.

When I look over at her, she's smiling, and it makes me smile, too, even though my mind's on overload.

We stopped by the cabin so Sonya could feed and walk Gus and grab a present she'd bought for Hanna and the baby. I don't have a gift, so we stop at the hospital shop and

I pick out a rattle and a teddy bear and some baby clothes and a bunch of flowers and a balloon—

And then Sonya makes me stop—"Enough, Quinn! There won't be room for it all!"—her hand on my arm, her laughter filling my ear and drifting like smoke into my chest. She steps onto her tiptoes and plants a kiss on my cheek, and I wouldn't trade this friendly, affectionate kiss for the one I had with her fifteen minutes ago, but also? It's really fucking nice.

We take the elevator up to Labor and Delivery and find Hanna's room. Easton's family is in there—a full house with the whole sprawling Wilder family—so Sonya and I line ourselves up on the wall outside and wait. She reaches for my hand and holds it tight. I squeeze back. I don't let myself think about what it means because if I do, I'll screw something up. I know that much.

"Hey," a voice says. Shane. He looks from Sonya to me to our linked hands and says, "Well. That worked quickly."

I scowl at him. "Don't think I'm going to thank you for being an ass," I say. "Not until you thank me for saving your life."

"Maybe we could call it even."

I shake my head, but our eyes meet for a split second. Just long enough for me to see that he's trying not to smile.

A minute later Tucker appears. He leans against the wall, grim, dark. Something's going on with Tucker. I wonder if he'd tell me what.

Preston's next, clutching a box of what looks like cigars. I hope they're chocolate, but knowing Preston, who's a whiskey-and-wine connoisseur, they're probably Cubans.

I try to imagine Easton smoking a cigar, but I can't see it. He's too wholesome.

"Am I too late?" Rhys asks, rushing down the hall toward us. It's the first time I've ever seen my lawyer brother look anything but buttoned up and put together.

We're all here. Together. Again.

Whatever else you can say about my grandfather, he managed that.

"Can we go in?" Rhys asks, gesturing at the door to Hanna's room.

"Easton's family's in there now," I tell him. "I'll check to see how things look."

I approach the door and peek in. Hanna is sitting up in the hospital bed, surrounded by women. I look for the baby in her arms, but she's not there—and then I spot her, in the arms of a big, bearded guy. Another bearded guy has his arm looped over that guy's shoulder, and Easton stands at his side, laughing and talking to him. They're unmistakably brothers and, equally unmistakably, they're all friends. Joking, jostling, jovially fighting over who gets to hold the baby next.

They remind me of us—not the us of now, awkward and still mostly angry, but the old us, the us that used to roam the woods and the scrubland, that played in the barns and other outbuildings, that nearly burned down the ranch house roasting forbidden marshmallows over the gas range's flame. The us that joked and teased—even if I often didn't get the joke—that wrestled and hugged—even if I almost always stood back from the fray. I still knew I belonged.

The bearded man passes the baby back to Hanna, and

people begin filing out of the room—two silver-haired women, arm in arm; one of the bearded men holding the hand of a blond woman; the other with a slim dark-haired woman.

"I met some of you at the wedding, right?" one says to me and my brothers. "I recognize Tucker and Shane." He holds his hand out to me. "Gabe Wilder. My wife, Lucy, my brother Clark, his girlfriend Jessa, my mom Barb, and my step-mom, Geneva."

Preston, Rhys, and I introduce ourselves. Preston remembers Gabe and Clark from school, and they do some speed reminiscing about particularly awful teachers. Sonya knows everyone, and she hugs Lucy and Jessa and congratulates the new uncles.

"We won't hold you up. Get in there and check out our gorgeous niece," Lucy says. "And make sure Hanna drinks water and gets as much sleep as she can. You guys should each take an hour and pace with the baby so Hanna can rest. She'll tell you she doesn't want it, but it'll save her life."

My brothers and I exchange glances. None of us has tended a baby for an hour in our lives. But I'm pretty sure if that's what Hanna needs, we'll do it.

As I watch the Wilders recede down that hall, Lucy's words sink in. We're all the baby's aunts and uncles now. Which makes them our family now, too, in a way.

I guess that's what a new baby does: makes family where there wasn't any before.

Huh.

When they're gone, we slip into Hanna's room. She beams at us and holds up our niece, wrapped tight as a burrito in a pink-and-blue-striped blanket. "Eloise."

It's our mom's name. My chest is tight. My hand rests there, like it's trying to make room for my next breath. I meet Hanna's eyes, and she nods at me, like she knows.

Then she beams at us. "All of you came!"

And for the first time since my grandfather's funeral, grief crowds me.

Because Eloise made Hanna into a mother. Easton into a father. All five Hott brothers into uncles.

But Granddad got us into this room together.

He made Hanna smile like that.

And he missed his chance to be a great-grandfather.

I'm still really *pissed at you,* I tell him. *You were a pain in all of our asses. But also:* Thank you.

"Who wants to hold her first?" Hanna asks, breaking my trance. She's tired and pale but beautiful.

We all exchange slightly terrified glances.

"Oh, come on, guys, she won't break."

But when I step forward and take her, I'm not sure Hanna's right about that. The baby in my arms is light as a feather and so little. And when she wriggles a hand free and waves it, and I take it in my own, her tiny bones feel as fragile as a bird's. Her eyes are closed. She has a button nose and a rosebud mouth. Her hair is as black as Hanna's, but her face is bright red.

She's perfect, and she feels just right in my arms.

My brothers press in on every side, stroking her hair, exclaiming. Jostling for their turns, giving me a hard time about not wanting to hand her over.

For a moment, I think: Maybe we could be *us* again.

27

SONYA

Quinn Hott holds baby Eloise in his arms, and my ovaries buy a crib and register for cute pastel animal sheets.

It's probably the forearms, on excellent display along the pink-and-blue-striped blanket. Or the chest that baby is currently cradled against.

Or maybe just the overall picture: Big, built, bearded, bedheaded dude and itty-bitty teeny helpless baby. Plus the soft look on Quinn's face, the way his gaze lingers on Eloise's pudgy cheeks and button nose…

Eggs, stand down.

Under the grumpy shell, Quinn has the hugest heart of anyone I've ever met. He's like a teddy bear that thinks it's a wolf. He clearly loves his sister. And, despite how complicated it may be, his brothers.

And this man, with his huge heart, for some reason…

Wants me.

"She's beautiful," Quinn says, voice both rough and soft,

and damn it, it's a bad idea to fall for this guy, but I don't think I have the self-control to hold out.

The other brothers want their Eloise time, and they're not shy about it, telling Quinn he's hogging her, reaching greedily for the baby while taking care not to jostle Eloise.

I hang by Hanna's side, watching the Hott brothers with her daughter. Hanna's watching, too, her eyes bright.

A nurse comes into the room, followed by a woman she introduces as the hospital's lactation consultant, and we're all unceremoniously ushered out. In the hallway, in the absence of Hanna and Eloise, the Hott brothers seem to stiffen up again, and one by one, they peel off with excuses. Preston and Rhys have work to do, Shane's headed to a party he got invited to this afternoon, Tucker wants to hit the hay early tonight.

Quinn and I take the elevator down and trek in silence across the hospital's big parking lot to where we left his rental car, a generic white sedan with California plates. He comes around to my side, unlocks the door, and opens it for me. He did that on the way to the hospital, too. I was too discombobulated from his kiss and Easton's call to appreciate it for what it was—yet another sign of his thoughtfulness. I climb in, and he strides around the car and slides in next to me.

He puts both hands on the wheel but doesn't start the car. Just...sits there.

"So," I say.

"So," he repeats.

"I've never seen Hanna smile like that."

He shakes his head. "I know. And I'm still mad at my grandfather, but..." He sighs.

"It's a good silver lining. I mean, what are the odds that you all would have come back for this birth if it weren't for that stupid will?"

He looks away. "If you'd asked me a few weeks ago, I would have said slim to none. But I've been doing a lot of thinking." He swallows hard. "It wasn't always like this."

"No?" I'm almost afraid to speak because I know Quinn's about to tell me something that matters to him. I feel like I'm trying not to scare a wild animal.

He shakes his head. "No. We were close as kids." He tilts his head. "Did you know we don't all the have the same dad?"

I shake my head.

He nods. "My mom went to LA straight out of high school and met Preston, Rhys, and Shane's dad. She was trying to make it as an actress, and he was a director—you know how that story always used to end."

"Yes, unfortunately."

"He was a rich, savvy asshole with a prenup, and she ended up with child support and nothing else, so she came back to Rush Creek. Very unwillingly, because my grandfather hadn't wanted her to go to LA in the first place, so it was kind of a belly crawl back to the family."

"Ugh."

"Yeah. Not that long after she got back, she got together with an old childhood sweetheart—Tuck's and my dad— and for a while it looked like she was going to be happy, but when I was barely a year old, he died."

"God," I breathe, my heart aching. "That's a lot."

"Yeah," Quinn says. "For a while it was just us—the kids, Mom, and Granddad. And Aunt Meryl. She was always around, too. Her marriage had ended, she didn't have kids, and we were all her family. Then my mom met Hanna's dad. Big man on the barrel-racing circuit, passing through...our mom fell hard. But he couldn't give up racing. Loved the work, loved the travel, loved the rhythms of the rodeo. Went back to the circuit. Broke my mom's heart—and Hanna's. Eventually died doing what he loved. It took years before Hanna even found out he was dead."

I remembered that. It had been a minor Rush Creek scandal, blown up into a story worth telling by the gossip grapevine. Eloise Hott taming a rodeo man...who turned out not to have been tamed after all. The third man she'd lost. No wonder it broke her heart. And I'd be willing to bet it would've hurt Quinn, too, because he'd definitely have been old enough by then to form a bond with the man who loved his mother.

He rests his palms on the wheel and looks straight ahead.

"I never knew Tucker's and my dad, and I wasn't as close to Hanna's dad as she was, but the whole thing still sucked. You can see why my brothers and I were close, right? Men didn't stick, my mom fell apart when they left. My granddad was gruff, prickly. Not a bad man, but a hard man. He always had to be right, and he was always harping at my mom about something. Always on one of us about something. So the five of us, six of us—Hanna most of the time, too—we were outside all the time, in the woods, getting into trouble. But also having each other's backs."

His face softens, his tone warms; I can *see* how much he loved that time and how much he misses it.

"I was on the outside sometimes, but I didn't mind it

because I knew I belonged with them. And if I ever forgot..."

His voice trails off, and he runs a thumb over the thick muscle below his other thumb, a gesture I've seen him make before. But this time, he holds his hand out so I can see what's there: a small white scar.

"We used Tuck's knife," he says. "Hanna wasn't there; I'm not sure where she was that day, but maybe doing something with her dad—it was when he was still around," he says offhandedly, like dads disappearing was an everyday occurrence.

And in the Hott household, it really was.

"It was a blood vow. You know, how kids do."

His eyes are on my face now. His tone is throwaway again. *How kids do.* And yet there's something in the stillness of his face, the way he's watching me listen to his story, that belies his casualness.

It *mattered* to him. It wasn't just a kid thing.

"Pres, Rhys, and Shane promised to change their name to Hott, which was Tuck's and Hanna's and my name, because our mom never married again after the first time." He takes a breath. "And we vowed that when we grew up, we'd run the ranch together."

It's hard to express how shocked I feel. It's the last thing I expected him to say. Five brothers who, to all outside appearances, had chosen careers as far removed from ranching as you can get. Who'd left Rush Creek as soon as they were grown and gone out of their way to come back only when circumstance absolutely required it.

Once upon a time, though, the Hott brothers had loved each other and the land enough to use Tucker's knife to nick their skin, to let their blood flow together, to vow that it was all for one and one for all, like the five musketeers.

"Quinn..." I say.

His eyes flick to my face, alarmed. "Don't," he says. Gently. "Don't be nice about it."

So much for the hug I want to give him; I wrap my arms around myself instead. "What...happened?" I ask.

He shrugs. "I don't know."

"You don't...know?"

"Preston left. He went to college, fell in love... He and Granddad fought over her. Granddad wanted him to stay and run the ranch. Kali was a city girl. In the end, Preston left and didn't come back."

I close my eyes, putting the pieces together. "And you said Preston was the one who supported you. The one who told you you'd be a great scientist."

He rubs both hands down his face.

"Yeah. Right after our mom died, there was a science fair. I'd signed up for it before she got so sick—"

His eyes are distant, remembering. Dark is falling now; the light in the car is starting to soften to gray.

"—and my granddad couldn't drive me. He had stuff to take care of on the ranch. He wanted me to stay home and help him. He made it pretty clear he thought the science fair was a waste of my time. Preston heard, though, and he found me crying in the barn and said, 'Get your stuff, Quinn. I'll drive you.'"

He shrugs. "It was the first thing since our mom had died that made me feel like it was going to be okay. So, yeah. That was Preston."

I close my eyes, grief-stricken. "And then he left you."

"Yeah." He turns away, staring out the car window.

"And you were?"

"Twelve," he says.

I can picture it. I mean, not completely, because it's hard to imagine the Quinn in front of me right now, the Quinn who fills this car with his shoulders and his broad chest and his headful of gorgeous hair, it's hard to imagine this Quinn as a twelve-year-old boy whose world got turned upside down.

But at the same time, I can. A boy whose brothers were his world, who'd lost a dad and another father figure and whose mother had died. Barely holding on to faith in something, to the nick in his thumb that meant he had a family. And then...

And then, piece by piece, he didn't.

"Quinn," I whisper.

"Yeah?"

"Who told you you weren't a people person?"

"I've never been..."

I shake my head. "But you said your brothers never made you feel that way. So someone said it to you. Someone's in your head."

He pushes a thick-fingered hand through his hair; my own fingers tingle at the remembered feel of those curls.

"Her name was Freya. We dated for two years, and I was going to ask her to marry me."

I think I must have known all along it was a woman.

"But you didn't."

He shakes his head. "No. I bought the ring, but before I could give it to her, she ended things. She said..." His voice is the rasp of a calloused palm over velvet. "She said she was a people person and I was an ideas-and-things person."

I bite down on my anger and frustration. "She was wrong." My voice matches his. Rough with the need to make him see himself more clearly. "She didn't see how big you love. She didn't see how deep. She had no fucking idea who you are."

I turn to him at the same time he turns toward me. There's pain and grief in his eyes, but something else, too. Want. Need. I touch his arm, slide my hand up and up, over his broad shoulder, my fingers slipping into his hair. Both of us groan as I pull him down into a hungry, open-mouthed kiss.

28

QUINN

I lose myself in Sonya for a long time, in the softness and generosity of her mouth, in the clutch of her hands at my hair and clothes, in noises she makes: moans and whimpers and gasps, especially when my hand slides up from her waist to cup her breast, my thumb gliding over her needy nipple.

"You like that, huh?" I ask her.

"Yeah," she moans.

"God, Sonya, I want to touch you everywhere."

"Then *do*," she says.

"Someplace where I really *can*," I say. "Where there's no gearshift and I'm not being"—I gesture at my lap—"strangled by my clothes."

But that gesture makes her look down at my lap, and she gets a naughty look on her face right before she palms me.

"Oh *God*, that feels— You should stop *right now*," I say, plucking her hand off me because, holy shit, I'm primed to go off. And I'd rather not do that while hogtied by my boxer briefs and jeans. Or before she does.

She gives me another naughty look and takes her hand away. "Let's go home," she says.

Home. It's scary how much I like the sound of that.

I start the car and drive toward the cabin. I drive fast, but it's still the most interminable fifteen minutes of my life, and I nearly break the steering wheel trying to keep my hands off her.

I pull up next to the cabin and stride around her side to let her out. She grabs my hand, and we run toward the front door.

She wrestles her key from her purse and fumbles the lock.

I take the key from her shaking hand, unlock the door, and hustle her over the threshold, slamming the door and backing her up against it.

"Okay?" I murmur, my lips inches from hers.

"Hell yes."

My mouth crashes down onto hers. For the first time I crowd my body against the whole length of hers, and *fuck.*

She feels so good.

She's the best of all the things: tall and strong enough to match me, to push back, to wriggle against me in a way that makes me want to tear all her clothes off right now. Or maybe leave her shirt wrapped around her wrists so she can't struggle so much.

And she's soft and curvy everywhere, and my hands can't get enough. I want to fill myself with her, and I do, palmfuls of her ass, yanking her tight up against me—

"Wait," she says, and *holy Jesus,* she is reaching into my

jeans, into my boxer briefs, working me free from my cloth chastity belt, and her warm fingers on me are the best thing I've felt in years. I lift her and press her against the door, notching my length against the vee of her thighs. She wraps her legs around me, groans, and tips her hips, rubbing herself against me.

I sweep her away from the door and toward my room. She laughs, arms around my neck, legs around my waist. When we get to my bed I deposit her there, and she holds her arms up, beckoning me. And who I am to refuse her anything? I crawl up over her, bracing myself, letting my hips sink down on hers, pulling another groan out of her.

"Too many clothes." She struggles with her top. I lift up a bit to let her take it off.

"Holy shit, Sonya, you're so fucking beautiful."

She's wearing a black lace bra that's mostly see-through, and I take her in, the silky sheen of her skin, the darker color of her nipples, the smooth, delectable, heaped-up curves of her breasts. I could stare at her for hours, except I can't because I need to put my mouth on her. She groans as soon as I do, at the touch of my beard and lips on the satin skin above the line of her bra.

"Quinn..."

"What do you want?"

"More."

I smile against her breast, pushing one bra cup down so I can draw circles with my tongue, spirals, narrowing in on my destination.

"Please," she groans.

I'm so hard it hurts. I'm trying to keep still, but it's impossible, my hips involuntarily grabbing small thrusts against the seam of her jeans. I close the spiral and take the tight peak of her breast in my mouth, teasing with my tongue, my teeth.

"Suck," she instructs, and *fuck*—

"You're bossy," I chide, looking up.

She's smiling. "I'm the boss," she teases.

"Nope," I say. "Not here."

I can tell she likes that because her hips tip up, seeking. Rolling. Her hand comes behind my head, pulling me hard down to her breast. I lift my hips and stroke her over and over, my length against her seam, while I suck and tease her nipple, working the other one through her bra with thumb and forefinger, paying attention to what makes her feel best.

"I'm going to come," she says, and then she is, yanking my hair so hard it hurts, jerking her hips up against me, choking out half words that definitely, gloriously include my name. I pull back so I can watch her face, and her abandon is so pretty that I almost lose it, too.

But I hang on because I want to be here, to witness all of this.

I settle on an elbow next to her and wait for her to come down. And worry, as one does, that when she comes to her senses, she'll be embarrassed or ashamed or regretful.

But when she opens her eyes, it's to smile at me.

"Hey," she says.

"Hey."

"That was—really, really good."

I grin.

"I didn't think scientists had a particular rep for being good at this stuff."

"Oh, we do," I say. "I mean, think about it. We understand chemistry. We're good at experimenting. We're very, very patient."

She's laughing. "You need *that* T-shirt."

"I do."

She rolls toward me. "Hey, so—you want a turn?" She puts her hand on my painfully hard erection, still held fast behind layers of denim and cotton. It surges against her hand, taking away my chance to lie.

"You know," I say, "I would like to be a big man and say, 'Nah, I'm fine, I just wanted you to feel good'—which is true as far as it goes, but the truth is? 'Fuck yes!'"

She's laughing again, and I decide it's my new favorite chemical reaction. And I'm going to make it happen every single time I possibly can, for the rest of—

For the rest of the time I'm here.

She reaches for the button of my jeans.

Something buzzes. My butt. I reach behind me and pull out my phone.

"Shit," I say.

"What?"

"Shane's in trouble."

29

SONYA

Quinn tries to convince me to stay in bed and wait for him, but I want to go with him. I throw my shirt back on, fix my touseled hair and smudged makeup, and wipe some stray lipstick off the corner of his mouth.

On the way, he tells me what he knows.

"He went from the hospital to a party. And I guess up to this point, he's been lying low. Somehow he managed to get out of LA without the paparazzi following him to Rush Creek, and people here have been pretty respectful about not putting him on social media. But tonight when he got to the party, someone posted a photo of him talking to a married woman, and the pissed-off husband showed up—"

"Oh shit," I say.

"Yup. And apparently there was a paparazzo. So he took off on foot and is hiding in some bushes on Wayfarer Lane."

"Yikes."

Wayfarer Lane is on a bluff, and it's the one road in Rush Creek that has houses you could describe as mansions. They date back to the gold rush, but they've been built up even bigger by wealthy newcomers.

"So our job is to drive slowly up Wayfarer Lane and wait for him to come running out and then bundle him into the car as fast as possible."

"Without getting arrested for loitering with intent," I point out.

"Right," he says, frowning.

"What about his car?"

"He says he'll figure that out tomorrow."

Quinn's obviously worried about Shane—and maybe a tiny bit annoyed at being pulled away from what we were doing.

Yeah. I mean, I didn't want to stop, either. I had a hand on Quinn's big, thick cock, and even through a couple of layers of fabric, I could tell that thing was going to be fun.

I'm still boneless from the orgasm Quinn gave me, which shook me to the core.

He might be right about scientists.

Or maybe I just really, really like him.

I close my eyes because that thought doesn't sit well with me. It doesn't pair nicely with reality, with a guy who has said, in no uncertain terms, that he loves his life in Boston, that he's leaving once he meets the terms of his grandfather's will.

"You okay?" he asks.

"Yeah," I say, but I'm not so sure. "Just still feeling some aftershocks."

He groans. "Not fair. I have to keep my hands on the wheel and my eyes on the bushes."

"That's what he said," I whisper, and he flicks an eye roll my direction.

A shadow separates itself from the vegetation and darts toward our car. Quinn stops, and Shane tries to open my door. Then sees me. Gets big eyed. Opens the back door instead and climbs in.

"Hi, Sonya," he says.

"Hey, Shane."

"Wasn't expecting to see you with my brother in the middle of the nigh—"

"Shut up," Quinn says genially.

Shane snorts.

"Can't stay out of trouble, can you?" Quinn growls at him.

There's a long silence from the back seat, and I turn around to see Shane staring out the window. Then he gathers himself. "Nope," he says cheerfully.

But the hesitation, the time it took for him to wind himself back up to light-hearted Shane, lands with me.

There's definitely more to Shane Hott than meets the eye. Which makes sense because there's a lot more to Quinn than meets the eye, too.

I'm betting you could say the same for all the Hott brothers. What were Quinn's words? *Filthy rich and ridiculously good at what they do.* I'd like to add: *and all a little more wounded than they'd like to admit.*

"Couldn't you get a better rescue?" Quinn asks him.

"Tucker had to go to Seattle for something. And Rhys and Preston are back in New York."

"They left?" Quinn asks. I hear the heaviness of his disappointment, even though he doesn't finish the sentence. They left *without saying goodbye.*

I close my eyes.

So much for the idea of a blissful brotherly reunion.

"They rushed out of town," Shane says, like he's heard the unspoken disappointment, too. "Rhys got called back in a hurry to appear in court. They took Preston's jet."

Still.

"Where am I taking you?" Quinn asks.

"Back to the Depot Hotel is fine," Shane says.

Quinn turns the car toward town.

The men are quiet, and I suddenly feel desperate to fill the dead air between them. "Was it a good party? Before things went south?"

"Didn't get much of a chance to take it in," Shane says. "And it doesn't matter much anyway. It would've been better than sitting in my hotel room by myself."

For the first time, he sounds dark and a little lonely. And now I'm sure of it: there's definitely more to Shane than meets the eye.

"So what happened? If you don't mind talking about it?"

"The usual," he says, and I can almost hear his shrug. "Got too cozy with a married woman."

The bright edge is back, like a mask he can put on and take off.

"That's what happened?" I ask. "Or that's what everyone will *think* happened?"

"What does it matter what happened if that's what everyone *thinks* happened?" Shane asks.

I want to tell him it matters a lot. That he's more than just his image. That he doesn't have to accept the way the world sees him.

That there are people who could be in his corner, like Quinn. Like me.

Maybe his other brothers, too, if the warmth I saw in that hospital room is any indication.

I open my mouth to say something along those lines, but at that moment, as we pull up in front of the hotel, Shane curses and ducks down. "Go around the block," he says. "That pap is there."

The pap in question is a twenty-something pasty guy with hair that needs cutting and a long-lensed camera around his neck.

We drive around the block, but when we finish our circle, the photographer is still standing on the Depot's Western-style front porch.

"I don't think he's going anywhere," Quinn says.

"Fuck."

"You can come back with us," I offer.

"I doubt Quinn would like that," Shane says, that same dark, naked tone in his voice.

Quinn's quiet beside me for a moment. Then he says, "Sonya's right. You're coming back with us."

"Don't be ridiculous," Shane protests. "I'm obviously…interrupting."

For an eternity, the only sound in the car is the slight flutter of the cooling system's fan.

Then Quinn snorts. "Yeah. You definitely are."

I hold my breath.

Quinn gives a half hitch of his shoulder, sighs, and steps on the gas.

"But you're my brother, and I'm not throwing you to the wolves."

30

QUINN

None of us has eaten, so I make a quickie Bolognese and some spaghetti, and Shane puts together a salad.

The three of us eat at her table. Sonya and I tell Shane about the product-development plan, and he tells us a little bit about the Hott Springs project he's been working on. Apparently Hanna and our granddad had always planned to convert one of the hay barns into a second smaller wedding venue, to increase the number of events the resort can host. Shane's been looking at costs and feasibility.

"When are you going back to LA?" Sonya asks.

He shrugs. "I don't know. I guess when I figure out what my next movie project is."

"What are the choices?" she asks.

"Unclear."

What's clear, from his tone of voice, is that he doesn't want to talk about it, so we both let it go, and Sonya and Shane talk about their favorite streaming shows on Netflix.

By the time we get Shane set up on the couch, it's late.

Sonya's brushing her teeth in the bathroom when I go to brush mine, but she waves me in. It's weirdly companionable, standing there together. We don't look at each other in the mirror. And then we do. Our eyes lock over our foaming mouths. Around her toothbrush, her mouth forms a small, inviting smile.

I raise an eyebrow.

"Hold that thought," she says, smiling.

I don't know what she has in mind, but it's not like there's any danger I'll *stop* thinking about what I want to do to her. It's been running through my mind nonstop since I watched her face go slack with pleasure.

I go back to my room, change into sweatpants and my *If you're not part of the solution, you're part of the precipitate* T-shirt, and get under the covers.

I'm almost asleep when my phone buzzes on the nightstand. It's Sonya.

If I were to sneak in there, would you kick me out?

Oh hell no, I reply. *But we have to be really, really quiet. Because the last thing I want is for my brother to hear any of those sexy little noises you make.*

I can be quiet, she promises.

A moment later, my door opens—soundlessly—and a shadow slips in. She shuts the door, tiptoes across the room, and crawls under the covers with me. I open my arms, and she comes close, warm and soft.

"You feel amazing," I whisper.

"You, too," she whispers back. She's running her hands all over me, her fingers and palms warm through my T-shirt. Her touch feels so good. "You're so...*hard.*"

I snicker.

"I didn't mean that. But that, too," she says, sliding a hand down my stomach to the elastic of my sweats, the only layer I'm wearing. She bumps the head of my cock, which has risen to meet her. She runs her hand over the thickness of it, using her thumb to trace the shape under the cotton. "May I?"

"Mmmm," I manage.

And then she's working my sweatpants down. I kick them away, and she takes me in her hand.

"Show me," she whispers.

I put my hand over hers, guiding her, and after a few strokes, she takes over. And she's good. Just tight enough, with a quick wrist and an excellent way of curling her thumb over the sensitive spot below my head with each stroke. I groan my appreciation, and she puts her other hand over my mouth, laughing.

"You were the one who said *quiet*," she murmurs, stroking me again, and holy shit, I'm not going to last if she keeps doing that.

"Hang on," I say. "Wait. Slide these down." I touch the waist of her sleep shorts, and she shoves them down with her underpants. We both shed our shirts, dropping them over the edge of the bed. "Put your leg over mine."

We're lying on our sides, looking into each other's eyes. My eyes have adjusted enough that I can see her, see the way her eyes darken with pleasure at my words. She likes being bossed. She does as I said, and I slide a hand between her legs, finding her already slick. I dip my finger and use it to circle her clit, reversing the spirals I teased on her breast earlier today. She laughs quietly, like she gets it, and I can't decide what I like most, the grip of her hand on my cock, the feel of her clit stiffening at my touch, or that laugh.

I settle my hand more firmly on her, entering her with one finger and then another. Her breath hitches and speeds, but she stays quiet. My fingers stroke in and out of her, my thumb on her clit now. Her hand moves faster on me, and I follow her rhythm. She rocks up into the touch, and I rock into hers.

"It's going to be really good," she murmurs.

"When you come?"

"When you fuck me," she whispers, and then she's coming, panting, arching, making nearly-but-not-quite-inaudible whimpers. Her hand tightens and twists on me, rubbing right over the most sensitive spot, and pleasure rockets up from the base of my spine, grabs me at the base of my cock, takes me over. I come so hard that the world goes blank for a second, at the last minute cupping my free hand to catch my release.

I collapse onto my back. She grabs a tissue from the box on the nightstand and hands it to me, then flops onto my chest.

"Was I quiet?" she asks. "I lost my head for a minute."

"Quiet enough. Was I?"

"Yeah."

She slips her hand into mine. It's a small gesture, but it feels so intimate and trusting. I squeeze it. "I want you to know," she whispers, "that I heard you when you said you don't do relationships. I get it. And I know you're leaving soon. But...I'm still glad this happened."

I want to tell her that even if this isn't a relationship, and even if I can't be what she wants, it's not casual to me. But I know that'll just confuse things. So instead, I put my arms around her and draw her as close as I can. And we fall asleep that way.

31

SONYA

"Um, guys, there's a big delivery coming in?" Lily says.

Quinn's sitting behind the desk; I'm in another chair behind him. We were about to look at sales numbers, but when we hear Lily's words, we practically take each other out in the rush away from our post.

"Will you...?" I'm already halfway to the hallway, Quinn on my heels, leaving the desk unattended with reckless disregard, gesturing at Lily to take it over.

"What the heck?" she asks.

"I'll explain everything. Just—watch the desk?"

"Yes! Go! Go!"

Quinn and I race each other out to the delivery entrance, Gus right behind us. Our boxes—both the product and the packaging, labels and boxes—are waiting for us.

As Quinn pulls out his penknife and cuts into the first box, Reggie appears.

"I heard there's some big drama?" she says.

"You're a drama *magnet*," I tell her.

"Yep," she says and leans against the edge of the big door. Mei saunters in a minute later as Quinn pulls a bottle of shampoo out and squeezes it into his palm.

He touches it, sniffs it, and nods, then does the same to the conditioner.

"What the fuck is that?" Reggie asks. "Drugs?"

"No. It's—" But I have to know something else first. "Is it okay?" I implore Quinn.

"Looks like it. I'll do some actual testing later."

"Thank God."

He touches my hand, and when I look up at him, he smiles at me. He knows. He knows what this means to me. It's not only a bunch of shampoo and conditioner. It's making my world right again. My throat closes up at the feeling of being seen that way. It's almost too much.

"It's *what*?" Reggie demands as Lily appears.

"You're supposed to be at the desk!" I cry at her.

"I left Catalina there. I wasn't going to miss whatever made you and Quinn dash out here."

I point to the bottle in Quinn's hand. "Hott Spot–branded shampoo and conditioner."

"Wait, what?" Reggie's eyes bug out. "That's so cool!"

Quinn and I had been trying to keep our project under wraps in case we couldn't pull it off, but obviously the cat's out of the bag now with pallets of product sitting in the storeroom.

He slices into another case and pulls out one of the flattened boxes. He hands it to me, and I assemble it.

"Those are great!" Reggie says. "I love the pink spot!"

We all admire our creation. When I look up, Quinn is

looking back at me, an expression I've seen only once before: the night he held his niece in his arms for the first time. Tenderness and affection—and something bigger, too. Wonder. Gratitude.

I love being on the receiving end of that look.

I want to enjoy every minute that it lasts because we're so close to the end. His last day is less than two weeks away. After that, he'll go back to Boston and do what he's supposed to be doing, developing treatments for life-threatening diseases. And he *should* be. The world needs him.

But for now, I am so glad to have him here, looking at me like I'm something...

Precious.

I tear my attention away from Quinn and discover Reggie staring at me oddly.

"How long has this been in the works?" she asks.

"I guess—almost as long as Quinn's been here."

"You should have said something," she says. "We could have helped out if we knew."

"Oh, no," I say. "It was an off-the-clock kind of project. I didn't want anyone else to have to give up work or leisure hours to help me with this half-assed plan."

"Sonya," Reggie says, somewhat sternly. "I've known you since you were six. I don't think I've ever seen you do something 'half-assed.' If you did it, you had your reasons."

"She did," Quinn says.

I turn and glare at him. He closes his mouth, a firm line. He obviously thinks I should tell them that we're doing this for Bella, but I never told them that Maura's pilfering had endangered Bella's start, and I don't want to get into it now.

"It looks like you still have a lot of work ahead of you,"

Reggie says. She raises her eyebrows, looking down at the cases in front of us. "That's a lot of labels to affix and boxes to assemble. And bottles to put into boxes. And boxes to close."

"Were you going to do a launch party?" Mei asks. "Because we could."

"I was—I was thinking two weeks from now."

A few days after Quinn's last day at the desk. Will he even stay for the party? If I asked him to, would he?

"So someone has to order food and drinks for the party," Mei says. "Unless you did that already?"

I shake my head. I hadn't thought that far yet.

Lily crosses her arms. "And decorations."

"I have streamers."

"Streamers are good," she says, "but we also need a helium pump so we can blow up the balloons."

"Balloons?" I bite my lip. They're escalating this beyond where I was thinking it would go.

"Tons of them. The whole room crammed with them. All black and white, except for a few hot-pink ones here and there," Lily says. "Just like the packaging."

"And we could do one of those Elf on the Shelf or Where's Waldo–style things for the kids," Reggie says. "But maybe more like, Spot the Spot."

This is sounding more and more like an epic amount of work. Panic bristles in my chest. Gus, flopped out beside me, whines.

"You know what," I say, "let's keep this super simple. Let Quinn and me handle the product stuff. I don't think we need a launch party. Maybe just a coupon in the newsletter."

Reggie, Lily, and Mei exchange looks. Then Reggie turns to me. "Up to you," she says. "You're the boss. But if you change your mind and you want to do something bigger, just pull us in. We're always here."

She tilts her head, eyes on mine.

"You just have to ask."

QUINN HELPS me carry the boxes inside, and we set them down in my office. They fill most of the remaining space. Gus finds himself a small sunny square, turns around a few times, and goes to sleep.

Serenity pokes her head in. "Let me see!"

I show her the boxes, and she whistles her approval and fans herself.

"Oh, Serenity," Quinn says, "some guy called today to make an appointment with you, but I told him we were full through the end of the year because according to your notes, last time he was a 'fucknozzle' about his eyebrows being red even after you used the wand and the roller." He rolls his eyes. "Man up, asshole. Eyebrows get red."

Serenity looks at me. "Can we hire him permanently?"

"I wish," I say.

Quinn blushes.

She shrugs and goes back to work, and Quinn and I finish moving boxes.

Then we're standing alone in my office.

"Thank you," I say quietly.

He shakes his head. "I just did the science. You had the business plan."

"There's no 'just' about what you did."

"As long as you know there's no 'just' about what you did, either."

We stare at each other for a moment, and then he steps toward me and pulls me into his arms. And God, he feels good—the strong enclosure of his embrace, the hard wall of his abs and chest against me. I think I moan.

But then he steps back.

"I have some news," he says.

"Yeah?"

"MedThena's clinical trial with the new drug was a success. We're going to have another product launch."

"Quinn, that's amazing."

He smiles. "Yeah. It's good news. But—"

The expression on his face makes my stomach feel like someone carved the Grand Canyon into it. Whatever he has to tell me, he doesn't want to say it.

And that means I don't want to hear it.

"It means I have to get back to Boston right after I'm done here. I can stay through Hott Spot's product launch, but then I'm done."

He's watching me so closely. I don't let it show, how it feels like a dump truck full of rocks. I know it's what he wants, what he *needs*...

But it's also the harshest reminder yet that he's leaving. Leaving Rush Creek, leaving *me*.

I can do this. I can be happy for him. His science is going to save more lives. He's going to go back to doing what he loves, not catering to the whims of a grumpy dead guy. Rush Creek, Hott Spot was never forever. *We* were never forever.

It was always only until he fulfilled the terms of the will.

His eyes search my face. I hold his gaze. "We knew you were leaving, Quinn. We did this knowing that it would end when you left."

This, I think. What even is *this*? What are we doing, and how did I let it happen?

"Thank you—for telling me." But that's as far as my voice will take me. It cracks then, betraying me. And strangely, that makes me laugh. The cat's out of the bag; I might as well be honest. "Quinn," I say, "I know you have to go. But...I don't want you to."

For the longest moment of my life, his face is shuttered, like the face of the stranger who first walked into my spa all those weeks ago. Then he shakes his head and laughs, too, a *life's too strange* chuckle. "I don't want to go."

My hands go around his neck, his mouth drops onto mine, and we kiss like we're running out of time.

"Your office..." he says. "Does it have a lock?"

I grin. "Absolutely."

Without taking his eyes off mine, he steps to the door and locks it. Then he stalks back toward me. It's easy to forget, because Quinn Hott is such a good man, that he's also a big man, and right now, he's set to maximum predator. Blue gaze fierce. Beard starting to grow a bit wild again, waves gone a little ragged. He's leonine. A lion that's hunting me.

He sweeps most of the contents of my desk onto the floor and sets me on top of it.

"Quinn...the desk. The camera—"

He looks at his watch. "It's lunchtime. I get thirty minutes. I've only used twenty-one."

Then he kneels and peels my leggings and underwear down.

"Quinn," I whimper as his mouth moves from my navel down over the slope of my belly.

"Is that a yes?" he asks, his fingers working to part me, spread me for his perusal.

"Yes," I moan as his tongue finds me, curling, teasing, stroking. "Except—"

He stops.

"I want you inside me," I tell him.

The color's already high in his face, but at that his pupils go dark as night. "God," he says. "I want to be there. But the first time my cock's inside you, it's going to be when we have lots of time to enjoy ourselves and we can both make as much noise as we want. I swear."

Then he goes back to work, his beard scraping the tender flesh of my thighs, tickling everywhere between my legs, and his tongue and two curled fingers doing the rest. He puts his hand up to cover my mouth when I go over the edge, and I suck his fingers, hard, in the same rhythm as the surges in my body.

Afterward, when we've put me back together, he tells me there's no time for me to return the favor.

"Which is okay," he says, "because I want to sit at the front desk all day thinking about your mouth on my cock later."

"What about Shane?"

Quinn grins. "He took off this morning and texted me that it was all-clear at the Depot, so we should have the cabin to ourselves again tonight."

"Mmm," I say and then remember: "Ohhh. I told Bella

I'd watch her grandkids tonight. She's gonna be out late for some kind of auction for their school. And if I have any time afterward, I was gonna look in on my dad. I haven't for way too long."

He drops a kiss on my forehead. "That's okay. There's no limit to the amount of time I'm willing to spend on this particular thought train."

"Tomorrow morning," I promise.

His grin gets even bigger. "I'm holding you to that."

"**W**ake up, Quinn."

The voice is a soft murmur in my ear, a vanilla-scented cloud of hair across my face. I reach for her, but she laughs and drifts away.

"You slept so late!" She hovers a few feet away, already dressed, in a tight hot-pink T-shirt and skinny black pants that stop at mid-calf. "I didn't want to wake you up, but we've gotta go."

"Go where?" I ask.

"It's a surprise."

"Okay, but what kind of where?"

"A where you'll like. It's a thank you for what you did. For developing the shampoo and conditioner. For saving Bella's job."

"I know lots of ways you could thank me for that," I say, rolling onto my back and eyeing the delicious package she makes in that outfit. As hot as she looks in a button-down blouse, this tee clings to her like a second skin. And her bra is too thin to hide her response to my suggestion. "It's 'tomorrow morning,' isn't it?"

She reaches out and, with a flourish, traces a finger over my morning wood through my boxer briefs, then dances out of reach, looking back over her shoulder at me, a tease in her eyes.

I catch her in the bathroom, stripping her out of her clothes and pulling her into the shower with me, where I press her against the tile and suck her pretty nipples while I tease her clit with one finger until she comes.

She drops to her knees.

"Sonya," I groan.

Her reply is muffled by my cock.

"I'm not going to last long," I grit out.

"Good," she grunts, her tongue working back and forth over the sensitive head of my cock.

And true to my word, I slap a hand hard against the tile a moment later, bracing myself while I come, strong, wracking spasms against the caress of her tongue.

Once we're both coherent, we grab breakfast, and then she drives us into Bend. When we get there, she leads me down an alley between a tall brick building and a lower stone one.

"Should I be scared?" I ask her as we approach a locked gate. Then I see the sign: *Houdini's Hours*. It's an escape room. She brought me to an escape room. "Seriously, Sonya? Are you *sure* about this? It's about the nerdiest way to spend seventy minutes you can possibly imagine."

"I'm actually very nerdy," she says primly.

I scowl at her, in her cute top and her satiny black pants, at her glossy corkscrew curls that I know took her at least twenty minutes to accomplish, and that was before she spent thirty minutes on her makeup.

"Looks can be deceiving!" she says in response to my skeptical look. "I read three reviews yesterday saying that you were *such a sweet boy*."

"Not a boy," I growl.

"No," she agrees. "You are definitely not."

I growl again, this time against the curl of her ear, her body sighing back against mine, and something is going to happen in this alley that might get us arrested.

"Hold that thought," she instructs me.

"I'm holding a lot of thoughts right now."

"I'll make it worth your while later."

"You're not making this any easier," I groan.

"I know," she says happily. "I like messing with you."

I tug her close, snugging her against my erection. She wiggles. I lean down and murmur, "I like being messed with."

She calls the phone number on the sign, and we're admitted by a twenty-something guy who explains the rules of the escape room to us. Eventually we're deposited into the starting room of the puzzle. It's configured to look like a modern-day game café.

"You found an escape room about board games," I say, staring at it.

She shrugs. "I thought you'd like it."

"Sonya, I freakin' love it."

But we don't have time to focus on that right now. We have to solve the puzzle. "Okay," I say, arms crossed, looking around. "I'm guessing we start...here..."

Our journey takes us across a landscape that looks like

Catan, requires us to play word games Code Names style, and finally forces us to string trains together in a Ticket to Ride–style puzzle to win the day.

I know way more about board games than she does, unsurprisingly, but it turns out she has hidden genius at both spatial concepts and word problems. And she's easy to work with, happy to step up if she knows an answer, but willing to hang back and play a support role when she doesn't.

It feels like we've done this together forever, and I love it. I love working with her. I love playing with her. I love solving problems—made-up and real ones—with her.

Fifty-three minutes later, when we're unleashed back into the main lobby, triumphant, I pull Sonya into my arms and say, "You do have a nerdy streak."

"Thank you," she says. "Coming from you, I know that's the highest possible compliment."

"Now I have something for you," I tell her. "It's also a thank-you present."

"*Ohhhkay*," she says. "Why do you need to thank me?"

There are so many answers to that, I don't know where to start. "I wouldn't have been able to fulfill the terms of the will without your help," I remind her.

"I wasn't going to stand in the way of that. I hate to break it to you, but I did that as much for Hanna as for you."

"I also wouldn't have had a place to stay without you."

"Mmm," she says. "Again, the situation forced my hand."

"Yes. But you were gracious about it."

Her mouth curves up. "Maybe I like you."

"Maybe you need to stop telling me why you don't deserve my thanks and come home to see your present."

That shuts her up, and we drive back to the cabin.

"Sit at the kitchen table and close your eyes," I say.

She does. I bring in my gift for her and set it on the table in front of her. "Okay," I say. "Open."

She shrieks when she does. "A sewing machine!" she says. "Holy shit, Quinn, you can't buy me a sewing machine. It's way too expensive."

"Actually," I say, "it wasn't."

"What the hell are you talking about?" she demands. "This is, like, a five-hundred-dollar machine."

"New," I say. "But this one isn't new. It belonged to Mrs. Jensen. I asked everyone who came into the spa if they knew of a sewing machine that wasn't being used, and Mrs. Jensen had one. She got it as a gift five years ago, used it twice, then went back to her thirty-year-old Bernina. I'm quoting. I have no idea what that means."

"Quinn," she says. "You asked all the clients about their sewing machines?"

"There's not that much to do at the front desk," I say, shrugging. "You have to keep yourself entertained. I should probably tell you, though, I did give her a year of free upper-lip waxes."

She burst out laughing. "You did *what*? Are you *serious*?"

"Are you angry?"

"Hell no," she says. "I'm—"

Her eyes are big. Shiny with tears. "God damn it, Quinn. Why'd you have to go and do something so fucking *nice*?"

I pull her up from the table and into my arms.

"Because you're so fucking nice," I say.

33

SONYA

Quinn's beard and breath brush over my ear, and all the strength goes out of my legs. I sag against him. "I don't want to pull you away from your new toy," he murmurs, but he does —I can tell he does from how hard he already is against me and the fact that he sounds like he's run a mile to reach me.

He swoops me up in his arms and carries me to his bedroom, where he sets me on the bed and crawls over me.

"Sonya," he says, kneeling up. He reaches back and, with one hand, tugs his T-shirt (*Never trust an atom. They make up everything.*) over his head. It takes my breath away —not only the flair of the action, but also the flex of every muscle in his upper body and what's revealed underneath the T-shirt: the broad swell of his pecs, the hair fanned out across them, the ridges of his abs, the V-dip of his hips. The place where dark curls arrow down into the waistband of his jeans. The thick bulge of his arousal under the denim.

"God, Quinn." I'm breathless. "I need—"

"Me, too." A moment later, he's over me, hands planted

on either side of me, mouth settling onto mine. It's a gentle kiss by Quinn standards—slow, languid, like he's asking me a question. *Like this?* And I answer back, *No, more, more, more, please more,* and then we're on fire. His tongue sweeping in, demanding, taking, merciless, me whimpering under his onslaught, grabbing handfuls of everything I can —hair, beard, shoulders, ass. Everything I touch flexes and tenses under my hands. He's so hard everywhere, and I can't get enough.

He's moving against me. I'm not even sure if he knows he's doing it. His denim-clad erection settles into the notch of my thighs, against the inseam of my leggings. He rocks there, faint needy thrusts that are lighting me on fire. Not just the motion and the friction—which, holy fuck, is bad enough—but the knowledge that he can't hold still, that what I do to him is just like what he does to me. Impossible to resist.

"I'm going to make you come," he says, pulling back and looking at me, wild eyed. His hair is a mess from the T-shirt operation; his beard needs to be trimmed again, which is— glorious. If I could go back, I'd tell Day One Quinn: *You're perfect. Don't change anything.*

His eyes hold my gaze, pinning me. "Then I'm going to fuck you. And then I'm going to make you come again. And only then am I going to come inside you. So fucking hard. So hard, Sonya. You're going to feel it for days."

I can't even answer. I can only hang on while he lowers his mouth to mine again, fierce and authoritative. I lift my hips, trying to get more, trying to get what I need, chasing the hot, tangled, twining urgency in my low belly.

"Quinn—" I'm trying to work my hands between us, to

get my own shirt off. I need his fingers and his mouth on me, and I need them now. He gets it, even though I'm incoherent with need. He levers himself up enough so I can work my shirt free. I throw it across the room, and neither of us even stops to laugh. He's already buried his face against me, rubbing his beard against the lace of my bra, working the cup down with fingers that are all strength and aggression until they find my nipple, and then they're all skill and finesse. A thumb over the sensitive peak, so soft and slow I want to beg for more. Like he knows it, he works me and works me without giving me what I need, and then I realize it was what I needed all along, the winding pleasure between my legs spiraling tighter and tighter.

He slides his big hand into my leggings, edges a thick finger into the seam of my sex. Finds me wet for him. He makes an incoherent noise deep in his chest, a grunt or a growl or a moan, I don't even know. He plays there, finger dipping and delving and teasing, drawing circles at my entrance, then nudging higher to slick my own wetness onto my swollen clit. I expect more circles, but instead I get soft and slow again, the way he grazed my nipple with his thumb earlier. He rolls to his side, freeing his other hand, and then he's giving me both. An easy, languid, back and forth over the tight peak of my nipple, another over the bud at the top of my sex, and it's so much, too much—

"I can't," I pant.

"If you really can't, I'll stop," he murmurs. "But I think you can. I think you can and you want to, and I think you're going to come so hard, Sonya, so fucking hard—"

Then I am, just like he said, like he conjured it, sensation rolling through my body, drawing the invisible cord tight between my nipple and my clit. He knows. He flattens his palm against my mound while his fingers fill me where I'm clenching, empty, and I thrust down against those fingers, wanting more.

He lets me ride it all the way through, and then he's rolling over, off the bed, shedding his jeans, freeing himself from his boxer briefs. His cock is beautiful, thick and smoky-skinned. He makes my mouth water. He opens the nightstand drawer and takes out a condom, rolling it on, and I'm wrestling myself out of my leggings and panties. They're still wrapped around one ankle when he climbs over me again, bracing himself on toned arms. I spread my legs in welcome, and he smiles at that.

Then the smile is gone, and he's nudging my entrance. "Okay?" he asks.

"Please," I beg.

The first thrust is so thick, long, and slow that I'm pretty sure my eyes roll back in my head. It's pressure—good pressure, the perfect slide, the perfect fit. I'm still swollen from my orgasm, and the sensation of his hard heat stroking there is bliss.

"Quinn."

"Sonya," he groans, dropping his head so his cheek rests against mine. "I'm—I want to—"

"It doesn't matter," I say. "It's already good. It's already the best ever. Everything else is gravy."

He doesn't laugh. He lifts his head and stares at me, eyes dark and lost. "I want to ruin you for everything else ever."

I don't laugh either. I just fuck back against his next thrust and the next one, the two of us finding a rhythm, his eyes never leaving mine. The two of us staring into each other's eyes, moving helplessly toward something we can't avoid and don't want to. I would have sworn I couldn't come again, but it's building for me, with the steady rhythm, and it only takes a few strokes that swivel and grind, that circle me and ride his hips hard up over my mound, before I'm calling his name, begging for one more.

He gives it to me, long and deep and thick, and I come hard, clutching him, feeling the moment when he freezes at the edge of his thrust, feeling the heady sensation of him throbbing deep inside me, coming.

He holds my gaze, holds it and holds it and holds it, his eyes full of affection and warmth. Then he rolls me over on top of him, wraps me tight, and buries his face against mine, panting for breath.

"I—think—you—ruined—me—instead," he says.

34

QUINN

We have a good week.

There's no other way to put it.

As if by agreement, we don't speak about the countdown to my departure. Ten, nine, eight, seven... The days tick away toward the moment when I will have fulfilled the terms of the will. But we don't say anything about it or about my leaving.

We just make love. A lot. Every chance we get.

We talk a lot, too. She tells me about her dad, who's been doing pretty well the last two years after a few relapses into problem gambling. She wonders aloud if the new girlfriend will be good for him or not. She shakes her head and grumbles, *He doesn't even like dogs.*

She tells me about her mom, how much she loved the salon, how much she loved the beauty industry. How she was the cookies-and-crafts kind of mom, the one who showed her love with food and fun projects.

I tell her about crashing around the woods with my brothers. About the time that I almost let Shane eat the poisonous mushroom (and my ongoing ambivalence about sparing him). She laughs. Hugs me. Says she knows I don't mean it. I admit she's right.

I tell her about my mom, how she was the quality-time-and-serious-talks kind of mom, the kind who showed her love by sitting a long time on the edge of your bed and stroking your hair until you could fall asleep. Listening if you needed listening to.

I tell her about loving the lab, about loving science, about loving the precision you need to give an experiment, and the patience. Things other people find hard but that come easily to me. She smiles and says she knows. She pulls me to her, and I am precise and patient until she shatters.

She tells me about loving the spa—and I tell her that on good days, when people keep their appointments and the sun is shining, so everyone's in a good mood, I love the spa, too.

The days tick down toward my departure. I Zoom into work meetings and weigh in on the coming product launch. Banks asks if I know what direction my research is going in next. I tell him I know, and he asks for a timeframe. I give him one.

I make plans to go back. I book flights.

But I find myself thinking: *What if I don't?*

That's what I'm thinking about right now, on my last Saturday and fourth-to-last day of this ridiculous arrangement. This travesty orchestrated by my deluded and probably sadistic grandfather who somehow, nevertheless, seems to have known *exactly* what he was doing.

I'm sitting at the front desk in Hott Spot, thinking: What if I *don't go back*?

"Cake?"

Somehow, I missed the door opening. I missed Nan from the bakery stepping into the reception area and approaching the desk. Now she's standing practically in front of my nose, holding out a plate filled with chocolate cake.

"It's my better-than-Robert-Redford cake," Nan says.

She's come equipped with a fork, which she thrusts at me, tines first. I gingerly take it, handle first.

"It's actually my better-than-sex cake," Nan says confidingly. "But for some reason people are uptight about older women thinking about sex, so *better-than-Robert-Redford* sells better. What do they think we do, quit after age fifty?" She clocks my expression and says, "PSA: We don't. And there are a lot of guys over fifty who are very glad about that."

"I imagine," I say. Then—because I need something to do—I help myself to a big bite of the cake, which, whatever you call it, is delicious. Rich, dark, soft, and loaded up with really fucking good frosting. I take another bite and another.

"Good, right?" Nan asks.

"Un-fucking-believable."

She grins at that. "Thank you." Then she sets down the plate and crosses her arms. "I hear a rumor."

Uh-oh.

"What's that?" I brace myself. Nan is notorious for being Rush Creek's resident gossip, and Sonya and I have done some very gossip-worthy things recently.

(That thing in the shower last night, for example. Where she had a foot up on the edge of the bathtub. And I had to bend my knees, but it was totally worth it because A) that fucking angle and B) the hot water falling down over us and the bath steamer she'd put in there—it was total sensory overload in the best possible way. You could have heard her yelling my name in town. Probably Nan did.)

"I heard you're leaving. To go back to Boston."

"Oh," I say. Surprised and maybe even disappointed; Sonya's and my shower shenanigans did *not* register on Nan's Richter scale. "Well. Yeah. I can't be the Hott Spot receptionist forever."

"No?" she says. "Hmm. I guess not. Well, we'll miss you."

I wait for something more. About how I'm eye candy or good at not losing appointments or she knows I was responsible for developing that new shampoo that Hott Spot is going to sell. Something. But she doesn't say anything else. She just smiles at me.

"Nan, I'm ready for you!" Serenity singsongs.

Nan goes back, and Sonya comes out, tote bag slung over her shoulder.

"Huh," I say. "Nan said she'll miss me when I go."

"Well, duh," Sonya says. "Everyone's going to miss you when you go."

"What do you mean *everyone*?"

She looks at me like I'm speaking French. "I mean Reggie and Mei and Catalina and Serenity and Lily and all the customers. Definitely all the customers. They adore you."

"And you?"

Her whiskey-in-candlelight gaze darkens. "Do you really need to ask that?"

She says it quietly but fiercely. I know she means it. I know she doesn't want me to go, but...

Does that mean she wants me to stay?

How can two sides of the same question feel so different?

"Are you sure you want me to come with you tonight?" she asks. "Hanna's going to have...some questions."

I'm babysitting tonight. For Eloise. And I asked Sonya if she'd come, too. Not because I don't trust myself around a baby.

I don't. But I'm sure I would have figured it out.

I asked her to come because of this countdown thing, because our time together is almost over, and I don't want to...

I don't want to miss any of it.

She's right. Hanna's going to give us a hard time when we show up together. Best case, she'll tease. Worst case, she'll demand explanations.

I don't have them.

"I'm sure," I say.

35

SONYA

"Wait," Hanna says. Hands on hips. Staring at us. Maybe...glaring. "Why'd you bring her?"

She says it accusingly, but if you've known Hanna a while, it's her way. She's blunt. Sometimes even a tiny bit careless with words.

Just like Quinn. The grumpy things both of them say are just...things. And I like it. How you always know where you stand.

Quinn's been honest with me all along. He's never pretended that there's a future for us. He's never tried to hide the fact that he's going back to Boston, back to his science and his life.

He's going to be leaving, right on schedule.

So I'm trying to stay in the here and now. Because the here and now—

It's so good.

It's so good with him. Every time. And all the in-betweens. The *lying in bed, hand in hand, staring at the ceiling* moments. The *I can probably manage not to ruin oatmeal if you make the eggs* moments. The *I'm going to kick your ass at Bananagrams—oh shit, you have weird skills* moments. Others, too. Him reading an advance reader copy of a chemistry textbook that a friend of a friend sent, while I sit at the kitchen table and figure out how to use the sewing machine to make a skirt out of the fabric Bella gave me for my birthday. Looking up periodically to see him not reading but watching me, a smile playing over his face— here, then gone, like a ghost.

And this one: Hanna gaping at me like I'm something gooey she touched on a subway pole.

"I don't suppose you have a spare item of clothing on you," Hanna says to me.

I stare at her.

"I know this guy who has a dog," she says.

"Don't," Easton says, covering Hanna's mouth with his hand. He yelps, jerking it away and laughing because she's clearly bitten him. They're so stinking cute together.

Easton rolls his eyes. "Don't believe anything she says. She's going to tell you that my brother has a dog that can predict, um, certain things by eating an article of your clothing. It's like a cult. It's a mass-delusion thing. You have to trust me—you don't want to get involved."

"I feel okay trusting you on this one," Quinn says.

"Good man," Easton says. "Are you going to let them in?" he asks Hanna. "Or just make them stand there all night explaining themselves?"

"They have a lot of explaining to do," she says grumpily.

Easton looks from Quinn to me and back again. "Ignore her," he says and holds the door open wide for us.

In the living room, he unbundles Eloise from his chest and hands her over to Quinn, who looks down at her with that helpless expression of love that slayed me in the hospital room. Easton and Hanna give us a lot of instructions about bottles and diapers, which I record as video on my phone in case I need them later. It boils down to the fact that there's an excellent chance that Eloise will sleep through their absence, but if she doesn't, she will cry, and we won't know why, and then we will try the same three things over and over again until she stops crying, and then we'll know what she was crying about.

When they've gone, Quinn lowers himself to their couch gingerly, Eloise still clutched in his big arms. I take my phone out of my pocket, set it on the coffee table, and follow suit.

Hanna and Easton's living room is cozy, with a bold-print area rug, the comfy blue-gray couch we've sunk ourselves into, and two matching armchairs. A coffee table that looks like it's made of recycled wood. Walls full of the outdoors—a poster featuring every variety of mushroom you can imagine, one of someone performing some death-defying ski jump, a canoer alone on a lake. A photo of Easton and Hanna together at their wedding, probably taken by Easton's brother, who's a world-class photographer.

It feels like home. Safe, and also dangerous, like something I could want if I let myself.

"Want me to take her?" I ask, gesturing to Eloise.

"Sure," he says. He hands her to me. She's heavier than I was expecting, a warm, solid weight in my arms. Surprisingly comforting against my body.

"You want to watch something?" I ask, gesturing at the TV.

He grins. "Next episode of *Chemical Reaction*?"

"I thought you hated it."

"I thought I did," he says, nodding. "I thought I hated everything about it."

His hands are in my hair as he says it, cupping my face. His eyes on mine.

"But I don't," he says. "I love it. And I can't stop."

His mouth touches down on mine, hungry, and I open to him, just as hungry.

On my lap, Eloise flails, frees a hand from her swaddle, and lets out an angry yell.

We pull apart, laughing.

"Guess we know what Hanna and Easton's sex life is like right now," I say.

"Gah!" he groans. "Don't talk to me about my sister's sex life, even if you're saying it doesn't exist!"

He rewraps Eloise in her swaddle, and we settle down to watch our show. He is merciless, relentless. *That's not a thing! That's not how you do that! Those things cost one hundred bucks a pop—no way she'd leave it sitting at the edge of the table.*

Those poor show writers. I bet they can feel his scorn from LA.

Until the hero kisses the heroine in the rain outside their lab. And then when I turn to sneak a peek at him, he's rapt, eyes glued to the screen, mouth a tiny bit open in adoration.

Oh, Quinn.

When the credits roll, he leans back into his corner of

the couch and gives a sigh of contentment. His expression still has the softness it wore during the kiss in the rain. I curl up in my own corner, Eloise drowsing on my lap.

"So you're a hopeless romantic," I say, watching him.

Startled, his gaze flicks across the couch to me.

"A secret people person and a secret hopeless romantic."

He shakes his head. "No." But a smile plays over his face.

"You want to tell me why you don't do relationships?"

He gives me a sharp look. It might be a warning. *Don't. Don't try to talk me into something I've told you I can't do.*

It hurts my stomach, and suddenly I want to turn back. I don't want to push Quinn, not right now, when everything feels so good.

"Forget that," I say. "Let's talk about whether Marianne is in cahoots with Malone."

A phone vibrates faintly, and Quinn reaches for his pocket, pulling his out. I watch his face as he swipes and reads. He frowns, and his eyes flick to my face. His expression shutters completely, and he slides the phone back into his pocket.

"What?" I ask, even though I know it has to be about his work.

"A work thing."

"What kind of work thing?"

"Banks—my partner—asking if I can come back a few days sooner."

I know what that means. It means he'd miss the product launch. "If you need to go," I say carefully, "you should go."

I mean, *If you need to go early, you should go early*, but I also mean something bigger, and we both know it.

"We haven't talked about it," he says. "My leaving. Or staying, I guess."

The *I guess* lands awkwardly, a dancer on the wrong foot. And Quinn's not looking at me. His eyes dart around Hanna and Easton's living room.

I remember another man with eyes that wouldn't settle on mine. Brandon's, when he came to tell me he was leaving. For good. That Rush Creek wasn't for him.

The thing was I'd already known. Maybe I'd known from the beginning, when I'd first laid it in front of him, the idea of him coming to live with me in Rush Creek. There'd been a wariness in his eyes that in retrospect I should have seen as a warning. A *don't do this—I can't do this—don't ask this of me.*

By the time Quinn's eyes come back to mine, the ache has landed permanently in my stomach.

And just then, there's another, louder vibration—from my phone on the coffee table. We're all such creatures of habits these days that I can't help turning my head. When I do, I recognize the bright green and the logo of the notification on my lock screen.

It's from my dad's credit card company. Well, technically, it's a jointly held card because my dad's credit was absolute shit after he lost the house and the salon and had to declare bankruptcy.

The notification is the alarm I set up to notify me if he transacts more than three hundred dollars in twenty-four hours. I never thought it would sound because he's savvy enough to figure out how to lose thirty thousand dollars while never spending more than a hundred a day.

But there it is.

Southwest ticket counter, Portland International Airport.

Thankfully my dad's airline account is configured to send me an email when he makes travel plans—a backstop we agreed on together—so unless he disabled that, I should be able to see where he's going.

I open my email. The destination jumps out at me like it's emblazoned in flaming pink.

Las Vegas.

36

QUINN

Sonya wants to go after her dad. She wants to drive to Portland right now, to stop him.

I look at my phone lock screen, do a quick calculation in my head. "You won't make it on time."

"I knew that woman was going to be a bad influence," she says, pacing back and forth in front of the coffee table while I hold sleeping Eloise. "I knew it. She's like a Vegas show herself. All those little dogs."

"I don't think there are little dog shows in Vegas," I say, unhelpfully. I deserve the glare she shoots me.

"God!" she says. "When was the last time I visited him?" She stares into space. "Weeks ago. It was that night you cooked for me. He could have been lying in his own filth. The cat could have eaten him."

"Does he have a cat?" I ask.

"No! But the neighbor's cat could have. Or any wandering cat. Or raccoon."

"That's—"

"Don't tell me it's unlikely," she warns.

"I would never." I set my sleeping niece in her bassinet, stand up, and cross to Sonya, figuring I'll wrap her up like the baby blanket is wrapped around Baby Burrito Eloise. And she lets me, but then she breaks loose again, pacing.

"I should go," she says.

"I don't think you can do anything tonight." Feeling a bit frantic myself, I pull out my phone and do a flight search. "Look. No more flights out. That was the last one."

"What have I been doing?" she moans. "I'm too busy to check on him? Or text him to ask if everything's okay?"

"You were living your life," I say. "You were trying to get Bella a job. You were—"

"I was with you," she says.

My stomach clenches.

I knew she was going to get there eventually. I was just hoping—

I was hoping she wouldn't.

She closes her eyes, then opens them again. "No," she says. "No, this isn't my fault. It's *not my fault*. I'm allowed to have fun. I'm allowed to have a life. I'm allowed to think about something other than whether my father is running off the rails." She stares down at her phone screen, like she can use laser eyes to burn away the offending notification.

"Okay," she says, taking a deep breath. "Okay. There's a ceiling on how much harm he can do. Thousand-dollar credit limit. A few hundred bucks in his bank account. Worst case, I can put a hold on the credit card if more charges start showing up. I planned for this. I've set things up so it's not the end of the world. I'll get him back on track again; I've done it before."

I smile because she's so Sonya. She already has a plan.

I let myself exhale a bit, too, because she's calming herself down. Walking back from that edge she walked up to: *I was with you.*

And then she says, "I've almost got Bella squared away. And you're leaving. So I'll be able to give him more attention. I'll have enough time to really get him solid."

"I don't have to go, Sonya. It's not the only choice. I could stay." The words come sailing out before I can think better of them.

She shakes her head. "You don't mean that. You hated small-town life enough to leave the last time around. And there's a good reason for that. What you do in Boston's important. You make people's lives better there."

"There are lots of ways to make people's lives better, Sonya. You of all people know that."

"It's not the same," she says. "You told me how much you love your work. You lit up when you told me. It was so clear that it's your happy place. This? Here? This is just your grandfather's lark. And don't get me wrong. It's been amazing. I've—"

She stops.

"I just—I don't want you to stay. Not if it means you giving up what matters most."

My brain freezes on *I don't want you to stay.*

A car scrapes up on the gravel outside; Hanna and Easton are back.

Shit.

"We don't have to decide this right now." I say it as calmly as I can so she doesn't hear the frantic edge.

She's staring at me, expression blank, like her mind's

going a million miles a minute behind her eyes, but she's not going to let me know what's in there.

Hanna and Easton are at the door, laughing outside. They tumble in, drunk on their taste of freedom, pink cheeked, happy. Hanna's eyes go instantly to Eloise, sleeping soundly in her bassinet. "Oh my God, you guys, did she sleep this whole time? Of course she did." She throws up her hands. "Now she'll be up every ninety minutes all night."

"Go get in bed," Easton tells her. "I'll take this shift."

"I love you." She says it in that laughing, off-the-cuff way you could fling at anyone, someone you'd just met in a grocery store, but it's so obvious it's true from the way she looks at him.

And I let myself admit it, now that it's slipping out of my reach...

I want that.

IT'LL BE BETTER *in the morning,* I tell myself. Because it's always better in the morning. It doesn't make sense to push a conversation like this late at night, when we're both tired. When we're both up to our ears in feelings. I won't make her talk.

But I think we're both craving connection because when I pull the car up outside the cabin, she climbs over the center console and straddles me. There's a kind of desperation in her kiss. Her hands in my hair wind tighter. Her thighs lock me in, like she doesn't want me to get away. It feels like reassurance. I groan and sink into the seat, letting her set the pace, which is a gallop. A headlong rush into pleasure.

She bites my lip and then soothes it with her tongue—does it again. Rubs her face against my beard, purrs. Licks my mouth, licks into my mouth, moans, tightens her hand behind my head again. Her hips shift, impatient, over me, finding where I'm thickening and starting to strain against my jeans. She makes a small, self-satisfied noise when she lines herself up the way she wants, then another sound of renewed desperation as she starts to chase pleasure.

I grab her hips, holding them still, because if she keeps going she'll take me over with her, and I want to be inside her. I want to be buried to the hilt in her warmth and reassurance.

"Inside."

I open the driver's-side door, point her toward the house. She disentangles herself unwillingly, hops to her feet, grabs my hand to hurry me up. Her impatience is cute. And very hot.

"I thought you meant inside me," she says.

"That, too."

"I love it when you get like this."

"Like how?"

"Short words. Practically grunting. Like a caveman."

I sweep her off her feet, over my shoulder, and carry her up to the house, and she's laughing, and I think, *It's going to be okay.*

I'm not sure how I get the door open or how I get inside, but I make it to my bedroom. I tumble her onto my bed, and she kneels up and crawls to the edge of the bed, plucking at my clothes. "Quinn," she begs.

Despite the way we started, it's slow. Languid. The slide of warm skin over warm skin, the tight clutch of our arms around each other, our mouths locked together like we're afraid to stop the touching and the connection. When I enter her, she cries out and clutches me tighter, holding my head so she can slick her tongue against mine. She feels so good everywhere, and I want it to last forever.

"Don't stop," she says.

As if there was any danger.

"Kiss me harder."

Happily.

"Quinn. Quinn."

"It's okay," I say. "I'm here."

She won't be soothed. She's wild with it. "Quinn," she says, over and over.

I meet her, thrust for thrust, matching her desperation with my own, trying to tell her that whatever she needs, I can give it to her, winding us tighter and tighter until we spiral over the edge together, clinging to each other, calling each other's names.

As I slowly ease us back down to stillness, stroking her hair, cuddling her close, she goes still and quiet in my arms. I realize something I've been trying to ignore.

I'm trying to hold on.

And she's trying to let go.

She's saying goodbye.

37

SONYA

I wake up the morning after babysitting for Eloise, and there's a weight in the middle of my chest. I sit up, reach for my phone, and check to make sure things look okay on the financial front. My dad has charged a hotel room, but that's it. No casino charges. I know that probably means he's using cash—or Wendy's money—but I still breathe easier when I see it.

I should have gone to Vegas last night, should have chased after him. I should be there, making things right.

I have the flights up and have clicked through to the cheapest one when my phone buzzes with a message from my dad.

Hey sunny girl, don't be alarmed if you stop by and I'm not there. On a quick trip with Wendy. Back this afternoon!

My exhalation fogs my phone screen.

Okay. Back this afternoon. So that's good. Whatever damage he's caused, it's done.

And I'll be better about keeping an eye on him after this.

I slide out of bed, bare feet pattering quietly onto the wood floor.

Quinn is sleeping soundly, so I let myself drink my fill of him: red-brown hair, thick beard and eyebrows, long-lashes casting shadows on high cheekbones. Mouth open slightly, lips soft with sleep. I want to bend down and kiss them, but I don't.

I don't have to leave, he said.

My heart leapt like crazy when he said it. I was ready to grab onto those words and reel them in. Reel him in.

Except it was too much like another moment. The one when Brandon agreed to give Rush Creek a try, for me. When he said that he thought he could do small town life... for me.

I can't do that again, let myself believe in happily ever after with someone who's trying me on for size. I can't talk a man into a life he doesn't want. Quinn loves being a scientist. He's good at being a scientist. And the world needs scientists. I can find another receptionist.

I can even find another lover.

Science needs Quinn.

I want to crawl back in next to him. I want to wrap myself around him. I want to hold him here, like I tried to last night, anchoring him to me the best I could. Like having him over me, inside me would be enough, when what I want is so much bigger than that. A place that's ours, a baby that's ours, a life that's ours.

Last night, when I said, *It's been amazing,* there was so much more I wanted to say.

I've loved every minute of it. Because I have. But the *L*-word felt too close to home. I was afraid if I said it out loud, the rest would spill out, too. How I love his bluntness and his honesty, his humor, how good he is with people while having absolutely no idea he is. How I love how he is with Gus. With Eloise. With his brothers, their slow dance back to each other. With Hanna.

How I've loved the way he takes care of me, the groceries, the dinners, the science on my behalf. The sewing machine, and more than that, what it stands for: Feeling seen. Feeling supported.

How much I love the feel of him over me, confident and alpha, and in me, strong and sure. How much I'll miss it.

I've loved every minute of you, I wanted to say.

But now I'm glad I didn't because it gives me more room to think. About what's best for him and what's best for me.

I need to go somewhere else to think. All I can think about here is how much I want to touch him.

I shower, do my hair, fix my makeup, grab breakfast, and feed and walk Gus, and still, Quinn hasn't moved. It makes me smile, the way he's sprawled out in the bed, the sheets tangled around his legs like someone arranged him for a photo shoot. Bare chest and abs and the thick V muscles at his hips—yum—and then, artfully hidden, the goods.

He's better than a suggestive photo. Better than art.

But he's not mine, and I have to let him go if that's the right thing.

I head for the spa, leaving Gus behind with Quinn. I figure I'll organize my office, maybe label some bottles and stuff them in boxes. Give myself some mental space. Figure myself out.

But when I get to the front door, my lizard brain immediately knows there's something wrong. There's water seeping under the door.

There's not supposed to be water in there.

I unlock the door, and my heart jumps into my throat.

There's water *everywhere.* It pours out in a torrent. I want to slam the door, but I couldn't even if I tried. The pressure of the water inside the spa is too much.

I circle around to the back entrance, where I unlock the service door and fumble my way to the breaker panel, killing the electricity. Then I make my way down the hallway by the light through the windows and from my phone, scoping out the situation.

Water pours in through the wall that runs between the reception area and the spa itself. A pipe must have burst during the night. I slosh around, trying to track the source, but I can't—it's somewhere in the walls.

The spa's a total mess. The product from the lowest shelves has floated away, leaving a layer of flotsam and jetsam on the water that's over my ankles in the reception area. There are soaps in the water and open testers, and some bottles are less watertight than others, so there's a lather of bubbles and grease and oil, too. Ugh.

Hands shaking, I put a call in to the plumber we usually use, Jenny Arden. She answers right away, and I tell her the situation. "I know you don't work Sundays…"

My voice is shaking, too.

"I'll be right there," she says.

I trudge through the water and debris to find garbage bags. I start discarding the trash—wet cardboard, ruined soaps, dry-clean-only scarves that I'm pretty sure aren't saleable. I start a list of ruined inventory, snap photos. It hurts to drop my products into the garbage bag.

I think of Bella, of how most nights she's up in the middle of the night to rein in her mother's wandering, of how caretaking is her more-than-full-time job.

I'm sorry, Bella.

Jenny shows up with her favorite assistant, Arin, and gets to work. I can hear the sound of tile cracking and wallboard tearing as the two of them go to town, which hurts, too. I have to put a call into Hanna, but I'll let her sleep. I know she went to bed late and was up every ninety minutes.

I'm trying to figure out if I can save the sea sponges when I hear, "*What the fuck?*"

I look up to find Quinn standing in the doorway. He takes one look around, then sweeps in, like Poseidon parting the seas, to make his way over to me. "What the *hell*, Sonya?"

"It flooded," I say.

"Yeah," he says. "I'll say. And when, exactly, were you planning to call me?"

"I—"

"You weren't, were you? You weren't going to tell me this had happened or let me know you needed help. You were going to stay here all day trying to fix this by yourself." He sees it on my face. "You didn't even *think* about calling me."

"I would have."

"When?"

But I don't have an answer for him.

He closes his eyes. Opens them again. "I'm lying to myself, aren't I?"

"What do you mean?"

"Here I am, ready to give up, well, basically anything and everything for you—and I'm not even the guy you call when your world falls apart."

But I don't call anyone *when my world falls apart,* I want to say. Except I don't say it because I'm stuck on something else he said:

Here I am, ready to give up anything and everything for you—

"Quinn," I say, "you have to know—I want you to know—I don't *want* you to have to give anything and everything up. Not for this." I gesture between us.

"Well, that much is crystal clear," he says in a tone I haven't heard from him since I first walked into the salon and found him sitting in my chair. Dark. Hard.

"Wait," I say. "Hang on."

He closes his eyes. Opens them again. "You have to stop, Sonya. You have to stop pushing people away and refusing their help and trying to do everything on your own. The idea of needing anyone scares the shit out of you!"

He's breathing hard.

I am, too. We're squared off in the water, staring at each other.

"Okay, guy in a glass house throwing stones." I cross my arms. "What about you? You're the one who's so ready to hear the worst from everyone that you can't even listen to what I'm saying. Maybe I'm scared of needing anyone, but you're scared of wanting *anything*. You're the one punishing yourself. You're the one telling yourself that there's no way I could want you to stay. You're the one who decided *all by yourself* that there's no way. What did you think that was last night in bed if it wasn't me wanting you to stay?"

Now I'm pissed. We stare at each other, heated, breathless.

And then Quinn raises a hand and rakes it through his hair, and his expression is so raw, it almost hurts to look at him. "I thought it was you saying goodbye!"

Oh.

Oh. Oh. Oh.

Suddenly everything makes a lot more sense.

Water is no longer rushing. I can hear it dripping now. It swirls around our ankles, and occasionally something drifts by. A ribbon. A coated business card. A pen. The room smells like the unleashing of every scent you can possibly imagine, all clamoring for attention.

And in the stillness, I hear his words echo back at me.

The idea of needing anyone scares the shit out of you.

I mean, he's not wrong.

Because, okay, science needs Quinn.

But so do I, if we're being totally honest, and...

I *hate* that.

I hate that I love that he cooks for me. I hate that I love that he grocery shops for me. I hate that I love that he knows me better than I know myself. And if he leaves now...

I'll have to get used to being on my own again, to being the only one who makes things happen and gets things done. To eating alone, shopping alone, cleaning up my own messes—alone.

Repairing my own spa.

And...

Seeing my own truths.

Because, yeah, he sees so much that I haven't wanted anyone to see.

I don't say any of that, partly because he's glaring at me so fiercely that I'm struck speechless with awe and lust, but mostly because I just got it, what Quinn and I talked about when I told him about Bella and the spa.

You can *know* a thing and not *know* it.

Like, for example, you can know that having your mom die and your dad fall apart made you feel alone in the world.

You can know that getting called home from college made you feel like if you don't take care of things no one will.

But you can also not know how much it sits down there at the bottom of your brain, ruining things for you.

And right now?

I can see it super clearly.

I can hear the voice in my head, the one that always says, *If you don't need anyone, they can't disappoint you.*

"Quinn," I say quietly at the same time as he says, "Maybe I'm not used to people thinking I'm worth it."

He stands there, hands in fists, head down. He looks like he did that first day, when I thought he was belligerent but he was just beaten down.

When he thought I was a control freak but I was just... desperately needing not to need anyone's help.

My eyes fill up with tears.

Because we're *not* the same people we were almost two months ago. We're different people.

We've changed each other.

For the better.

"Oh God, Quinn," I say. "You're so fucking worth it."

Slowly—too slowly for my tastes—that raw pain on his face softens to something more like...wonder.

"You're completely right about me," I tell him. "I *am* still punishing myself for letting everyone down. And on top of that, I'm terrified that if I depend on you..."

"That I'll let you down," he finishes for me. "Because your mom did, even if she didn't *mean* to."

"No, of course she didn't," I say, reasonably, because everything about death and trauma is reasonable, right? *Not.*

He shakes his head. "But your dad *could* have done a better job of being there for you."

"He sure as fuck could have." I sigh.

We stand there in the water up to our calves, starting to shiver because it's *cold* water. Still facing each other like we're about to draw swords and have it out.

So much like—and so much unlike—that first day.

And then all of a sudden, we both start laughing. Like, *doubled over, belly laugh* laughing. Because look at us. We're ridiculous.

"It's like pop-up therapy, but with aromatherapy—"

"Aromatorture," he groans through his laughter.

"—and, like, with the water—" I gesture. "I don't know, like a water birth. Water aromatherapy therapy..." I'm laughing too hard to talk.

"We could offer paddleboard yoga in here," he offers, barely able to get it out. "Isn't Hanna planning to add massage and yoga this year?"

"Yeah."

"Maybe we leave the water, and—"

Just then Jenny comes out from the back, holding a rubber seal, and finds us, doubled over laughing. Her eyebrows go up, and I try to rein in my mirth.

I take one look at Quinn, also trying to keep a straight face, and collapse into laughter again.

When I finally pull myself together and apologize for losing it, Jenny shows me the broken seal. "I'm honestly surprised. The seals aren't very old, are they?"

"Less than two years."

"New construction," she says with an exasperated groan. "The quality these days sucks mud. Still. Seals should have lasted longer than that. Might want to have a lawyer look at the warranty. Meanwhile, I'm going to pump as much water as I can out of here for you," she says.

"Thank you," I say. "You're a lifesaver."

She shrugs. "Least I can do. You have a lot of work ahead of you. You have people to help out?"

I'm all ready to say, *It's not a big deal—I've got it.* But right then I look up and see the expression on Quinn's face. I flinch. It's *ferocious.*

Don't you dare, it says.

He's not always ferocious, of course. He's also gentle. Supportive. Warm. And if you do right by him, you earn *all* the smiles.

And I want the smiles. I want them more than I've ever wanted anything.

"Yes," I say, not taking my eyes off his. "Yes. I do."

38

QUINN

It's kind of a toss-up, which one of us is more miserable about actually having to make the phone calls to ask for help. But we don't let each other back down. Sonya stands over me while I call Shane and then Tucker. Neither of them hesitates a split second when I tell them what I need.

Then I cross my arms and stare her down while she calls Hanna and Easton. Next, she phones Reggie, deputizing her to reach out to Mei, Bella, Serenity—whoever isn't busy on a Sunday. She must apologize twelve times for disturbing her people on their day off, and I can hear Reggie on the other end saying, "Shut *up*, Sonya, you know we'd do anything for you."

There are tears streaming down Sonya's face when she ends that call. I open my arms, and she walks in, resting her cheek against my chest in a way that makes the center of me crack open. I stroke her hair and tell her we're going to fix this.

Sonya and I still have a *lot* to talk about, obviously, but we've got a spa to salvage first.

Shane's there ten minutes later, with Tucker in tow. My actor brother crosses his arms and looks at the disaster that's Hott Spot's front room. Then he pulls out his phone.

"What are you doing?" I ask.

"Checking the weather."

"The—weather?"

"That desk," Shane says, pointing at it. "You're supposed to sit at it for three more days."

"Oh *shit*." The terms of the will had completely slipped my mind in the chaos of this situation.

"That hadn't even *occurred* to me," Sonya says.

"Yeah, well. I sign a lot of contracts with no maneuvering room in them," Shane says with a big sigh. "And even though I have people who are supposed to read them for me, I've gotten pretty good at the legal stuff. And I'm guessing Wiggles—"

"Weggers," I correct, laughing despite myself, despite the situation.

"—is going to be a hard-ass about what exactly it means to 'sit at that desk.'"

"*Seriously?*"

He nods. "You met the man. He was born with a legal code in his hands. So first order of business is to get you set up so you can still conduct business for the next three days."

"How are we going to do that?" Sonya asks, looking around at the wreckage.

Shane consults his phone. "You're in luck," he says. "The weather forecast is glorious. Step one is to figure out how to unmoor the desk from where it is...and then we can drag it outside."

Jenny's pumped out as much water as she can, and even though now the front room—and most of the rest of the spa—looks like a post-storm beach, it's easier to see what needs to be done.

Tucker, Shane, and I inspect the desk and work out how it's anchored and what we need to do to A) remove it and B) reestablish a base for it so it can stand alone. Tucker heads out to grab the lumber and paint we need, Shane goes to borrow tools from all the townspeople he has so far befriended, and I get to work on relocating the computer, emptying the drawers, and otherwise making the desk easier to move.

While I'm working, the door opens and Reggie, Mei, Serenity, and Lily spill in, carrying garbage bags, gloves, sponges, mops, pails, a shop vac, and lots and lots of rags. There's another woman behind them, and from the way Sonya flies at her and the woman pats her hair while she cries, I figure that's got to be Bella. The five of them jump right into cleanup, each of them taking part of the interior of the spa—Lily in the main spa area, Reggie in the salon, Serenity in the treatment rooms, Mei dealing with hall-ways, and Bella on bathrooms.

Hanna's next. "Eloise is with Easton's mom," she says, waving away my objections. "I have at least an hour and a half till I'm needed for the next feeding." Easton's hot on her tail, still arguing with her that this isn't how she should be spending her energy.

You can imagine how well *that* goes over.

But before that argument can get any more heated, the

door opens again and disgorges Gabe Wilder, Lucy Wilder, and two of—I assume—Gabe and Easton's brothers—one wearing a fly-fishing T-shirt and the other with a camera around his neck.

"Well, shit," Gabe says, looking around. "This is a hot mess. What do you need?"

Reggie has appointed herself the head of the volunteer squad, and she's obviously more than happy to direct the activities of three large, extremely competent men. In short order, Gabe runs off to get drywalling tools and supplies, Brody heads to the flooring shop in Bend for new tile, and Kane starts photographing the chaos for insurance purposes.

Sonya has set herself up in her office, which is mostly salvageable, except for the carpeting, one shelf of books, and a stack of files she left on the floor. Thankfully, most of the boxes of Hott Spot–branded shampoo and conditioner were out of reach of the water. One case of the unassembled boxes was ruined, and first on Sonya's list is reordering those on rush. She's also inventorying all the damaged product and placing orders for replacements.

In the early afternoon, a familiar man steps through the front door with an equally familiar blond woman in tow. It takes me a minute to place them. Then I get it.

It's Sonya's father and his girlfriend, Wendy.

"We stopped at the bakery for a snack, and Nan said the spa flooded," he says.

I have no idea how news reached Nan that quickly, but obviously I'm not even slightly surprised.

Sonya's father doesn't look like a man who's blown a fortune at the tables in Vegas—if there's such a look. He and Wendy are holding hands, and concern for Sonya is written all over their faces.

"Where is she?" he asks.

"In the back," I say, pointing, and then, for both their sakes: "She—she saw the credit card bill. You. In Vegas."

His eyes widen. "The— Oh *shit*. I forgot about those alerts. Please," he says, opening his hands, palms up, like a sign of surrender. "Whatever you think, it's not that. I wasn't gambling."

"He wasn't," Wendy says.

I stare at them for a long time, and they hold my gaze without flinching.

Maybe they're full of shit, maybe I'm a sucker, but they're so earnest, I have to take their word for it.

I lead him back to the office.

"Sonya," I say.

She looks up from where she's hunched over her computer. Her expression is bleak, but when she sees her dad there, it gets even bleaker.

"Sunny," he says. "It's not what it looks like."

"Oh, really?" She stands, glaring at him, hands on hips. "I got the credit card notification."

"I was in Vegas," he says. "But not for the reason you think."

He holds up his and Wendy's linked hands, showing her the twin gold bands. "We got married," he says.

39

SONYA

I'm pretty sure I stare at my dad for a full minute before I can talk.

"You got...married?"

"Wendy and I got married."

He's beaming at me, full of pride, full of his joy, and I try to swallow my anger and frustration, my *Oh my God, did you really scare the shit out of me so you could get married in Vegas without even* telling me you were going to*!*

There's a moment when I almost do what I always would have done. I almost give him a big hug and tell him he's doing great and that I'm proud of him and *Congratulations* and *Wow, I'm so happy for you guys* and all that jazz.

And then a small movement out of the corner of my eye pulls my attention back to Quinn. He's still standing behind my dad, arms crossed. His face is neutral, thoughtful. He's watching us, his eyes moving quietly from my face to my dad's to Wendy's and back again.

He doesn't say anything, he doesn't signal to me. He's just there.

In case I need him.

And I think of all the people in the spa right now who are here to help me because I asked them to be.

Who've always been here, ready, willing, and able to help me—if I asked them, like Reggie said.

"You scared the crap out of me," I tell my dad. "I was sure you'd gone off the rails again."

The smile falls off my dad's face. "Sunny," he says, "I'm so sorry. I didn't think—"

"No," I agree. "You didn't. You made me an afterthought."

The anger's died to a dull flame, a burner set to low, and in the still space in my own chest, I can see myself clearly. How ever since my mom died, I've been trying to make everything okay for everyone else because...

Because the people who were supposed to make it okay for me were *both* gone.

"And the worst part is," I tell him, "I've always been an afterthought for you. You *left* me after mom died. You might have been literally there, in the room, but you were gone. And every time you fell off the wagon, you left me again. And I'm done. I'm done always being here...when you're not."

My dad's mouth is open. Wendy's, too. They're both staring at me.

"I'll, uh, leave you two for a sec," Wendy says, dropping my dad's hand and hustling to the door.

Quinn takes one more look at me, his eyes asking, *You okay?*

"Yeah," I say, like he's asked it out loud.

His eyes rake over my face, as if satisfying himself I

really am okay. And whatever he sees there must be enough because he gives me a nod and the slightest, Quinn-iest smile and slips out after Wendy.

"Sunny," my dad says. His voice breaks. "I'm sorry. I'm sorry I fell apart. I'm sorry I wasn't there for you. I'm sorry I made you find another place besides our house that was your safe haven. And most of all I'm sorry—"

My dad is crying.

"I'm sorry I took that safe haven away from you."

"Dad..." I say.

Apparently I'm crying, too.

It shouldn't matter, after all these years, but some wounds don't heal until you clean them out.

"You should've hated me for that," my dad says, his shoulders shaking.

"What would that have accomplished?"

"It would have been just punishment for my losing everything that mattered to you."

"Dad," I say. "Dad. I think we both probably need to stop punishing ourselves. If we're going to figure out how to, you know, do this. Be family to each other."

"Do you still want to...?"

His expression is anguished enough that it's easy to understand what he's asking me. Whether I still want him in my life.

"Yes," I say. "I'm your kid. You're my dad. But we're gonna have to change some things up. I've been punishing myself, too, without calling it that. And leaning too hard on you needing me, too. Leaning too hard into taking care of you as an excuse for not..." I think of Quinn's words. "For

not letting myself have nice things. But now, I guess—well,
I guess I'm done."

He nods.

I tip my head to one side. "No more groceries or
cleaning."

He shakes his head. "I should have told you years ago to
stop. But I—" He closes his eyes. "I was afraid if you didn't
think I needed you that you would stop coming by."

"Oh, Dad," I say. "Good grief."

I go to him then and let him give me a hug, and even
though there weren't enough of them when I needed them,
I do love his hugs. So much. We cry a little in each other's
arms, and then I step back and say, "Also. That money you
were offering. You need to use it to throw a wedding reception for you and Wendy so I can celebrate with you."

"You got it," he says. "Just tell me what you want—"

"I want to not have to do anything, decide anything, or
help with anything," I say.

He smiles at that. "I can definitely do that."

I give him a big hug, and he hugs me back. His arms are
warm and strong, and for the first time in a long time, I feel
like the kid, not the parent.

It's a good feeling.

Sometimes it's not about getting what you need but just
about asking for it.

"You want to come out front with me?" I ask him, swatting my tears back.

"I need a minute," he says. He's still crying.

I hand him a box of tissues. "Take your time."

I leave him there and head toward the front of the spa,
but Wendy intercepts me.

"Hey," she says. "Just so you know, there's a prenup. It was his idea. He didn't want to have access to my money. He thought it would be a temptation. But that doesn't mean I won't use that money to take care of him. I'm here now. Whatever he needs, whatever you need, I'm here for both of you."

"It's fine," I say. "We're fine. We've been doing okay—"

And then I hear myself.

Well, shit. I'm probably going to have to get a lot of therapy before I don't want to push away help.

But I can do this. Now. Today. I can make a start.

I say, "Actually, scratch that." I take a deep breath. "Thank you." I smile at her. "I'll give you the instruction manual for Dad care. It's mostly: *don't give him the Wi-Fi password* and *don't go near Vegas*."

She winces. "I'm sorry about that."

"No, I get it," I say. "But maybe—different vacation destinations from now on."

She smiles. "I can handle that."

She reaches a hand out, like she wants to touch my cheek. Or pat my hair. Shake my hand. She stops short of touching me, her hand suspended by my face. We both stare at it, then make eye contact and kind of...laugh.

She drops the hand and gives me a wry smile. "Too soon?"

Then we *really* laugh.

That's the moment when my dad comes out of my office and joins us in the hallway. He looks from one of us to the other, and he smiles—not victorious or knowing, just a smile.

He looks happy.

It makes me happy...and also a little sad because it's almost exactly the way he used to look at my mom, and I miss her. Today is obviously going to be like that.

"Congratulations," I say. "I'm really happy for both of you."

"Thanks," Wendy says.

My dad gestures around him at the wreckage. "Put me in, Coach," he says.

"Put *us* in," Wendy says.

"We're fine," I say reflexively. "If you guys want to head out—"

And then I clap a hand to my mouth.

"Or," I say quietly, "you could head down into the locker room area and ask Lily—she'll be the one bossing everyone else around—what you can do."

They smile at me and go.

Then I just kind of *stand there.*

Because it's been quite the day.

"You know, you're so much like her."

Reggie and Bella have stepped into the hallway.

"Your mom," Bella continues. "You're so much like her. She didn't like to ask for help, either. We always had to make her accept it. When you were born, we all showed up to do her laundry and help her clean, and she tried to make us leave. But we wouldn't. She *hated* every minute of it. And that's nothing compared to—"

They exchange glances, and then Bella says, "She really didn't want help when she was sick. I still wonder if we shouldn't have pushed so hard. But—"

I shake my head. "She needed you," I say. "We needed you. *I* need you."

Tears fill my eyes.

"Oh, hon," Bella says. "We miss her, too."

She pushes the stray strands of hair off my face and brushes a tear away. "She was great to work for."

"Not as good as you, though," Serenity says, stepping out of the treatment room where she's been working.

"Nowhere near," Lily calls from the bathroom, before she appears.

"Me three," Reggie declares.

"Y'all..." I say, tears spilling.

Reggie hands me a paper towel, and I swipe at my eyes.

"Hey," I say, my voice damp. "If the offer of help with the branded-product release party is still open—"

"Don't be ridiculous," Reggie says roughly. "Of course it's still open."

They all wrap their arms around me in a giant group hug, a cloak of invisibility, giving me a minute until I can stop crying.

40

QUINN

It takes us way longer than I expected to build a new base for the desk and separate it from the wall, which we need to do carefully, not with a Sawzall or an axe like I suggested at first. Shane rolled his eyes at me when I mentioned those blunt instruments, reminding me that we needed to be able to reinstall the desk once we could reopen the spa, and he was right, of course.

It's late afternoon by the time we get the desk free, and I'm glad that the flood happened on a Sunday and not another day of the week when my absence from the desk might have given Weggers an excuse to declare my receptionist gig an outright failure.

But when we go to move the desk, we discover that it won't fit through the front door. We stand there frozen, surrounding the desk, as it blocks the spa's entrance.

"Turn it on its side," a voice says.

Preston appears in the doorway, with Rhys right behind him.

My mouth drops open.

"It's the nice thing about having a private jet," he says. "You can get places fast."

I don't seem to be able to talk. At all. Which is fine because my brothers never needed me to do much talking.

"Shane said you could use some help," Preston says. "Let's go ninety degrees this way."

And before I can protest, he, Rhys, Shane, and Tucker get the heavy desk flipped onto its side. Then we all maneuver it through the door and out onto the lawn. We tip it up and square it to the building. I replace Arthur Weggers's spycam, and Rhys comes out with my rolling swivel seat on his shoulder and plants it in front of the camera. The chair's unsteady, and the wheels won't move on the grass, but I sit down in it anyway and give the finger to Weggers.

Brody Wilder appears in the door, looking at us like we've all taken the fast train to dumbassery—which, from an outside perspective, we clearly have. "There's a desk on the lawn," he says, eyebrows up.

"Long story," Rhys says. "Our grandfather left us this land. But we have to..." He stops. "Let's just say the desk has to be here."

Brody nods. "Family," he says, shrugging. "I get it. Hey —can I get a couple of you to help me and Easton with wet insulation?"

My brothers scramble to follow him inside, except for Preston. He stays outside with me. He runs his hand idly over the surface of the desk, looking like a man who has something he wants to say.

He stares out toward the Cascade Mountains. "This whole thing has had me doing a lot of thinking," he says. "I wish I could say I had the best reasons for leaving...but I think about the best I can do is—I was young and a stubborn SOB. Maybe more stubborn than Granddad."

I raise my eyebrows.

"I'll tell you the whole story sometime," he says. "It's not pretty. But...I guess what I'm trying to say is I'm sorry I left."

"You don't mean that," I say. "You left because of Kali."

"That's one way to look at it," he says. He turns away. Stares far off.

"Pres?"

When he turns back, his expression doesn't look like anything I've ever seen on his face. He looks wrecked. Broken. And then a curtain drops down, and he's Preston again. Stern, blank. "I don't know," he says. "I'm still not sure if I could have done anything differently. But—I wish I could have—"

He stops.

"You wish you could have what?"

He shakes his head. "Forget it. It's just, I was so fucking stubborn. And I left you all. You, especially. I think the others could've fended for themselves—"

"I fended fine," I say grumpily.

"Yeah," Preston says. "I know. But I feel like it, I don't know, cost you more."

I don't try to argue with him because maybe it's true.

"You showed up today."

"It doesn't cancel out," he says.

"No," I agree. "It doesn't. But it was something. And it meant something to me."

Preston's shoulders soften. Just a hair. "I want to keep showing up."

"Okay," I say. "As long as you know I'm not going to hang my hopes on it, not yet."

He laughs, a short, hard unamused sound. "Maybe we experiment and see how it goes?"

"Now you're speaking my language."

As warm brotherly moments go, it's probably not the best one history has ever recorded. But I touch the scar at the base of my thumb anyway. I used to do it all the time as a kid. Reminding myself of what mattered. And when I look over at him, he's doing the same thing.

"Hey."

Rhys stands in the doorway. "We could use you guys. Can one or both of you make a building-supply run? I'll give you the insulation specs."

"Sure," Preston says.

After Pres has been dispatched, Rhys comes back out to stand by me. "You know," he says, running a hand over the desk's surface. "You probably didn't need to move the desk out here. I think we could have claimed *force majeure*—an act of God that keeps you from fulfilling your side of a legal contract."

I look at the desk, and at my brother. I shrug. Because I can't wish today had played out any differently, even at its most absurd.

"Yeah," he says. "No point in sweating it now."

"Any progress on disputing the will?" I ask him.

He doesn't quite make eye contact. "Uh, yeah. About that."

I raise my eyebrows at him.

"I mean, we could, but..."

"But?"

"It doesn't feel completely fair to Hanna," he says. "Since it's clear Granddad did all of this with her in mind."

I don't argue with him about that. I just say, "So, what, we cross our fingers and..."

"And hope that whatever he dreamt up for the rest of us is less disruptive than what he dreamt up for you."

But it's funny—I'm not sure I can exactly hope that. I hope that what my grandfather has dreamt up for my other brothers is *exactly* as disruptive as what he did for me. I hope it shakes them out of their ruts and makes them look at themselves more sagely and, most of all, puts them face to face with...

With love.

Oh God.

Oh God, oh God.

I rake my hand through my hair and try not to hyperventilate.

Because I knew I wasn't ready to leave. I knew I wanted to be with her. But I haven't let myself think it. Not that word.

It feels huge and terrifying, but at the same time, it's absolutely fucking clear to me that I have no choice but to love Sonya.

41

———

SONYA

Amanda, Easton's sister, who runs a catering business, shows up around dinnertime with a giant feast, a completely amazing hearty Italian meal she lays out on the Hott Spot desk—now on the front lawn. Lasagnas, big bowls of spaghetti and meatballs, huge green salads, hot, fragrant garlic bread.

Everyone grabs food, everyone digs in.

The dog walker, who I'd called earlier in the day to look in on Gus a couple of times, brings him by, and he trots around, investigating all the new people and smells, finally settling down with his nose on Quinn's sneaker. I watch them together, feeling an impossibly big warmth in my chest.

"What's the status report?"

It's Nan at my side.

"We'll be open every day this week for retail, hair, and a few services," I say. "And Gabe and Easton think we'll be able to open everything else by Thursday."

"I made a GoFundMe for you," she says, holding out

her phone. "And in case anyone needed incentive, we told people if they showed us their donation receipts for any amount, we'd give them a slice of better-than-Robert-Redford cake."

I look down at the screen, expecting to see a few hundred dollars in donations, but my jaw drops when I see the total. $7,291.

"People like you," Nan says. "They like you and they like the spa and, I will be honest—" She shoots a look in Quinn's direction. "They *really* like the Hott guy at the front desk. Do you think those other brothers could take a turn, too? There are five of them. Maybe mix it up a little?"

I'm pretty sure she's not actually expecting an answer, so I just say, "*Thank you.*"

My heart is so full of what's happened today, the number of times I've said thank you, the number of times I've kept myself from saying, *It's fine, we'll be fine.*

But not only that. My heart is full now watching Quinn, who's standing in a small circle. Hanna. Easton. Gabe. Brody. And all four of his brothers, shoulder to shoulder, chatting and—

Laughing. They're *laughing.*

Even Quinn.

People go back to work after dinner, but most tasks are waiting on orders that need to come in, so after a while, people start drifting away. And finally, right around the time the Oregon summer sun finally goes down, everyone's gone. It's just Quinn and Gus and me.

We lock up the spa and stand outside by the desk. It's the first time since the flooding that we've been alone together, and neither of us knows what to do with our hands. Or feet. Even though our fight this morning ended with us laughing together, I still feel like things are unresolved. And I want to fix them.

"We did it," Quinn says.

"I mean technically *they* did it," I say, gesturing in a sweeping circle to encompass all the people who helped.

That makes him smile. "But only because you asked them to," he says.

I mull over what it means to me to do something for someone else, how it takes me outside myself and makes me feel better and freer.

"It's weird..." I say. "But I think sometimes asking for help is a gift to the people who love you."

"Yeah."

We're both quiet. Quinn's a mess. His clothes are wet and covered with sawdust and bits of paper and all kinds of grime. His hair looks like someone ran a vacuum cleaner over it. And his beard needs a trim so badly it makes my fingers itchy. But it only adds to the appeal.

He looks like a guy who'd spend the whole day trying to help fix what's broken in my life.

"I want you to stay," I say. "I'm sorry I didn't do a better job of saying that. As a wise man said, it scares the shit out of me to need anyone. But I want to try, and you're the one I need. You're the best kind of people person I know, the kind who pays attention and *sees*. You're the best man I know."

"Sonya..." he says, his voice breaking.

I reach for him, and he wraps me up in his dirty, grimy arms, and I don't care at all because it's absolutely the best place to be in the whole world.

When he releases me, he holds my hands. "I totally get

why it scares the shit out of you to need anyone. You haven't
had a good track record of the people who count coming
through for you. And it also makes total sense to me
because—as a wise woman said—it scares the shit out of
me to want anything." He closes his eyes and opens them
again, and they're steady and warm on my face. "But you're
totally worth it. If being scared is what I have to do to have
you in my life, I'm in. I love you. I love working behind this
desk together. I love sitting on the couch together. I love
eating dinner together. I love watching bad, unscientific TV
together. I love reading while you sew and—" Gus noses his
thigh, and he bends down, smiling, to stroke my dog's head.
"I also love Gus. So I thought the three of us—you, me, and
Gus—could officially move in together and be a family."

My legs are wobbly. I sit down in his desk chair, and it
tips over backward. My arms and legs flail out, and I'm
falling through space—

Gus barks, alarmed.

Quinn catches me and sets me upright.

"The chair's not very good on grass," he says.

"I love you, too." I'm crying for, I don't know, probably
the third time today, but this is the best time because he's
cupping my face and thumbing away my tears and smiling
down at me. "All the things you said—I would say them,
too, except I'm so, so, so tired."

That's when he sweeps me out of the chair and into his
arms and strides off toward home.

It's not a short walk, and he carries me the whole way,
Gus trotting behind us, even though I'm protesting most of
the time—*I'm fine, I can walk, I'm not* that *tired.*

"I'm not listening," he says a few times, and after a while I give up because it feels *so* good to be held.

We get back to the cabin, and he carries me inside, straight into the bathroom, where he hands me a makeup wipe and my toothbrush loaded with toothpaste and watches me with a stern expression until I'm done. He turns on the shower, helps me out of my clothes, strips his own, and bundles us both under the water, where he helps me wash off the dirty flood water and other nastiness still clinging to my hair and skin. His hands are sure and competent, his skin steaming hot everywhere I touch him, but I'm so tired I'm content to let him keep things chaste.

When we're both passably clean, he towels me off, picks me up, and deposits me onto my bed. He helps me into my pajamas, gets into his own, then pulls the covers up over me and crawls in.

"You're not naked," I protest, but he just smiles at me because I'm almost all the way asleep already. What I want to show him about how I feel will have to wait for morning, but I'm okay with that because I know I *have* the morning... and the morning after that and the one after that.

It feels like such a lovely, big, wide open span of time, and I settle my face into the crook of his shoulder and let him wrap me up in warmth and sleep.

42

QUINN

I sit at my desk for the next three days on the front lawn of Hott Spot. The first day I get a bad sunburn on my nose, the tops of my ears, and the nape of my neck. Then Sonya sells me a good sunscreen.

"We could brand a Hott Spot sunscreen," I suggest.

She hugs me.

Hotts and Wilders come and go from the spa for the next few days, finishing up repairs. We reopen for haircuts and waxes right away and for the rest of our services by Wednesday. On Thursday, I give Weggers one last middle finger and say goodbye to my spot at the front desk, while Sonya reopens the hot springs and main spa area.

Between insurance, Nan's GoFundMe, and the seal manufacturer's eagerness not to be sued, all the costs of the flood destruction are covered. Product trickles back into the retail area, and by Friday, my brothers and I are able to reinstall the desk inside.

Saturday is the product launch party.

News of Hott Spot's disastrous flood circulated far and

wide on social media. Brides who'd soaked in the springs with their bridesmaids or gotten their hair done by Sonya encouraged their Rush Creek–area friends to stop by the party to buy something in support of Hott Spot and Hott Springs Eternal.

Easton's sister, Amanda, and her company Around the Table supplied us with gorgeous platters of fresh fruit, crisp veggies, five different dips, six kinds of cheese, fancy crackers, and warm chocolate chip cookies. There's a big table with drinks, including champagne, and people are standing around chatting, eating, and drinking. We've opened the hot springs for the day for free dips, and there's a steady stream of people into the springs, many of whom return to the main desk with damp hair and make appointments to come back.

As Lily promised, the main room is crammed with balloons, all black and white, except for a few hot pinks ones here and there. Mei is holding a Spot the Spot contest for kids, who run around the space searching for pink dot stickers.

And I've been behind the desk, ringing up purchases as fast as I can. Lily had to jump in to help, and even so, we're barely keeping up with demand.

By all measures, the launch is a huge success.

Sonya brings me a plate filled with food.

"I figured you wouldn't get a chance to eat if I didn't bring it to you," she says.

"You're probably right about that," I say, my mouth already full of some wild-ass cracker jammed with raisins and seeds, topped with brie.

"You holding up okay?"

We're in a small lull, and I smile at her and tug her close to my side. She leans her head against me, and it gives me the same thick, warm feeling that being close to her always does: the world is a good, safe place while we're in it together.

"Hey. I talked to Banks today, and he likes the idea of my starting a West Coast—well, West Coast-ish—office for MedThena."

"Quinn!" she says. "That's so cool!"

"There are a few irons in the fire already from the previous two launches, but after that, I'll basically have carte blanche to strike out with some new R and D."

She gives me a big hug, and I lean down to plant a safe-for-work kiss on her.

A moment later I almost choke on the most amazing chocolate chip cookie I've ever eaten because the woman who's stepped up to the register is Eva Scott, the actress who played my favorite character of all time on the short-lived cult sci-fi classic *Bridge*. She's dressed like an ordinary person, but she's too striking-looking for everyday life, with a kind of glow from within most people don't have. I shoot Sonya a sidelong *Is that really her?* glance, and she gives me a tight private nod.

"Hi," I say, smiling at Eva and taking the bottle of shampoo and conditioner from her, ringing them up.

"Hi," she says, smiling back. She leans an elbow on the counter. "Are you Quinn Hott?"

My mouth falls open. "Uh. Yes."

"You invented the ALS drug my dad took," she says. "It gave us a lot more time with him than we would have had. Thank you." And then she does something I'm totally not expecting: she gives me a big hug, while Sonya looks at me wide eyed over the top of her head.

Then Eva gathers up her stuff, turns, and walks out of the store. My gaze snags on my brother Shane, who's standing in the middle of the store, watching her. He watches her all the way out the door, then turns and glares at me. He strides over.

"You didn't tell me you knew her."

"Oh, *her*?" I shrug. "Yeah."

I don't tell him I just met her thirty seconds ago because something is under my brother's skin and...

Well, I'm enjoying it.

"If I'd known, I would have had you introduce us," he mutters, grumpily.

"Wait," I say. "Are you *jealous*? That I'm *hugging friends* with her?"

"No!" he says. "Why would I be jealous?"

Sonya and I trade sidewise glances.

"Of course you wouldn't," I say. "Nah. No way. I mean, why would a famous movie star who gets any woman he wants be jealous of a grubby mad scientist?"

He glares at me again.

Well. This is going to be fun.

EPILOGUE
QUINN

Sonya and I are watching *Chemical Reaction* a few weeks later when both our phones vibrate simultaneously on the coffee table. Gus jumps up, barking, then settles back down at our feet.

Yes, we're still living in the cabin together. We're looking for a place we can call our own, but we're not in a huge hurry to vacate this one because it's so convenient to work —and because we have some sentimental feelings about it.

We're both in therapy—separately. It turns out that if you ignore your abandonment issues, they don't actually go away. My therapist likes to say, "That which you ignore goes in the basement and lifts weights," and Sonya and I have some world class bodybuilders in our brain cellars. But it's actually fun because we often do our therapy homework together, or at least cheer each other on. Well. Sonya cheers. I grumpily prod. And it works for both of us.

I'm no longer staffing the front desk at Hott Spot—no surprise there. But I did work a few days longer than my two months so I could train up Bella for her new job—

which she seems to absolutely love (because who doesn't love working for Sonya?). The spa's the most popular it's ever been.

The investigation closed without catching up with Maura—which sucks—but as soon as it was closed, insurance awarded the spa a big chunk of the lost revenue, and Sonya was able to pay herself back the salary she missed when she was scrimping to hire Bella.

She got her car fixed, too.

Meanwhile, we're working on expanding the branded product line to include versions for dry hair and oily hair.

Sonya put survey card into the boxes, with a QR code so people can easily respond and get ten percent off their next service, and that'll help us know where to go next with development.

If we're successful with that, we could potentially sell it to other salons so they can brand it...which means a huge untapped revenue stream for Sonya and Hanna.

On top of that, I'm thinking I might introduce some special formulations for certain situations, like breast cancer and perimenopause and alopecia. A lot of women asked me about those things when I was working the front desk, and I wished I'd had better choices for them.

I get now what Sonya was saying about giving people ways to take care of themselves. I've talked to so many people over the last few weeks, and I'm learning that yes, it matters whether the product in question does what it promises. But even more? It matters that it makes you *feel* like there's some magic in your life. Maybe it's the placebo effect, maybe it's just having a sense of hope.

But I know she's right when she says that Hott Shot isn't

only in the beauty business. We're also in the business of making life less difficult.

"Wait," Sonya says. "What's this?"

She holds up her phone and shows me the text.

Please report to Arthur Weggers's office at 9 a.m. Tuesday morning.

I look down at mine and discover an identical message there. Along with texts from all my brothers and Hanna—variants on *WTF* and *Haunted from beyond the grave* and *Whose number's up* now?

"Why would *I* have to report?" Sonya asks.

"I don't know," I say. "You don't have to, obviously, but—"

"But if I don't, Hanna gets screwed?" she asks.

"Potentially."

"He seemed like such a harmless old man," she says.

I shake my head. "Clearly," I say, "you did not know him well."

We crowd into the office that was the original scene of the crime: Hanna and Eloise, Easton, Preston, Rhys, Shane, Tucker, Sonya, Aunt Meryl, me. We're all here.

"All accounted for?" Weggers asks, puffed up with his own importance, as usual.

"Yes, Mr. Wiggles," Shane mutters, sending us into choking fits.

I'm never going to stop hearing his name that way.

"Shane, I have a letter for you to read," he says, pulling a folded sheet out of an envelope with so much excessive ceremony that it's hard not to think he's going to give himself a papercut across the face.

Shane, ever the actor, holds out his hands like a tray so Weggers can deposit the precious document into them, then—channeling Weggers—opens the letter with a flourish.

"'Famous is as famous does, Shane Hott,'" my brother reads.

He looks up at us, shaking his head.

I remember what it was like to be there. All my siblings looking back at me, confused. Amused. It feels like a long time ago, back before I knew they'd fly across the country, wade through dirty water, and wedge a heavy desk through a spa door for me.

Thanks, Grandfucker, I think, reaching for Sonya's hand, clutching it tight. She squeezes back.

Shane goes on:

Hott Springs Eternal has done a good job at putting itself on the local map, but to attain the kind of success Hanna and I envisioned—

"This is *not my idea!*" Hanna says. "I told him to leave you guys alone! I said he was going to piss you off! I said he had to get over the fact that you were your own people and needed to do your own things!"

"It's okay, Han," Preston says. "Nobody thinks this is your doing. You're not devious enough for this kind of bullshit."

"Please keep the interruptions to a minimum," Mr. Wiggles says imperiously.

I have to believe something very bad happened to him when he was a teenager.

I also have to believe my grandfather knew exactly what he was doing when he picked Weggers to be his agent of destruction. He would have said to himself, *I need a guy who won't give an inch on the rules. Who'll enforce my whims even if they make zero sense. And who will annoy my grandsons more than even I could have.*

"Carry on, Shane," Weggers says with a royal wave of his hand.

To attain success Hanna and I envisioned, Hott Springs Eternal will need a wedding that garners national, or even international, attention.

A celebrity wedding.

You, Shane Hott, celebrity, are perfectly positioned in your well-connected LA life to recruit a celebrity couple to be married at Hott Springs Eternal. You have six months to make a celebrity wedding happen.

"No," Shane says.

I look at Sonya. She smiles at me—big, bright, buoyant.

I smile back. "Accept your fate, dude."

Who knows, maybe it'll work out as well for him as it did for me.

ACKNOWLEDGMENTS

Welcome to back to Rush Creek! Readers, I adore you. You're the reason I do what I do, and your support means so much to me.

I hope you've loved meeting the Hotts as much as I've loved writing this book.

Well. Not the whole time.

This one was actually kind of a doozy, which means the acknowledgments are going to be extra long.

I started this book three different times, with three different brothers as the hero. I wrote pages and pages of outlines and synopses, and tens of thousands of words—no exaggeration—before I realized—TWICE!—that I was on the wrong track.

Then Quinn showed up... and the rest is history. Once I knew Quinn was the hero, I wrote the first draft of this book in six fevered weeks.

Several people bore the brunt of my unfortunate early missteps. Christine D'Abo listened patiently—as she always does—as I explained why nope, nope, nope, that was the wrong brother (twice). Dylann Crush lay awake in a conference hotel bed alongside me and helped me figure out the perfect beginning to a book that will, sadly, never exist.

Being an author's friend is NOT for the faint of heart.

But the real hero of this story, as you might guess, was Mr. Bell.

Mr. Bell endured more hours of misbegotten plot bunnies than anyone should *ever* have to confront, and never once complained.

Mr. Bell also came up with my favorite conceit in this whole series, the idea that the Hott brothers receive their marching orders from their Granddad via drip-release letters. In this age of AI-generated plots and premises, it feels important to acknowledge that my ideas don't always spring perfect and full-grown into my head... but they all come from interactions with other people—not AIs.

Unless there's something Mr. Bell isn't telling me.

Sometimes he does seem too good to be true.

Similarly, the flood in the salon is Christine D'Abo's brainchild. And every time I re-read that scene where they're standing up to their calves in water, I want to hug her. She's also the one who came up with the idea of the rocks in *Wilder At Last*. If that made you cry, go buy Christine's Thirty Days series.

My therapist gave me the phrase "that which you resist goes in the basement and lifts weights," but says she's pretty sure she got it from someone else, so I don't have to credit her. It's such a good phrase. I mean, it's so freaking true. Ignore your BS at your own peril.

As always, I am deeply indebted to my early readers, who made the book I finally wrote so much better through their insightful comments. These include Rachel Grant, Susannah Nix, Audrey Nelson, Brenda St. John Brown, Christine D'Abo, and Gwen Hernandez.

Alyse Boncado, one of my readers and a newsletter subscriber, owns a spa and did an expert read for spa- and salon-related storytelling. She gave me lots of great suggestions. Any remaining unrealistic spa or salon material is either my error or...quite likely...a flight of authorial fancy.

Huge thanks also to the author friends who support me on a regular basis—those I've already mentioned, as well as Liz Alden, Christina Braver, Cheryl Cain, Julie Farley, Christy Hovland, Claire Marti, Kate Davies, Kris Kennedy and many, many more, including but not limited to the authors of the Corner of Smart and Sexy, RAM Rom Com, Wide for the Win, Awesome Babes for Good Things, and my ongoing newsletter swaps.

Thank you to my agent, Emily Sylvan Kim, and my sub rights agent, Tina Shen!

Thank you, Mandi Andrejka of Inky Pen Editing, and welcome to Rush Creek. I'm so glad you reached out to me after you read *Sleepover*, and I've loved your care, thoughtfulness, and thoroughness on this book.

Thank you, XPresso Book Tours, especially Giselle, for the cover reveal and release blitz!

Hugs and kisses for my not-author friends who support my imaginary worlds with so much love and patience: Aimee, Darya, Ellen, Elizabeth, Lauren, Molly, Soomie, and Tracey.

To BellGirl, BellBoy, and Mr. Bell (again, because it cannot be said enough), there is nothing more comforting and wonderful than coming home to you. You may not technically be my found family, but I've "found" that you're the best family I could ever have imagined. I love you all so much.

Any errors of fact or insensitivity relating to representation are mine and mine alone. If you note any, please let me know so I can fix them, apologize, and learn to be better.

ALSO BY SERENA BELL

Wilder Adventures

Make Me Wilder

Walk on the Wilder Side

Wilder With You

A Little Wilder

Wilder at Last

Hott Springs Eternal

Hott Shot

Hott Take

Under One Roof

Do Over

Head Over Heels

Sleepover

Returning Home

Hold On Tight

Can't Hold Back

To Have and to Hold

Holding Out

Tierney Bay

So Close

So True

So Good (2022)

So Right (2023)

New York Glitz

Still So Hot!

Hot & Bothered

Standalone

Turn Up the Heat

ABOUT THE AUTHOR

USA Today bestselling author Serena Bell writes contemporary romance with heat, heart, and humor. A former journalist, Serena has always believed that everyone has an amazing story to tell if you listen carefully, and you can often find her scribbling in her tiny garret office, mainlining chocolate and bringing to life the tales in her head.

Serena's books have earned many honors, including a RITA finalist spot, an RT Reviewers' Choice Award, Apple Books Best Book of the Month, and Amazon Best Book of the Year for Romance.

When not writing, Serena loves to spend time with her college-sweetheart husband and two hilarious kiddos—all of whom are incredibly tolerant not just of Serena's imaginary friends but also of how often she changes her hobbies and how passionately she embraces the new ones. These days, it's stand-up paddle boarding, board-gaming, meditation, and long walks with good friends.

www.ingramcontent.com/pod-product-compliance
Lightning Source LLC
Chambersburg PA
CBHW051247210726

48287CB00002B/388